NOT SO
NICE GUY

NOT SO NICE GUY

USA TODAY BESTSELLING AUTHOR

R.S. GREY

Entangled Publishing, LLC
644 Shrewsbury Commons Ave., STE 181
Shrewsbury, PA 17361
rights@entangledpublishing.com

Amara is an imprint of Entangled Publishing, LLC.

Visit our website at www.entangledpublishing.com.

Edited by C. Marie
Cover design by Elizabeth Turner Stokes
Edge design by Elizabeth Turner Stokes
Stock art by erouleanwar/Shutterstock, RZN_desing/Shutterstock, and Haali/Shutterstock
Interior design by Britt Marczak

ISBN 978-1-64937-884-2

Manufactured in the United States of America

First Edition May 2025

10 9 8 7 6 5 4 3 2 1

Chapter One

Samantha

This morning, we're having sex inside the army barracks again. It's hot and heavy. The enemy is advancing—we might not make it out alive. Explosions rumble in the sky and in my pants. I'm sweating. Ian started out wearing camo fatigues, but I ripped them off with my teeth. That's how I know I'm dreaming—my mouth isn't that skillful. In real life, I'd chip a tooth on his zipper.

My alarm clock fires another warning shot. My waking mind shouts, *Get up or you're going to be late!* I burrow deeper under my covers and my subconscious wins out. Dream Ian tosses me over his shoulder like he's trying to earn a Medal of

Honor and then we crash against a metal bunkbed. Another indication that this is a dream is the fact that the fleshy part of my butt hits the corner of the bunk yet it doesn't hurt. He grinds into me and the frame rattles. I scrape my fingers down his back.

"We're going to get caught, soldier," I moan.

His mouth covers mine and he reminds me, "This is a war zone—we can be as loud as we want."

A staccato burst of machine-gun fire erupts just outside. Heavy boots begin stomping toward the locked door.

"Quick, we'll have to barricade it!" I implore. "But how? There's nothing useful in here, just that standard-issue leather whip and my knee-high combat boots!"

He hauls me up against the door and we lock eyes. The wordless solution suddenly becomes clear: we'll have to use our own writhing bodies as a sexy blockade.

"Okay, every time they kick the door, I'm going to thrust, got it? On the count of three: one, two—"

Just as my dream gets to the good part, my phone starts blaring "Islands in the Stream" by Kenny Rogers and Dolly Parton. Cool 80s country pop serenades me at max volume. There are synthesizers. I groan and jerk my eyes open. Ian changed my ringtone again. He does it to me every few weeks. The song before was another silly throwback tune by two old kooks.

I reach out for my phone and bring it beneath the covers with me.

"Yeah yeah," I answer. "I'm already showered and heading out the door."

"You're still in bed."

Ian's deep, husky voice saying the word "bed" does funny things to my stomach. Dream Ian is blending with Real Life Ian. One is a hunky lieutenant with arms of steel. The other is my best friend whose arms are made of a metal I've never had the pleasure of feeling.

"Dolly Parton this time? Really?" I ask.

"She's an American treasure, just like you."

"How do you even come up with these songs?"

"I keep a running list on my phone. Why are you breathing so hard? It sounds like you're over there fogging up a mirror."

Oh god. I sit up and shake off the remnants of my dream.

"I fell asleep to reruns of *M*A*S*H* again."

"You know they've continued making television shows since then."

"Yes, well, I've yet to find a man who titillates me like Hawkeye."

"You know Alan Alda is in his 80s right?"

"He's probably still got it."

"Whatever you say, Hot Lips."

I groan. Just like with Major Houlihan, that nickname annoys me...kind of.

I sweep the blankets aside and force my feet to the ground. "How long do I have?"

"First bell rings in thirty minutes."

"Looks like I'll have to skip that 10-mile morning run I was planning."

He laughs. "Mhmm."

I start rummaging through my closet, looking for a clean dress and cardigan. Our school's employee wardrobe requirements force me to dress like the female version of Mr. Rogers. Today, my sundress is cherry red and my cardigan is pale pink, appropriate for the first day of February.

"Any chance you filled up an extra thermos with coffee before you left the house?" I ask, hopeful.

"I'll leave it on your desk."

My heart flutters with appreciation.

"You know what, I was wrong," I tease, affecting a swoony lovesick tone. "There *is* a man who titillates me more than Hawkeye, and his name is Ian Flet—"

He groans and hangs up.

Oak Hill High School is a five-minute bike ride from my apartment. It's also a five-minute bike ride from Ian's house. We could make the morning commute together, but we have drastically different morning rituals. I like to roll the dice and push the limits on my alarm clock. It thrills me to sleep until the very last second. Ian likes to wake up with the milkman. He belongs to a gym and he uses that membership every morning. His body fat percentage hovers in the low teens. I belong to the same gym and my membership card is tucked behind a beloved Dunkin' Donuts rewards card. It leers out at me each time I make a midday strawberry frosted run.

Those barbaric contraptions at the gym intimidate me. I once sprained my wrist trying to change the amount of weight resistance on a rowing machine, and have you seen all the different strap, rope, and handle attachments for the cable machine? Half of them look like sex toys for horses.

Instead of subjecting myself to the gym, I prefer my daily bike rides. Besides, there's really no fighting my physiology at this point. I'm a twenty-seven-year-old woman still riding the wave of pretend fitness that comes naturally with youth and the food budget of a teacher. The only #gains in my life come from binge-watching Chip and Joanna Gaines on *Fixer Upper*.

Ian says I'm too hard on myself, but in the mirror I see knobby knees and barely-filled B cups. On good days, I'm 5'3". I think I can shop at Baby Gap.

When I make it to school (ten minutes before the first bell), I find a granola bar next to the thermos of coffee on my desk. In my haste to make it to school on time, I forgot to grab something for breakfast. I've become predictable enough that Ian has stowed snacks in and around my desk. I can pull open any drawer and find something—nuts, seeds, peanut butter crackers. There's even a Clif Bar duct-taped under my chair. My arsenal is more for his own good than mine. I'm the hangriest person you've ever met. When my blood sugar drops, I turn into the destructive Jean Grey.

I scarf down the granola bar and sip my coffee, firing off a quick text to thank him before students start filing into my classroom for first period.

Sam: *TY for breakfast. Coffee is LIT.*

Ian: *It's the new blend you bought last week. Are your students teaching you new words again?*

Sam: *I heard it during carpool duty yesterday. I'm not sure when to use it yet. Will report back.*

"Good morning, *Missus* Abrams!" my first student sing-songs.

It's Nicholas, the editor-in-chief for the Oak Hill Gazette. He's the kind of kid who wears sweater vests to school. He takes my journalism class very seriously—even more seriously than he takes his crush on me, which is saying something.

I level him with a reproving look. "Nicholas, for the last time, it's Miss Abrams. You know I'm not married."

He grins extra wide and his braces twinkle in the light. He's had them do the rubber band colors in alternating blue and black for school pride. "I know. I just like hearing you say it." The kid is relentless. "And may I just say, the shade of your dress is very becoming. The red nearly matches your hair. With style like that, you'll be a missus in no time."

"No, you may not say that. Just sit down."

Other students are starting to file into my class now. Nicholas takes his seat front and center, and I avoid eye contact with him as much as possible once I begin my lesson.

Ian and I have drastically different jobs at Oak Hill High.

He's the AP Chem II teacher. He has a master's degree and worked in industry after college. While in grad school, he helped develop a tongue strip that soothes burns from things like hot coffee and scalding pizza. Seems stupid—SNL even spoofed it—but it got a lot of interest in the science world, and his experience makes the students look up to him. He's the cool teacher who rolls his shirtsleeves to his elbows and blows shit up in the name of science.

I'm just the journalism teacher and the staff coordinator for the Oak Hill Gazette, a weekly newspaper that is read by exactly five people: me, Ian, Nicholas, Nicholas' mom, and our principal, Mr. Pruitt. Everyone assumes I fall into the "if you can't do, teach" category, but I actually like my job. Teaching is fun, and I'm not cut out for the real world. Hard-hitting journalists don't make very many friends. They jump into the action, push, prod, and expose important stories to the world. In college, my professors chastised me for only churning out "puff pieces". I took it as a compliment. Who doesn't like puffy things?

As it is, I'm proud of the Gazette and the students who help run it.

We start each week with an "all-staff meeting" as if we're a real, functioning newspaper. Students pitch their ideas for proposed stories or fill me in on the progress of ongoing work. Most everyone takes it seriously except for the few kids who sought out journalism for an easy A—which, off the record, it is. Ian says I'm a pushover.

I'm talking to one of those students who fall into that second category now. I don't think she's turned in one assignment since we got back from Christmas break. "Phoebe, have you thought of a story for next week's newspaper?"

"Oh, uhh…yeah." She pops her gum. I want to steal it out of her mouth and stick it in her hair. "I think I'm going to ask around to see if the janitors are like, banging after hours or something."

"You leave poor Mr. Franklin alone. C'mon, what else you got?"

"Okay, how's this...*School Lunches: Healthy or Unhealthy*?"

Inwardly, I claw at my eyes. This type of exposé has been done so many times that our school's head lunch lady and I have worked out a system. I keep students out of her kitchen, and in return, I get all the free tater tots I want.

"There's no story there. The food isn't healthy. We all know that. Something else."

There are a few snickers. Phoebe's cheeks glow red and her eyes narrow on me. She's annoyed I've called her out in front of the entire class. "Okay, fine." Her tone takes a sassy and cruel edge like only a teenage girl's can. "How about I do something more salacious? Maybe a piece about illicit love between teachers?"

I'm so bored, I yawn. Rumors about Ian and me are old news. Everyone assumes that because we're best friends, we must be dating. It couldn't be farther from the truth. I want to tell them, *Yeah, I WISH*, but I know for a fact I'm not Ian's type. Here are four times this has been made clear to me:

- He once told me he's never imagined himself with a redhead because his mom has reddish hair. *HELLO, MOST GUYS HAVE MOMMY ISSUES! LET ME BE YOUR MOMMY ISSUE!*

- He's only ever dated tall broody model types with wingspans twice as long as mine. They're like female pterodactyls.

- We're both massive LOTR fans and guess what—SAM IS THE BEST FRIEND, NOT THE LOVE INTEREST.

- Oh, and then of course there was that one time I forced myself to dress up as slutty Hermione (his weakness) for Halloween and tried to seduce him. He told me I looked more like frizzy-haired Hermione from the early years and less like post-pubescent Yule Ball Hermione. Cue quiet meltdown.

Ian and I became friends three and a half years ago, close to 1300 days if some loser out there was keeping count. Upon accepting teaching positions at Oak Hill, we were placed in the same orientation group. There were fifteen new hires in total, and Ian immediately caught my eye. I can remember the first time I saw him, recalling specific, random details more than anything: how big his hands looked holding our orientation handbook, how tan he was from summer vacation, the fact that he towered over the rest of us. My first thought was that he should have been incredibly intimidating what with the sharp blue eyes and short, slightly wavy brown hair, but he cut away the pretense when he aimed a smile at me as our eyes locked over the crowd of new teachers. It was so disarming and easygoing, but most importantly, it was seriously sexy. My heart sputtered in my chest. He was the boy next door who'd grown into a man with a chiseled jaw and solid arms.

He was wearing a black T-shirt I focused on as he made his way toward me through the crowd.

"You're a Jake Bugg fan?" he asked. "Me too."

I responded with a poorly executed, "Huh?"

His Crest smile widened a little further and he pointed down at my shirt. *Oh, right.* I was wearing a Jake Bugg concert T-shirt. We struck up polite conversation about his last US tour, and I kept my drool in my mouth the entire time. When it was time to get started, he asked if I wanted to sit with him.

For a week straight we endured instructional videos about sexual harassment and workplace protocol together. While choppy VHS tapes from the 90s played on a rolled-in TV stand, Ian and I passed cheeky notes back and forth. Eventually, we just pushed our desks together and kept our voices barely above whispers as we got to know each other. We had so much to talk and joke about. Our words spilled out in rapid-fire like we were scared the other person would go up in a POOF and disappear at any moment.

We didn't pay attention through the entire orientation, but the joke was on us.

They gave us a test at the end of the week and we both failed. Apparently, it was an Oak Hill first. The test is ridiculously easy if you had paid the least bit of attention. We had to retake the orientation class for a second time and our friendship was cemented through the shared embarrassment and shame.

At the end of the second week, we celebrated our passing scores with drinks—Ian's idea. I tried not to read too much into it. After all, we were both inviting plus ones.

That's when I met the girl he was dating at the time: a gazelle-like dermatologist. At the bar, she regaled us all with interesting stories from the exam room.

"Yeah, people don't realize how many different types of moles there are."

She gave me unsolicited advice such as, *"Due to your fair skin, you really ought to be seeing someone for a skin check twice a year."* She, by the way, didn't have a visible pore or freckle on her. When we both stood to use the bathroom midway through the evening, my inadequacies multiplied. Our size difference was obscene. I could have fit in her pocket. To anyone watching, I looked like the pre-teen she was babysitting for the night.

The only silver lining was that I had her check out the smattering of freckles on my shoulders while we were waiting for the stalls to open up. All clear.

At the time, I was dating someone too. Jerry was an investment banker I'd met through a friend of a friend. This outing was only our third date and I had no plans to continue seeing him, especially after he droned on and on about Greek life back at UPenn.

"Yeah, I was fraternity president my junior and senior year. HOO-RAH."

Then he proceeded to holler his fraternity chant for the entire bar to hear. I think he thought it was funny, but I didn't feel like I was in on the joke. I wanted to press a red button and exit through the roof. Ian's eyes locked with mine over the table, and it felt like he knew exactly what I was thinking. He could tell how uncomfortable I was, how much the situation made me squirm. We both proceeded to fight back laughter. My face turned red with exertion. He had to bite his lip. In the end, I caved first and had to excuse myself to go to the bathroom again so I could crack up in private.

Ian's date later told him she was concerned I had an overactive bladder.

By the time lunch rolls around at school, I'm ready for a break. My journalism classes are interspersed with on-level senior English classes. It's not my favorite part of the job, but it's the only way Principal Pruitt can justify keeping me on full-time. The students in these classes are already checked out, blaming their late homework and poor quiz scores on senioritis. I type the illness into Wed MD to prove it isn't a real thing. They don't look up from their cell phones long enough to listen.

Most of them wouldn't be able to pick me out of a lineup.

Last week, one kid thought I was a student and asked for my Snapchat.

Ian doesn't have this problem. His classes are filled with overachieving nerds, the kids who've already been accepted to Ivy League schools but still feel the need to take 27 AP classes. Most of them intimidate me, but they treat Ian like he's their Obi-Wan.

"Tell us more about the tongue strip, Mr. Fletcher!"

"Bill Nye's got nothin' on you, Mr. Fletcher!"

"I wrote about you in my college admissions essay, Mr. Fletcher. I had to pick the one person who's inspired me to pursue learning the most!"

I sit down for lunch in the teachers' lounge and puff out a

breath of air, trying to move the few strands of hair from my forehead. They are evidence that I've tugged at my ponytail in distress too many times this morning.

Ian slides into his designated seat across from me and his positive energy clogs the air between us. It could also be his delicious body wash.

"Let's see it," he says.

"It's not my best haul."

I've got a cheese stick, pretzels, grapes, and a peanut butter and jelly sandwich.

He has a multi-layer turkey sandwich with avocado and alfalfa sprouts, sliced watermelon, and almonds.

Without a word, we start the exchange. I take half his turkey sandwich. He takes half my PB&J. My cheese stick gets divided in two. I let him keep his nasty almonds—they aren't even salted.

"Let me have some of your pretzels," he says, reaching over.

I slam my hand down on the bag, effectively cracking most of them in half. Worth it.

"You know the rules."

His dark brow arches. "I have chocolate chip cookies from one of my students back in my classroom. His mom baked them as a thank you for writing him a rec letter."

In the blink of an eye, my threatening scowl gentles to a smile. My dimples pop for added effect. "Why didn't you say so?"

I turn my bag of broken pretzels in his direction.

Even though the teachers' lounge is packed, no one sits at our table. They know better. We're not rude, it's just hard for other people to keep up with us. Our conversations involve a lot of shorthand, code, and inside jokes.

"All-staff go well?"

I try for my best local news anchor tone. "Ian, *is* the food in our cafeteria healthy?"

He groans in commiseration.

"Yeah, then I had another student try to threaten to expose our relationship."

"You mean the one that doesn't exist?"

"Exactly."

"All right. All right!" Mrs. Loring—the drama teacher— shouts near the fridge, cutting through the noise in the lounge. "Guess what today is…"

"The first of the month!" someone shouts enthusiastically. "Confiscation Station!"

For the next few seconds, there's an overwhelming amount of applause and chatter. Confetti might as well be raining down from the ceiling.

"Okay. OKAY! Settle down," Mrs. Loring shouts excitedly. "Does anyone have late entries?"

Ian stands and withdraws a crumpled note from his pocket.

People clap like he's a hometown hero returning from war.

"Snatched it up during first period," he brags.

A few female teachers act as if they're going into cardiac arrest as they watch him cross the room. Mrs. Loring holds out her mason jar and he drops it inside.

He reclaims his seat across from me and suddenly, it's time for The Reading.

On top of the fridge in the teachers' lounge sits a medium-sized mason jar, into which we drop notes we've seized from students during class. The moon waxes and wanes and that jar fills up. At the first of every month, Mrs. Loring interrupts our lunch for a dramatic reading.

It might sound cruel, but don't worry, we keep the notes anonymous. No one knows the source except the confiscator. As a result, Principal Pruitt doesn't really care about our ritual. It's good for our morale. Think of it as team bonding.

Mrs. Loring swirls her hand into the bowl like a kid searching for candy on Halloween, and then she comes up with a neatly folded note.

I turn to Ian, giddy. Our gazes lock. Last year I sat in while he did an experiment with his students. He burned different elements to show that they each produced a different color flame. Calcium burned orange, sodium burned yellow. The students were amazed, but then so was I, because when he burned copper, it produced a dark, vivid blue flame—the exact color of Ian's eyes. I've kept a little bowl of shiny pennies on my nightstand ever since.

Mrs. Loring clears her throat and begins. She's the best person for the job. There is no half-assing on her part. She's a classically trained actor and when she reads the seized missives, she affects different accents and performs with a convincing earnestness. If I could, I'd bring my parents in for an evening showing.

"Student #1: Hey, did you see that [name redacted] sat by me during first period?"

"Student #2: YES! I think he likes you."

"Student #1: We're just friends. He's not into me like that."

"Student #2: C'MON! YOU JUST NEED TO GO FOR IT! Next time you hug, push your boobs up against him. That's my secret weapon."

A smattering of snorts interrupts the reading before Mrs. Loring restores order.

"Student #1: Let's say that actually works—what if it changes everything? What if it messes up the friendship?"

"Student #2: Who cares? We're about to graduate. You need to getchasome."

"Student #1: Okay, sleezeball. I, for one, actually think it's possible to have guy friends without banging them all."

"Student #2: You're delusional. It's only a matter of time before best friends of opposite sex morph into LOVERS."

The bolded final word, read with overblown dramatics, produces uproarious laughter. But, at our table, there is conspicuous silence. Crickets. The note parallels my life too closely. I fidget in my chair. Heat crawls up my spine. I've broken out in hives. Maybe I'm having an allergic reaction to Ian's turkey sandwich. In fact, I wish I were—anaphylactic shock sounds wonderful compared to this. It feels like someone just transcribed the thoughts and words of the little angel and devil on my shoulders.

I hate this game.

I hate that Ian is trying to get me to meet his blue-flame gaze, probably trying to make some *friendly* joke.

When lunch is over, I'll stand and make a break for it. I'll decline his invitation to accompany him back to his classroom for cookies, and when we part ways, I'll try hard to keep my tone and my gaze calm. He'll never know anything was wrong.

I've had to tread lightly for the last 1300 days. Ian and I have a relationship that depends greatly on my ability to compartmentalize my feelings for him at the start of every school day and then slowly uncork the bottle at night. The pressure builds and builds all day.

It's why my dreams are filthy.

It's why I haven't dated anyone else in ages.

This whole tightrope walk is getting harder and harder, but there's no alternative. For 1300 days, I've been best friends with Ian Fletcher, and for 1300 days, I've convinced myself I'm not in love with him. I just really, really like pennies.

Chapter Two

Ian

Sam and I have been friends for a while now—so long, in fact, that I know she isn't into me. Here are four times she's made that perfectly clear:

-She once told me she feels nervous whenever we're too close. *"You're the bull and I'm the china. You could probably sit on me and squash me to death."* The last guy she dated was short enough to fit into her jeans.

-She goes for boring business types, guys who spend their first month's paycheck on an expensive frame for their MBA certificate.

-I once overheard her on the phone swearing to her mom

that we were *"never, ever, ever going to be more than friends."* It sounded like a Kidz Bop version of Taylor Swift.

-Oh, and there was the Halloween party last year when she dressed up like Hermione and I tried to kiss her and she laughed in my face...and then puked on my shoes.

Today is Wednesday, which means Sam is already at my house when I get home from soccer practice. I'm the head coach of Oak Hill's men's JV team. We're undefeated, and Sam's never missed a game even though sports aren't really her thing.

"Please say you've already started dinner, Madam Secretary," I say when I walk in and drop my bag.

"It's in the oven, Mister President."

She's at my kitchen table, hunched over with her back to me. I can't tell what she's doing until I get closer and lean over her shoulder.

She's sprinkling glitter onto poster boards, adding the finishing touches to bright neon signs. They say, GO OAK HILL SOCCER and COACH FLETCHER IS #1! Construction paper and glue and markers litter my table. It's a complete mess.

"Are those for the game tomorrow?"

"Wow, aren't you the master of deduction," she teases before catching a whiff of my sweat and pushing me away with her hip. "Go shower. You stink. Dinner will be ready in 15 minutes."

I don't argue. I worked out with the team today and I'm sure I smell terrible. I walk into my room and yank off my shirt. I never bother closing the door as I undress because Sam never bothers to look.

Every Wednesday, she and I have a standing commitment: *West Wing* Wednesdays, hence the nicknames.

This tradition started out differently. In the past, it included other friends and significant others. The friends have either moved away for jobs or had children. Our significant others have disappeared too. It's not a coincidence. None of Sam's boyfriends have ever liked me. It could be that I'm not very buddy-buddy with them. I don't let them drink my beer. I kept calling the last one Biff when I knew his name was Bill. It always ended up making him irrationally angry, which made it easier for me when I had to watch him kiss her good night.

When I walk out of the bathroom after my shower, Sam has set out our dinner plates on my coffee table. We share a Blue Apron subscription and switch off making the meals. Tonight, she's also filled our glasses with cheap boxed wine and has included a bowl of reanimated tater tots courtesy of the lunch ladies at Oak Hill.

Sam props her hands on her hips and glances up at me. We're wearing the same *West Wing* t-shirt that promotes a mock 1998 presidential campaign for Bartlet. I ordered us the same size. It fits me fine. On her, it's a boxy dress. She's a pipsqueak—a beautiful pipsqueak, though I know if I told her so, she'd scrunch her nose and blurt out a change of subject. *Tater tots are getting cold!* On some level she has to know she's attractive; I'm sure enough guys have told her so over the years. She has high cheekbones and a full, feminine mouth. Her fair skin and dark red hair and large blue eyes are the stuff of castles and fairytales. If she went to Disney World on vacation, small children would group around her like a mob, staring up with doe eyes and begging for photos.

She's caught me staring.

Her head tilts to the side. Mine follows.

"What is it, Mr. President? An emergency? Do we need to head to the Situation Room?"

I lick my thumb and drag it aimlessly across her cheek, her forehead, her chin.

"You just had some glitter on your face," I lie.

I move around her and take a seat on the couch, trying to refocus my brain. I'm hungry for food, not Sam.

"Looks good."

"It's tandoori chicken." Her accent turns hoity-toity and British when she continues, "I've chosen a robust red for pairing and only the finest tots of the potato variety."

She takes a seat beside me, her feet propped up on the coffee table. I know she's wearing shorts under the t-shirt, but every week, the illusion plays dirty tricks on my brain. I'll have to take another cold shower once she leaves. My infatuation with Sam is a major drain on our planet's supply of freshwater.

We've finished all of the seasons of *West Wing* once already. We could move on to a new show, but there's comfort in tradition. Besides, it's not like we watch it that closely. Usually we're doing other stuff too, like now: Sam's done eating and is back at the kitchen table finishing up her poster boards.

Her phone is sitting on the couch beside me and it lights up with a notification from a dating app. The accompanying sound effect grabs her attention.

"Did I just get a match?"

I check. Some guy named Sergio sent her a message.

"I don't know why you bother with this crap."

She huffs out a sigh of annoyance and marches over to grab her phone from the couch. "Maybe because I'd like to get laid every now and then. I'm basically a sexless nun without all the perks of the convent."

My dick stirs and I ignore it. I've gotten pretty good at it by now.

"Well I'm not sure this Sergio is up to the task. He looks like he waxes his eyebrows."

"So? That sounds like a great first date idea. Mine are overdue."

I quirk my eyebrow at her, so she deflects.

"Besides, who are you to judge? The girls you date wax themselves from head to toe. You probably have to tie their smooth, frictionless bodies down so they don't slide off the bed during sex."

I smirk. "I might tie them up, but not for that reason."

She mimes a hearty puke session. "Gross. How did we get from *my* Tinder success all the way to you romancing plucked chickens and hairless cats?"

"You're right, back to Sergio. Is he really your type?"

"Leave him alone and turn around. This is the part where I'm supposed to send him nudes, right?"

I lean forward and drop my foot from its spot on my knee. Now she's standing between my legs. I'm nearly her height sitting down. Her phone is still in my hand and I scroll through a few of his photos. "Hmm, he's short. A lot of short guys are like Chihuahuas—all bark, no bite."

One delicate brow arches in challenge. "Oh, so you're

saying you're all bite?"

Our conversation is veering into dangerous territory. I want to reach out and slide my hand around her thigh then drag it higher until it disappears beneath her shirt...trace the curve of her ass...

Instead, I sit back, putting much-needed space between us. "I'm just saying, any guy who takes selfies and waxes his eyebrows is going to be selfish in bed."

"That's fine, I've always felt I was more of a giver. Also, I don't remember asking for advice."

She looks down at her phone, and a deep, angry line forms between her brows when she realizes I messaged Sergio back for her.

Sergio: *Hey QT*

Samantha: *How many children would you like to have? I'm thinking 10.*

"*Ian!*"

"He addressed you with *letters*. I thought the prerequisite for Tinder hookups was to at least be moderately clever. He abbreviated a five-letter word."

She turns back to the kitchen table. "I'm ending this conversation now."

🍎

don't date much anymore. I can't remember the last time I enjoyed spending time with a woman who wasn't Sam. I guess it was my mom when I was back home for Christmas. Cool story.

Part of the reason why I'm alone is that I'm tired of trudging through the same fight. In past relationships, it was always the same ultimatum: girlfriend or Sam. I always chose Sam, and they always followed through on their threat to leave.

Maybe I should start using dating apps too.

It's a few days later when I ask Sam to check over my Tinder profile while we're alone in the copier room at school.

She groans in annoyance.

"You're doing it all wrong. You're supposed to say something witty, not just boring details about your life, and there are hotter pictures you could have chosen."

She deletes the words that took me five seconds to type.

"What's wrong with telling them I'm a chemistry teacher?"

"You're supposed to say it in a witty way, like 'I teach chemistry, let's see if we have any between us.'"

"That's really bad. Honestly, the worst."

"And you didn't even include a shirtless photo. What's the point of all that gym time if you aren't going to flaunt the results?"

"I don't have any shirtless photos of myself."

Who does?

She snaps her fingers like she's got the perfect solution. "What about when we went to the beach last summer? There was that photo of us together on Facebook. My aunts gushed over you for days, and I unfortunately mean that in the literal sense. When I told them we were just friends, one of them asked me for your number."

"Oh, perfect. Let's skip Tinder and just hook me up with her then."

"She's 68."

"First date at Luby's? Senior discount?"

She shoves my phone back against my chest and shakes her head. "You know what? Now that I think about it, I don't think you should do the dating app thing. It'll be overwhelming for someone as pretty as you."

"You use them," I point out.

Her expression makes it clear she thinks I'm teasing her. I want to haul her up onto the copier and prove my point. Her ass would press against the glass, the bright light would scan past. I'd laminate the copies and hang them up in my shower.

"It's different," she says as she sighs, almost sounding sad.

"How?"

"I'm not everyone's type. Your face is deemed universally good-looking."

I sidestep her compliment.

"Did Sergio ever respond to you the other day?"

She scowls up at me. "Yeah, he told me we wouldn't work out even after I tried to clear up the mess you made. Why are you smiling like that?"

"Oh, I'm just thinking of what I'm going to eat for lunch."

After school and on weekends, I'm usually with Sam. We spend 99% of our time together. This seems odd to my parents and our other friends (the one or two that have stuck around), but it happened gradually. Weekly dinners became biweekly dinners, and so on. At this point, we're codependent. I can't remember the last time I had a meal for one—oh wait, yes I can: it was that time I bought myself Jimmy John's on the way to Sam's apartment a few months back.

"Shit, I should have brought you something," I said right as she opened the door and glanced down.

"No, it's fine. I have plenty of food here to eat."

She joined me on the couch a few minutes later carrying a plate that contained the following: one carrot, a moldy piece of cheese, and half a slice of expired lunch meat. It was turkey, from the looks of the sad pale color.

"How's your warm sub?" she asked, reaching for the carrot.

Obviously, I tore my sandwich down the middle and gave her half. Lesson learned.

We usually have a lot of grading to do on school nights: essays and edits for her, chemistry exams and lab reports for me. Tonight, though, I've talked her into going to the gym with me. She hates it so much. In the car on the way there, she works her way through an entire monologue about how it's commendable that I care so much about my physical health and well-being, but she thinks it's more important to focus on the mental and emotional health benefits of a sedentary lifestyle.

"Why do you think there's a whole genre of clothing called

athleisure? I'm not alone."

I push her into the gym and we start to head our separate ways. We've tried to work out together, but it's too distracting. I'm actually here for a purpose, while Sam just wants to talk and sip on a drink from the smoothie counter. She also likes to wear tight workout tops and yoga pants, and maybe I find that a little more distracting than the conversation. She steps back and sends me an over-the-top wave. "If I don't meet you back here in an hour it's because I'm hiding in a corner somewhere crying! Have fun!"

A beefy gym rat hears her as he walks by and offers up a greasy smile. "Are you new? I can take you through a few machines if you want. My name's Kevin. I work here."

Her eyes go wide and she looks petrified.

"Oh, no thank you, Kevin," she says firmly and quickly before turning and breaking out in a run-walk in the opposite direction.

Kevin looks to me for an explanation, but all he gets is a scowl.

Tonight, Sam's opted for a workout class led by a spunky pink-haired teacher. For an hour, I work out on the machines while stealing glances of her inside the studio near the back of the gym. Glass windows stretch from floor to ceiling. There are a dozen other women dancing and kicking and pushing up alongside her, but Sam's near the back and it's easy to watch her through the glass as she tries desperately to keep up. She's really not so bad. What she lacks in physical strength, she makes up for in enthusiasm, her red ponytail swinging wildly.

I finish up on a machine and drag a towel across my

forehead as the teacher takes them through some cool-down stretches. Sam steps her legs out into a V and bends forward at the hips so she can reach down and touch the ground. Her butt is displayed in the tightest pair of black stretchy pants she owns. I need to stuff my towel into my mouth and bite down.

The bicep machine closest to that back studio has had a steady line for the last hour. The machine is rusted and old and yet everyone wants a turn. The guy there now isn't even pretending to use it. There are no weights hooked up, and he's just tugging at the limp rope while he gawks at Sam. I want to wring his neck.

Sam's upside-down head falls between her legs as she stretches, and when she sees me looking, she grins and waves enthusiastically.

"Hi!" she mouths.

The guys hovering near the bicep machine jerk their gaze in my direction, and when Sam turns away, I wave them off. They scatter like cockroaches.

I'm in the middle of leg presses when she finds me later. I have headphones in so I don't notice her until she's right there, a few inches away, sweaty and breathing hard.

I reach up and cut my music, but I continue with my set. She watches, eyes studying my legs like they're wild animals, about to pounce.

"How was the class?" I ask, dragging my gaze slowly down her flushed cheeks and neck, down the front of her tight black top. She looks up and I jerk my gaze away before she catches me.

"Really fun, actually. Did you watch?"

Was I that obvious?

"I think I might've seen some in passing."

She tries to hide a little smile. "So you saw when we did the cardio dance stuff in the beginning?"

Yes.

"No, must have missed it."

"Ugh! It was my favorite part! Anyway, I'll definitely go back. I hate doing the machines out here, but that class didn't even feel like a workout. I mean, obviously it was…" She pinches her sweaty tank top for proof.

I pause my leg presses and reach for my water.

"See, feel. I think I got stronger just in that one class."

She's holding up her flexed bicep. I don't think it's a good idea to touch her right now.

"Ian! Appreciate my gains!"

"I can appreciate them from here, macho man."

She reaches out for my hand and places it on her bicep. She feels delicate and warm. My hand closes around her upper arm, not tightly, but it feels strange…intimate. I watch her smile waver and I nearly say, *You asked for this, remember?*

She jerks away and rubs her arm like she's trying to expel cooties from her skin. "Swole, right?"

I humor her. "You better watch where you aim those things."

"How much longer do you have?"

"Just one set of these."

"Okay, continue. I'll just stand here and watch."

I arch a brow, but true to her word, she watches quietly as I finish out my last round of leg presses. In fact, she's staring so intently I have to grind my molars together to keep from pulling her down on top of me.

Apparently, I'm not the only one struggling. She fans her face and I aim a mocking smile in her direction.

"*What*?" she groans. "I'm overheated from the class!"

"I didn't say anything."

She doesn't buy it. She throws her hands in the air and turns away, offering me another glimpse of the rear view that's been killing me all night.

"I'm waiting in the car!"

"You'll need the keys. They're over here in my bag."

She doesn't turn around as she sends a wave over her shoulder. "I'll just wait outside then!"

Like hell.

I cut my last set short and take off after her.

On the way home, she's silent until we pass her favorite ice cream shop and she insists we go in. While we're sampling flavors she turns to me, blue eyes staring straight at my chest. "Just to be clear, I wasn't checking you out back there. I was considering the possibility of moonlighting as a personal trainer, now that I'm a gym rat."

"Noted."

"And sure, I was sort of impressed by you, that's all. You're an impressive guy."

Still, her gaze won't meet mine.

"Sam?" I say, trying to ease whatever weirdness is happening between us. "You're impressive too—so impressive. Really, how'd you get so impressively...impressive?"

She pushes me playfully, turns to the kid on duty, and tells him I'll be buying her three scoops of chocolate-chocolate-chip ice cream with rainbow sprinkles on top.

"In a waffle cone—oh, and with a cherry on top!" she adds, turning to face me. "Impressed?"

🍎

The next morning, I wait for Sam outside the main conference room. We have a staff meeting with the rest of the upperclassmen teachers. Today, Sam's wearing a delicate yellow dress. I flick the lapel.

"Very prim and proper."

"Uh huh, save it. You hate this dress. The last time I wore it, you told me I looked like I was headed to my first day of kindergarten."

I did tell her that, but it was because it looked so good I needed to keep her from wearing it again, for my sake, and that of all of Oak Hill's male staff members.

These staff meetings are brutal, and Sam and I usually end up passing the time by playing tic-tac-toe underneath the table. We've only been caught twice. Now we're more careful.

Today, George, our vice principal, is running the show, and it takes him 15 minutes to get everyone to quiet down. He started teaching the same time we did, but he turned administrative when a well-paying position opened up. Deep down we all know he's just one of us, though. As a result, he's never really commanded the respect he deserves.

Like right now, he's trying to get volunteers to run a sex-ed course. They usually do this sort of thing in middle school, but apparently the district thinks our upperclassmen are in need of a refresher course.

No one offers their assistance, and then Sam's arm shoots into the air.

"Why doesn't Ian run it? He can present the abstinence portion based on firsthand experience—or lack thereof."

Everyone laughs and I smile good-naturedly. One of the PE teachers catches my eye, positions her hand like a telephone against her ear, and mouths, *Call me.*

George frowns. "Very funny, Ms. Abrams. Still, I'll take the recommendation. Ian, you'll head the course. Would anyone else like to volunteer to help him?"

Every hand attached to a single female teacher hits the air except Sam's. The PE teacher puts both her hands up and shakes them wildly.

George grins. "Well, what a wonderful sight to see so many eager beavers this morning!"

"*Literally,*" Sam whispers to me.

I smile.

"Tell you what, I'll just leave it up to Ian to decide who he'd like to accompany him during the course."

There are audible groans as everyone realizes at once who I will drag down with me.

Sam tells me my Cheshire grin is unbecoming.

Chapter Three

Sam

At the end of the staff meeting, Ian and I stand at the same time. Today, in my flats, I make it to the middle of his bicep. I'm made aware of this when we try to move around one another and my nose smashes against muscle. It hurts as much as if I'd just walked into a brick wall.

"*Ow*, Jesus."

He reaches out to stabilize me and I stare intently at his chest before wriggling free.

No. There can be no touching, not if I'm expected to maintain the status quo: *friends*, with a capital F.

"Ms. Abrams, may I have a word with you?" George asks

from the front of the conference room.

I don't know who he's kidding with all the formality. I've seen him shotgun light beer after an intramural kickball game.

Ian mumbles something about my yellow dress I don't quite hear.

"What was that?"

He shakes his head. "Want me to wait with you?"

I smile. "Think I'm in big trouble for the abstinence comment?"

"Either that or we're busted for tic-tac-toe again. You shouldn't have thrust your fist in the air after that last game."

"I'd just won the third and final sudden-death showdown. What was I supposed to do? Win with grace and aplomb?"

"Aplomb? You humanities teachers use the most bizarre words."

"Ms. Abrams?" George calls impatiently.

Ian tugs on the end of my loose braid. "Good luck. Don't hesitate to bribe him with a case of Natty Light."

I feign a look of grave concern. "Okay, and I'll tell him tic-tac-toe was your idea."

Turns out, I'm not in trouble. George has a task for me.

"As you've probably heard, Jen is going on maternity leave earlier than expected, so her long-term sub is arriving tomorrow morning. I'd like you to show her around, y'know, give her the lay of the land."

I hiss. "Oh man, wish I could, but I'm on carpool duty."

His time as an administrator has clearly taught him some tricks, because he's already prepared for my go-to excuse. "I've already got someone covering for you this week and next."

I grin, flipping through my rolodex of get-out-of-jail-free

cards. "Ooh, I could use that time to prepare for the sex-ed thing—"

"Prepare? All the material comes from the state. You're just there to put a condom on a banana and answer questions."

My brain trips up, and I run out of options. *You win this round, George.*

"Fine. What's the sub's name?"

"Ashley. I'll tell her to meet you at 7:30 tomorrow morning."

True to his word, the long-term sub is waiting for me outside the main office bright and early. She's overdressed in a black blazer with a matching pencil skirt. She looks like she's going to represent me in a Supreme Court case. Looks wise, I can't help but notice that she'd fit right in among Ian's old girlfriends. Blonde and tall, there's no way she's a day over twenty-three.

Apparently, she thinks the same about me, only younger.

"Excuse me, student, do you know where I can find Ms. Abrams?"

When I tell her who I am, she blushes at her blunder.

"Oh my gosh, I'm sorry. It's just, you're so...petite."

I straighten my shoulders. For the record, I'm not *that* little.

"Right, well, I'm supposed to give you a tour, so let's get going."

The high school is massive, and it's easy to get lost. I decide to keep it simple and avoid places like the band hall and theater room. She'll never remember it all, so I just stick to what's important.

"That's the server room. The campus IT guy sells weed out of it, I've heard." We turn down another hallway. "And here's the art room. You'll notice that the art supply room smells a lot like the server room," I hint with a wink and a nudge.

Ashley's childlike eyes widen, and I think maybe I should have taken her to the band hall instead. She looks horrified.

"Err, just kidding. Come on, I'll take you to your classroom."

Our tour is over pretty quickly, but it's not so easy to shake Ashley. At lunch, she's at my classroom door waiting for me. She's ditched her black jacket and looks marginally less stuffy. In her hand is a monogrammed Vera Bradley lunchbox.

"Mind if I eat lunch with you?"

I know Ian will groan when he walks in and finds her at our table. He hates new additions, thinks they mess with the sacred casualness of the lounge. Still, I shrug and smile. "Sure thing."

When we arrive, I take my seat and start lining up my food. Today's provisions include leftover spaghetti, green beans, and half a Hershey's bar. We'll fight over the chocolate for sure.

Ashley's hand hits my arm and she pinches hard. "Oh my god, *who is that guy?*"

I don't know who she's referring to because my focus is on her fingers. She's about to tear my skin off. I extricate my arm and sooth the ache. All the while, Ashley straightens her shoulders and fluffs her hair. Her finger brushes against her front teeth to confirm nothing is lodged there and then she smiles extra wide. I follow her gaze and find Ian over in line for the microwave. It looks like he brought leftover spaghetti too. That's what happens when we eat the same dinners most nights.

"Is he a teacher?" she asks, all breathy and bothered. She sounds like she's having a hot flash.

"That's just Ian."

Just Ian is the biggest understatement of the century and Ashley knows it. He looks like a Hollywood actor trying to portray a normal teacher, and he's not even doing that great of a job. Her gaze cuts to me and she frowns, deeply confused about how a man as handsome as him could have a modifier like "just" before his name.

"Do you know him?"

"Yeah. He and I are good friends." *Best* friends.

"Oh, okay." Her smile slowly spreads even wider, and it makes my stomach hurt. "Is he single?"

NO. No. Nah. Nope.

I look down at the table and force the truth out. "Yes."

A record screeches to a halt as all eyes whip over to me. Forks pause midway to mouths. Gazes widen. Birds turn their heads to look and smack into buildings.

A chair grinds beside mine and I glance over my shoulder to find the Freshman Four staring in my direction. They're the popular posse all grown up—the teachers who run the cheerleading and drill team programs at Oak Hill. They also have never met a Botox needle they didn't like.

Their leader, Bianca, leans her eyelash extensions closer and hisses, "Wait, I thought you and Ian have been dating for like...ever?"

I turn in his direction, worried he can hear this conversation. Thankfully, the PE teacher has engaged him in some kind of discussion over near the microwave. She's the only woman I've ever seen who could challenge him in the height department.

"Yeah. What are you talking about saying he's single?" her minion, Gretchen, chimes in. "You've been dating for years!"

"What?" I shake my head adamantly. Cold sweat breaks out on my brow. "No we haven't."

"Are you serious?"

"We all just thought—"

Clearly, there's been a misconception about us. Because we're friends and we spend so much time together, everyone naturally assumes we're an item. I am horrified to think this rumor has circled back to Ian. What if he thinks I perpetuated it?

"No, no, Ian and I are just friends."

Gaping mouths shift into curling pleased grins. My words are a waving checkered flag. Game on.

Ian joins us a few minutes later and I want Ashley to disappear so we can talk in private. I need to tell him what just happened and make sure he knows the truth. I did not ever once tell people we were dating. I have no idea how the rumor got started.

Ashley introduces herself and her hair shines like sunlight. "I'll be here for a few months. I'm subbing for Mrs. Baker while she's on maternity leave."

"Cool. Nice to meet you. Sam, what kind of trade package can I put together for that Hershey's? I really need it today."

"What? Oh." I nudge the crinkly wrapper to his side of the table. "You can have it."

"Really? I'm willing to part with these Cheez-Its—your favorite."

I've lost my appetite and I can't look at him, instead I shake my head and focus my attention on my spaghetti noodles. "Thanks, but I'm not that hungry. Just take it."

"Where are you from, Ian?" Ashley asks with dialed-up enthusiasm.

"Here. Sam, why are you being weird?"

I laugh an octave too high, like *ha-ha-ha what in the world are you talking about?* I know I'll have to meet his eyes so I can maintain plausible deniability. My gaze pings from my spaghetti, to Ashley, to the ceiling, to Ian, then back to my spaghetti. There. Nothing's wrong.

"A hometown boy, that's cool!" Ashley replies. "I grew up about an hour away in a small town called Frisco."

"You're hardly touching your food," Ian points out to me.

I inhale a mouthful of spaghetti to prove him wrong. I chew and chew, but the food stays lodged in my mouth. I'm forced to wash it down with a dramatic amount of Ian's water.

Ashley continues on, oblivious to the fact that no one's

paying her any attention. "Yeah, Frisco is okay, but Oak Hill is so much nicer. Maybe you can show me around sometime. So what do you teach?"

"Chemistry."

Her hand hits his arm. "No way! That was my favorite subject in college."

I want to ask her to name a single element from the periodic table. One. Also, I want to stick my fork in the back of her wandering hand.

A shadow suddenly falls over our table and I glance up to see the Freshman Four looming over us like vampires. They're smiling at Ian, fangs out, ready to suck.

"Ian! Hey!" Bianca says like they're old friends who talk all the time. "We were wondering—when's your next soccer game?"

He frowns, deeply confused by the question. "Next Thursday."

Bianca claps. "No way! That's perfect. We don't have cheer or dance practice that day."

"We'll be in the stands! Look for us!" Gretchen says a little too enthusiastically.

Bianca elbows her out of the way and smiles.

"Soccer? Are you a coach?" Ashley asks.

Bianca's gaze slices to her. "And you are?"

"Oh, um, I'm Ashley, Mrs. Baker's new sub."

"Since when do we let subs into the lounge? Anyway, Ian, let us know if the team needs any snacks. We can bring those little orange slices and Gatorade!"

"I'll make homemade granola bites!" Gretchen volunteers.

"Stop being desperate, Gretchen," Bianca hisses.

The rest of lunch is a complete shitshow. Ian barely has time to eat his food as he's inundated from all sides by single white females. I always thought the idea of a guy needing to shoo women away with a stick was hyperbole, but Ian looks like he could use a broom right about now. I feel bad for him, but I feel worse for me. Before this lunch, Ian's popularity was on a low simmer. Women still clambered for him, but they kept it at normal, restrained levels. I realize now it's because they assumed he was off the market, and my stupidity might as well have just pasted a *for sale* sign over his right dimple.

What the hell have I done?

Chapter four
Ian

Every year the Oak Hill choir does a fundraiser in the two weeks leading up to Valentine's Day. For $5, they'll deliver a single red rose to a student of your choice. $10 and they'll deliver a rose and a candy bar. For $20, your unsuspecting crush gets all that plus a teddy bear, and for $50, they will assemble the jazz choir to serenade the person of your choosing smack dab in the middle of the school day.

It's ridiculously disruptive.

Teachers aren't supposed to get involved, for obvious reasons.

Still, Sam and I have abused the system for the last three years.

The first year, I had them sing "I'm a Barbie Girl" to her during her first period. She got me back with "I Like Big Butts".

Last year, we mixed it up. She had them perform an original poem she'd written, mostly to amuse my chem students. It featured lines like *Don't be so Boron, Mr. Fletcher, or one day you'll find all your students Argon.*

For the kids, it's fun and probably a little cringey, but also a bit confusing.

"Why are you and Ms. Abrams sending valentines to one another?"

Who cares. It's the best $50 I spend all year.

Because of our knack for torturing one another, the choir kids know we're easy targets. This year, I've already had a handful of them hit me up for a donation. I keep sending them away. I haven't thought of the perfect song yet even though Valentine's Day is only a week away.

During fourth period, another boy in an OHHS Choir t-shirt knocks on my door. He's carrying two teddy bears and five roses.

"Another delivery, Mr. Fletcher!"

My students cheer.

"How many girlfriends do you *have*?" one bold teenager asks, sounding impressed.

I remind the class they only have five minutes left for their pop quiz. There are audible groans and then pencils start flying across paper.

The choir student gets the idea and tiptoes into my class to deposit my gifts discreetly. I brace for the worst, but fortunately, they're not all for me—only half. I add the flowers to a coffee cup on my desk and the bears get tossed in the pile by my bag. To an unsuspecting passerby, it looks like I have a fetish for plush.

My collection has been growing out of control over the last few days. At first, I assumed Sam was pranking me. It makes sense; the quartet isn't all that funny anymore. I thought this year she had changed tactics, but then I started reading the accompanying notes.

The gifts aren't from Sam, they're from other teachers around the school. Today's lot is from Bianca and Gretchen. Bianca has even taken the time to kiss her card with red lipstick so when I open her note, it accidentally smears across my thumb. My face is a mask of disgust as I wipe my finger on the edge of my seat. *Get it off, get it off.*

The choir student turns to leave but I grab hold of the back of his shirt. He stumbles and I right him.

"How much longer is this fundraiser going on?" I ask, desperate.

"Another week," he replies, whispering out of respect for my students taking their quiz. "Hopefully we'll meet our goal and then we can all fly to Disney for nationals and compete on the main stage!"

He says "main stage" with stars in his eyes. He's mistaken my desperation for curiosity.

I nudge my chin toward the leftover roses and bears in his arms. "Who are those for?"

He grins. "Abrams. We're not supposed to take notice of this sort of thing, but you two have the highest number of admirers so far this year!"

"What? Who? How?"

His smile falls and I realize I'm gripping his shirt so hard, I stretched out the collar. I let go and smooth it out. I should probably stop touching him now.

"What do you mean?" he asks.

He's nervous. His wistful tears have turned into fearful ones.

I lead him out of the classroom so our conversation isn't overheard.

"So those gifts are for her?"

He nods slowly.

"Let me read her notes."

His eyes are two round saucers as he clutches the gifts to his chest. "You can't! I'm honor-bound to protect the sanctity and privacy of—"

I pry one of them out of his shaky grasp. The kid will need counseling after this encounter.

Roses are red.

Violets are frilly.

You're the hottest teacher at Oak Hill.

Let's Netflix and chill-i?

That scholarly piece of verse was penned by Logan, the defensive coordinator for the football team. I'm not too worried, because I know Sam well enough to be sure she won't be wooed by an offer of sex and stewed meat.

"Hand me the next one."

"Mr. Fletcher, please! Have you lost your moral compass?!"

He checks back and forth down the long hallway, nervous to be caught as my accomplice.

I rip it out of his hand. The next note is marginally better because it's not masquerading as a poem.

Happy Valentine's Day, Samantha!

Maybe you and I can grab coffee sometime if you're up for it?

That one is from the photography teacher, Malcolm. He's Sam's type, in that he barely reaches my elbows.

"How many notes have already been delivered to her?"

"I-I don't k-know," he stammers. "I was only put on delivery duty this morning!"

Her collection is probably as full as mine.

Shit.

I know Sam has had her fair share of admirers at Oak Hill. She's the perfect blend of sweet and sexy. She's nice to everyone. She smiles and remembers birthdays. Her brand of humor is addictive, and it's the combination of these qualities that puts her squarely on every male's radar. For a long while now, there's been a rumor going around that we're dating, and I made a point to never confirm or deny it. It made my life a lot easier if people thought we were a couple. That all changed yesterday. I don't know what she told Ashley during lunch, but since then, I've had three guys come to my classroom trying to glean information about Sam.

"What's her favorite flower?"

"What's her favorite color?"

"Is she into chocolate?"

What the fuck kind of question is that? Are there people walking around this planet who *don't* like chocolate?

"How much do you have left for your personal fundraising goal?" I ask the kid while he moans about probably being kicked out of the Cupid Corps.

My proposition is understood immediately and he regains his composure so quickly, I'm convinced he has a future in Broadway.

"$250," he states with an even, no-nonsense tone.

"That's a lot of money to try to make the old-fashioned way. How good are you at keeping secrets?"

He shrugs, feigning boredom. He inspects his fingernails. Good. He gets it.

"Every time Ms. Abrams gets something from an admirer, deliver it to me instead. Every delivery gets you $20."

His brow arches. "I know you're on a teacher's salary, but I think you can do better than that."

I wish it weren't against the rules to smack students.

"$50."

He reaches out to shake my hand. "Pleasure doing business with you, Mr. Fletcher."

I justify my actions by telling myself my monetary contribution is going to charity. Those pimple-faced kids will get to sing on the main stage because I can't stand the idea of Sam having coffee with another man.

By the time my free period rolls around, I have four more bears for myself and five for Sam. I have the accompanying love notes stuffed in my desk drawer. I feel itchy about my deception, especially when she walks in and eyes the collection amassed behind my chair.

Her brows perk up. "Quite a few admirers you have there. I've only had one paltry rose delivered today."

What the hell? How did the rose sneak through? Kids these days can't be trusted for shit.

"Who was it from?" I ask, continuing to grade pop quizzes as if her answer doesn't interest me.

"PE teacher."

"Mrs. Lawrence?"

"Yup. You're not the only one she's into."

I smile, pleased.

"Gonna go for it? You never struck me as someone who might play for the other team."

She picks up one of the bears and looks at it longingly. "You know what, Fletcher? I just might."

🍎

That weekend, we have to attend a housewarming party at Principal Pruitt's place. It's not our idea of a good time. Sam meets me at my house beforehand and when I open the door to find her wearing a red dress, I decide I need a shot of Fireball. I pour one and Sam insists she needs one too. I hope we don't keep going shot for shot, because she's about half my bodyweight.

She's extra smiley tonight, a real charmer. Everyone in our group at the party is hanging on her every word. She looks so hot in her dress. It's not too low-cut, but even still, my mind fills in the gaps. I excuse myself to get us drinks and spot Principal Pruitt manning the grill. He's wearing a loose Hawaiian shirt and a plastic lei around his neck. He tips his Corona in my direction, but under no circumstances will I be getting sucked into a conversation with him over the subtleties of different wood chips for grilling. I motion toward the drinks and he shoots back a thumbs-up.

I'm surprised there's alcohol at this party. It's not a school-sanctioned event, but all the staff is here. I suppose it makes sense, though—with the Hawaiian shirt and free beer, Principal Pruitt is trying hard to be the cool dad of the administration.

"Maaan, that superintendent is so stiff, but you can come to me about anything," he said last week after a district meeting, clapping me on the shoulder. *"I always want to have relaxed, open channels of communication between myself and my staff."*

I should tell him saying phrases like "open channels of communication" makes him sound more like a suit and less like one of us.

I'm popping the top off a beer when Logan, the football coach, steps into line behind me.

"Hey man, cool shirt," he says with a bro nod in my direction.

I wasn't going to come tonight, but Sam insisted we had to show our faces. While I napped on the sofa, she yanked clothes out of my closet for me. The simple blue shirt was her doing and doesn't really warrant a compliment.

"What's the brand?" he asks. "Calvin?"

"Who?"

"Klein. Anyway, I saw you came with Samantha tonight. You two are just friends, right? That's the word on the street."

I respond with exactly half a nod and half a shake of my head. The gesture gives me a believable story in case Sam asks me about this conversation later.

"I don't know how you do it, man. She's so bangin'."

He says this while looking at her, and I have no choice but to follow his gaze. Her red dress is spaghetti-strapped and cuts off at the middle of her thighs. She brought a jacket with her but left it in my car since it's unseasonably warm for early February. Maybe we should move north, somewhere with chunky scarves and puffy jackets you have to zip to your chin.

Her red hair is piled high in a wavy ponytail and her cheeks have a rosy tinge to them. Her skin is glowing. She asked me in the car if she should add lipstick in her signature shade of red—side note: I now start drooling at the grocery store in front of the Red Delicious apples—and thankfully she listened when I responded with a gruff no.

"Jeez, fine. No lipstick then. Why are you driving so fast? I thought you didn't want to go to this thing."

I was driving fast because I had to keep my right leg straighter than usual to hide...well, she just looked great in the dress.

Logan clears his throat, and it's obvious he's waiting for me to give some kind of response. He wants me to acknowledge her hotness, but I don't.

He doesn't leave.

I take a swig of my beer and he rubs the stubble on his jaw.

"So yeah, anyway, could you help a brother out? What kind of food does she like, what kind of music does she listen to—y'know, insider information."

Abso-fucking-lutely.

"She's a big fan of that fermented shark stuff from Iceland, and her music tastes are pretty specific, mostly polka-pop and yodeling."

My tone is hushed like I'm in on a conspiracy.

"Damn, freaky." He grins. "What kind of guys is she into?"

"Gentle. Meek. Don't make her laugh. She wants a serious poet type."

His eyes light up. No doubt he's considering the shitty stanza he penned earlier. It's still stuffed in my desk drawer. I smell chili on his breath.

"What else?" I ask.

"If I ask her out, where should we go?"

"The zoo. She adores seeing animals in cages."

She hates it. If she weren't scared of the consequences, she'd figure out a way to set them all free.

"Really? Isn't that a little too kiddie for a date?"

"Sam's a kid at heart."

That's my first piece of truth.

He nods, taking in my information with a big smile. This guy really thinks he's going to get Sam—*my* Sam.

"All right, cool. Really appreciate it, man."

I'm on my way back to her when I get intercepted by another guy—the photography teacher, Malcolm. He really is small. He and Sam could fit together nicely on a twin-sized mattress, and there'd be room for a Husky at the very end.

"Hey, Ian. I was wondering…um, did Samantha mention my note or anything to you by chance?"

"Note?" I sound truly perplexed.

"Yeah. I sent her one of those Valentine's gifts from the

choir kids." He rubs the nape of his neck like it's a nervous tic. "It was a stupid idea."

"Ohhh, now that you mention it, I did see some crumpled up paper in her recycling bin yesterday."

He frowns, bummed. I want to feel bad for the guy, but I don't. You know what's hard? Try having a crush on her for three years and then come talk to me.

"Maybe she didn't get it yet. Maybe the crumpled paper was something else."

"I dunno, those little Cupids are pretty prompt with their deliveries."

I'm hoping he'll feel disheartened by the amount of competition and move on. Instead, he smiles like the nice guy he is. "You know what? Maybe I'll just ask her out in person. My therapist is always telling me to step out of my comfort zone."

What the...? He sounds serious, like he's really going to ask her out—and worse, Sam might actually say yes. She once told me she thought Malcolm took "pretty cool pictures". What the hell is going on? I need to know what Sam did to tilt us out of the perfect state of balanced homeostasis we've been in for the last few years.

When I make it back to the group, I pass her a lemonade and she acts offended that I didn't get her a beer. I offer her a sip of mine and her face contorts with disgust after she samples it.

"Ugh. Bleh. Tastes like cat pee. I just don't understand how you do it."

I don't know how you do it, man. Logan's words echo in my head.

"Come here, I want to show you something."

She follows me away from the group and I lead her toward a small garden near the toolshed so we're out of earshot from the rest of the party. It's early February, so nothing in the garden is green. Principal Pruitt still needs to clip away the dead plants from last season.

"What'd you want to show me?"

"Oh, this." I thump on the side of the shed. "Isn't it cool? Bet Principal Pruitt can fit a lot of tools in there. Anyway, you know how a lot of people at school always assumed we were dating?"

My question throws her for a loop. Her dark blue eyes widen then squint up at me in confusion. "Yeah, pfff, so ridiculous right? Why? What is this about?"

I drag a hand through my hair, unsure of how exactly to explain this. "Well, now people seem to think otherwise."

"Oh, well, yes." She looks away as if calling the conversation to mind. "That new girl Ashley asked about us and I told her we were just friends."

I internally groan and she gulps down half her lemonade. I think she's scared, and a moment later, when she starts rambling, my suspicions are confirmed.

"Listen, if you've heard I've been propagating rumors that we're a couple, I haven't! I mean, that's…yeah…" Her cheeks are the same color as the cherry red lipstick in her bag. Her fair skin means her emotions bloom right on the surface, and usually, I like it. Right now, I love it. "Obviously…I haven't been doing that."

Right—*I* have.

"So I guess everyone overheard your conversation with Ashley?"

She rolls her eyes as if exasperated. "The teachers' lounge has never exactly been known for privacy. It's why the Freshman Four came over and asked about your soccer game. I think they all have crushes on you."

"Shit. I kinda liked the misconception."

"Because everyone left you alone?" She frowns. "Are you mad at me for blowing it?"

I don't know...maybe. I'm definitely angry, but I can't tell why. Suddenly, I feel like I'm at the starting line of a marathon and the pistol was just fired, but I'm not ready to run. My laces are untied. I haven't stretched. For three years, I've sort of just been walking around in track shoes, calling myself a runner.

I'm scared of what will happen if I try to sprint now, but even more scared of what will happen if I don't.

Too bad.

The race for Sam has begun whether I like it or not.

Chapter five
Sam

I've been to every one of Ian's soccer games. He's the head coach for the JV team and takes the gig pretty seriously. The soccer program at Oak Hill is actually pretty well known across the state, and they haven't lost a game in two years. Even so, JV games aren't all that exciting. The fans usually include four or five overzealous parents, one stoner kid who was going to be out under the bleachers anyway, and me. I've never missed one of Ian's games because I know if I were involved in any kind of extracurricular activity (pfff, hilarious), Ian would be there to support me too.

Today, however, the bleachers are filled with half a dozen

female teachers, including the Freshman Four. They're sitting on the bottom bleacher in a little pack, forming a makeshift cheering section. One of them made a sign with sparkly glitter just like the one that now sits crumpled up under my feet. They're treating this early season game like it's the World Cup finals.

They chant, "Ian, Ian, he's our man. If he can't do it, no one can!"

The overprotective moms in attendance glare, unhappy that their motherly enthusiasm is being eclipsed by horny teachers. The referee tells them to stop disrupting and my grin is so wide, I think it'll stay there permanently. Then Bianca stands up and takes Ian an ice-cold Gatorade, a lemon-lime love potion. I want him to swat it out of her hand, or better yet, untwist the cap and dump the contents on her head. Instead, he takes it and offers her a warm smile and thanks. When he takes a sip, it feels like I'm watching them make out. I fight the urge to fire up the groundskeeper's riding lawn mower and chase her around the field.

Ian goes back to coaching, and Bianca walks back to her friends with swaying hips and a gloating smile. They all high-five her and she says proudly, "That's how it's done."

I stomp a little harder on my poster.

The last week has been nearly unbearable as I've watched teachers fight for Ian's attention.

To all of them, he's been my toy for the last few years, and now that I'm not playing with him, why shouldn't they get a turn? If we were on a kindergarten playground, I'd stand on their chubby necks and demand they leave him alone. The teachers would drag me off to the principal's office and I'd kick and flail, promising swift retribution for anyone who touched him while I was in the slammer.

A camera flashes from the edge of the bleachers, momentarily blinding me.

I turn and spot Phoebe, from my first period, aiming her lens right at me.

She waves and announces loudly, "Just getting photos for my newspaper assignment!"

Wonderful. She's finally decided to do some actual work and it's at my expense.

The game lasts for a short eternity. They go into overtime. Ian looks hot as hell on the sideline in his coach's jersey. The Freshman Four are champing at the bit. The wind keeps whipping my poster board and flecks of glitter lodge themselves in my eyes. By the time Ian and I are walking to his car after the game, I look like I've been crying.

"You didn't use the signs," he points out.

I glance down at where I have them folded under my arm. "Oh…yeah. They're silly. I didn't want to be a distraction."

I try to stuff them in a trashcan we pass by, but Ian insists he wants to keep them. "You spent a lot of time on them."

"Not that long," I say, quick to clarify in case it saves me from looking desperate.

I don't want to seem like I'm in the same boat as the Freshman Four—who, by the way, catch up to us in the parking lot and ask Ian if he wants to go with them to dinner to celebrate winning the game. They don't extend the invitation to me, going so far as to say the restaurant they picked only has tables that accommodate five people. *That's the best lie you can come up with?*

I open my mouth to let out the string of curse words I've been holding in for the entirety of the game, but Ian quickly declines their offer and drags me off to his car.

"Everything copacetic over there?" he asks as we drive home.

I have no clue what he's referring to. Oh right—in the last few minutes, I've grumbled and yanked on my seatbelt when it wasn't cooperating, fiddled with the air conditioning because it was too cold and then too hot, and adjusted the sun visor up and down half a dozen times before giving up altogether.

"Fine. Just hungry."

He buys this excuse. "All right, I'll feed you, but then I have a special request."

I keep my scowl aimed out the window and grunt in response.

"I need your help."

"With what?"

"I was having a tough time motivating my guys at the beginning of overtime, so I promised if they won this game, I'd dye my hair blue."

My attention whips back to him. "What?!"

He's wearing a small teasing smile as he stares out the front windshield.

"Just temporarily. I already bought some stuff that should wash out within a week."

"You'll look ridiculous."

No he won't.

"It's all for morale. Sometimes you have to be unconventional."

"Okay, but why do you need my help?"

"I don't want it to look stupid and uneven."

So that's how Ian ropes me into helping him dye his beautiful brown hair a shocking shade of electric blue. As soon as we get home from the game, he showers while I transform his kitchen sink into a salon.

When he steps out of the bathroom, steam billows out with him. Time slows. The sultry sounds of "Let's Get It On" by Marvin Gaye play in my head. He's barefoot, wearing athletic shorts and a t-shirt. His short hair is damp and a few strands are plastered to his forehead. His eyes are bluer than blue when he assesses me coolly.

"Ready for me?"

DEAR GOD YES.

I gulp and remind myself of his actual meaning.

"Sure thing."

I pat the chair and tell him to take a seat.

"The instructions say to start with damp hair, so step one is complete."

He leans his head back and stares up at me. The position reminds me of that iconic upside-down Spiderman kiss with Tobey Maguire and Kirsten Dunst.

His lips are so inviting.

"Okay, now what?"

I realize he's asking me a question a second too late. "Huh?"

"What next?"

"Oh." I swallow and turn my attention back to the box.

"It says to drape a towel over your clothes so they don't get stained."

He stands back up and yanks off his T-shirt.

Whoa!

"It didn't say strip!" I shout, covering my eyes.

He laughs and grabs a kitchen towel to drape over his broad shoulders. It's not quite big enough, so he's forced to grab one from his bathroom. When he walks back out, he explains, "I like that shirt, don't want it ruined."

"I'll be careful," I insist, peeking at him from between my fingers. "You can put it back on." I withhold a desperate *please*.

"This is easier."

I force out a resigned sigh and drop my hand.

He sits, leans his head back again, and closes his eyes. It's a gift. He's saying, *Here, take your fill, and I won't even watch you while you do it.*

Ho ho ho, Christmas has come early.

I've seen Ian shirtless exactly 23 times. Half of those occurrences have been innocent in nature: beach days and pool parties. The rest have been stolen glimpses of him while he's changing in his room. Yes, that's right—sometimes, I'm a sneaky little voyeur. I just can't help myself.

Still, this feels different. He's never just been shirtless like this around me. At the beach or at the pool, we're outside and there's room for my desire to swell and expand. Here, in his kitchen, it dwells like a physical presence.

My gaze skates gently across his abs and I note the grooves like a toddler counting up her blocks. One, two, three, four, five, six...I wonder if his skin would feel hot or if it just looks that way because it's tan.

I pinch the collar of my shirt and tug on it, trying to

increase airflow.

It's like we're in a pressure cooker.

He peeks one eye open. "Are you going to start today, or...?"

"Yes. Obviously." I grasp blindly for the instructions and shake them out. "I'm just giving you time to change your mind about ruining this thick head of hair. Your mom is going to kill you—and me."

He smiles. "Wouldn't happen. She likes you too much."

Then he closes his eyes again and this time, I am dutiful and stay on task.

I put on the nitrile gloves and pick up the bowl of blue dye. After a concentrated breath, I dip my fingers in the goop and start to disperse it across his hair. At first, I try to keep my distance. I'm standing as far from him as possible, bent at 90 degrees to reach his head, but my lower back aches in protest after a few seconds. I'm forced to step closer, but apparently it's not close enough because Ian laughs and reaches for me.

"You're getting it everywhere, c'mere."

His arm loops through my legs and around my left thigh so he can tug me toward him. Either he underestimates his strength or I'm just weak because when he pulls, I lose my footing and collapse against him, and worse, I can't steady myself because my hands are covered in blue goop. We're connected whether I like it or not. My hip hits his shoulder. My thigh is brushing his bicep. My boobs are inches from his face. He squeezes my leg to help stabilize me and his fingers are touching the sensitive skin above my knee. For a second, it feels like he's skimming them back and forth on purpose.

My entire body clenches in anticipation of what will happen next. We've never been this close for this long.

My breath is held hostage in my chest. His eyes are still closed.

My mouth is open, and I'm about to whisper his name like a question, but he pushes me back to standing on my own before I can. His arm drops from my thigh then his hands go right back to resting on his abs.

I force a slow, steady exhale I hope he can't hear.

After that mishap, I'm The Flash through the remainder of the dye job. I run my fingers through his hair, saturate the strands, and try to stay calm during the parts where I have to lean over his body to get to the other side of his head. I can feel his breath on my neck. A fireworks show makes its way down my spine.

If he's affected by our proximity, he doesn't let on. He could be napping for all I know.

When I'm finished, I step back. "Okay. Now we're supposed to let it sit for a few minutes."

He opens his eyes and offers me a devilish grin. "How do I look so far?"

I sigh, slightly annoyed with the results. "Not nearly as dorky as you should. Half the team is probably going to copy you."

"So I'm a trendsetter?"

He chuckles and turns to stare up at the ceiling. His fingers drum on his abs.

I rock back on my heels and reach for my blue-fingerprint-stained glass of water.

"What should we do while we wait?" I ask.

"How about I do you now?" he suggests.

I spew water all over the counter and break out into a violent coughing fit. Ian cycles from amused to concerned as he realizes I might actually be choking. Embarrassed, I turn to walk away, but he pinches my shirt and pulls so I plop down backward onto his lap. He slaps my back until the coughing subsides.

"Okay, I think I'm good," I say, trying to stand up and run out into traffic, but now his hands are on my waist, holding me in place.

"Did you think I was coming on to you?" he says to the back of my head.

We're too close for comfort, but the lack of eye contact has made him bold.

"I just misunderstood the question," I answer, feigning calmness.

"*Interesting.*"

I roll my eyes. "Oh please. Obviously I didn't think you wanted to like…*do me.*"

His fingers dig into my hips, and I think he can feel my pulse respond.

"Hmm, but it seemed plausible enough to inhale half a glass of water."

"Whatever. I was just woozy from the noxious hair dye fumes."

I try to wiggle out of his hold, but he doesn't let me.

I give up and hold stock-still, afraid the slightest movement might turn this friendly, lifesaving lap-sit into a $10 lap dance. The thought sends a new flush to my cheeks.

"I don't smell fumes, just your body wash. You've used the

same scent for three years."

He doesn't sound like he's trying to be funny. He sounds feral.

"I'll change it if it bothers you," I say, breathless.

"Don't."

I'm having wild ideas: *Maybe I should turn around and kiss him. Maybe I should finally find out what he tastes like.*

I catch our bizarre reflection in the window in front of me and an alarm whirs in my brain. *STOP THIS! STOP!*

I jump up and clap my hands. The noise is like a freight train, interrupting the tension building between us. "Oh! Time to rinse your hair!"

It's only been like two minutes, but he doesn't question me. He shakes his head and looks away.

After rinsing off in the shower, we see it was a success.

Ian's hair is blue.

My cheeks are still red.

Everyone at school goes crazy for Ian's new do. It's such a cool, shocking shade that the students call him a badass and the female teachers now think he has some untapped wild side. In the teachers' lounge, they whisper about him looking like a rock star.

I'm glad the color isn't permanent. His constant workouts mean he has to shower frequently, and soon, he'll be back to generic ol' Ian. Of note, I find that if I call him words like generic in my head, it's easier to make it through the day.

Here's how it works: *Oh, him? That's just plain ol' Brad Pitt. Meh.*

See? I bet you don't even think Brad Pitt is hot anymore.

As the blue fades from his hair, Ian's collection of valentines grows more out of control. He donated two large trash bags full of teddy bears the other day. The children's hospital called the local news and they tried to film a feel-good puff piece about the gesture. *Local Teacher Bears Gifts for Sick Kids.* Thank god he declined an interview. The last thing I need is for him to go viral. Can you imagine the YouTube comments?

Granny330: *Back when I was in school, teachers could still spank students—I wouldn't have minded so much if it were him doing it!*

SoccerMom88: *I think we need a few more parent-teacher conferences...*

TeachersPetXOXO: *Van Halen's "Hot for Teacher" anyone?*

He donated the roses as well—to me. I didn't want to accept his crummy secondhand flowers, but he insisted. They're stinking up my entire apartment. Every time I look at them, I'm reminded of my competition. After only a day, I decide to toss them and tell him they were carrying a fungus.

Thank god Valentine's Day is this weekend. The fundraiser will be over soon, and those choir dweebs will get their trip to nationals—Ian's admirers have made sure of it.

The only downside is that the end of the fundraiser brings with it the most lovey-dovey holiday of the year, the one I'll get to endure alone for the third year in a row.

Fortunately, I have a busy few days ahead of me to distract me from my bleak and desolate future.

Ian and I have to run that sex-ed course on Friday, then we have the Oak Hill Valentine's Carnival on Saturday morning, and finally, as if my life couldn't get any sadder, Ian surprised me by announcing he signed us up to chaperone the Valentine's Day dance on Saturday night.

"You're kidding me."

"What?" he asks, feigning innocence. "Do you have other plans?"

"I might."

"Valentine's Day is only three days away," he points out, oblivious to how pathetic I feel in this moment.

"Yeah, well...Logan came by my classroom earlier and said he wanted to talk to me. Maybe he's planning on asking me out."

It's a stretch, but still, it feels good to let Ian know I'm not a hopeless loser. Logan probably just wanted to chat so he could convince me to give extra credit to one of his players, but I don't have to admit that to Ian. In fact, I can tell him anything I want.

"Logan?" he asks, displeased. "Football coach Logan? Never met a tub of glossy hair gel he didn't like Logan?"

I will admit, Logan's hair is sort of crunchy, but I force enthusiasm when I reply, "He seems nice enough."

"No. Come on, you're chaperoning the dance with me. I'll treat you to dessert afterward."

Looks like that's how I'll be spending Valentine's Day this year: with my plain, un-sexy, definitely-doesn't-turn-me-on platonic pal, Ian—oh, and a couple hundred high school kids.

Chapter Six

Ian

I've decided to finally pursue Sam, but I haven't had the courage to actually get to the pursuing part. For days, I've wavered back and forth on the best plan of action. You can't just be friends with someone for three years then turn to them one day over lunch and ask them out on a date.

Sam would laugh and assume I was joking. My pride can't take that.

No. I have to employ tact, have to seduce and tempt her organically, like the other day in my kitchen when she was dyeing my hair. I knew there was something there, we were both just too afraid.

"I think I'm going to ask Sam out on a date," I tell my mom on the phone Wednesday night.

"OH MY GOD."

She drops her phone in shock and the screen shatters. She can't call me back. This is why I don't tell her things.

A few minutes later, I get a call from my dad's number. Apparently, she stole his phone so we could continue our conversation.

She's sniffling and when I push the subject, she admits she's been crying.

"I'm just so happy. You two have been dancing around each other for years and I truly can't imagine a more perfect woman for you."

"She hasn't said yes yet. In fact, I haven't even asked her."

"Oh, she will. Believe me, she's going to say yes, and who knows?! By this time next year, I might have myself a daughter-in-law! AND GRANDBABIES!"

Obviously it was a mistake bringing my mom in on my plan. I usually keep her on a strict need-to-know basis as it makes my life a lot easier. In an attempt to be a better son, I thought I'd tell her about Sam.

The next day, she won't stop texting me.

Dad: *At the Apple store! They're replacing my screen. This is Mom by the way. Have you asked Sam out yet? Let me know how it goes! *confetti emoji* *heart-eyes emoji* *champagne emoji* *bride emoji* *groom emoji**

baby emoji
baby emoji
baby emoji
baby emoji
baby emoji
baby emoji
baby emoji

I don't text her back.

She persists.

Dad: *Can you even imagine? I hope the children get her hair!!!*

Dad: *Mom again. About the hair, your children would look good with your hair too, I would just really love a little girl who looks like Sam.*

A few minutes pass.

Dad: *Now I feel bad saying that. You're cute too. Really.*

Dad: *Son, it's your father. I need my phone back. Please tell your mom you'll call her back when you have a minute.*

Dad: *Also, what the hell are you waiting for?*

Not him too. I wonder if I should block them, but they'd probably just get new numbers. I'm tempted to call AT&T and have them cut text messages from my contract. In fact, I would if I wasn't currently on the phone with Sam.

We're talking through our curriculum for the sex-ed course tomorrow morning. Most of it's preplanned for us, but Sam wants to be extra prepared.

"Why don't you just grab a condom or two from your house for the demonstration?" she asks. "Oh wait, will they still unroll if they're all expired and dried up? Don't want to embarrass ourselves in front of the kids."

"Hilarious. Make sure to bring your 55-gallon barrel of lube."

"Ha. Why me—don't you keep any around?" she asks, truly perplexed.

"I don't usually need it."

"Oh because the women who make it to your house are just little gushing Niagara Fallses 24/7?"

"24 is a stretch. I'd say it's only during the act, so, three, usually four hours."

She snorts. "Ooookay Casanova, let's hope you're keeping these mythical moist maidens properly hydrated. Jesus, I hope you offer them a Gatorade on the way out."

I lean back on my couch and smile up at the ceiling. Bantering with Sam is my favorite part of the day.

"What else do you think we should bring? Some of your heavy-duty, gas-powered vibrators?"

"To save space, I'll just bring the small one. I named it Ian—just a coincidence, no relation."

We're joking, but the idea of her naming a vibrator after me (even if it's anatomically incorrect) makes my stomach squeeze.

Usually, I'd back off and steer us back toward friendship territory.

Tonight, I decide to push it. It's called recognizing an opening when you see it.

"How often do you use him?"

I catch her audible intake of breath.

"Ha ha. Ian, c'mon, we need to focus or we won't have anything to tell the kids in the morning. So far we're just going to unroll a condom onto a banana—which, despite how common that seems to be in sex-ed pop culture, I've never actually done. What if it breaks? The boys will be turned off of safe sex forever."

"Just let me handle it."

"Do you think we should make up a rap or something, just so the lesson is more easily digested?"

"Absolutely," I reply, deadpan. "I'm going to go out on a limb and assume you've already come up with something."

"Oh, yeah. I mean, nothing major."

Then she immediately breaks it out.

"My name is Sam and I'm here to say,
sex can be fun in a healthy way.
You've got your condoms, lube, and some toys,
but just say no to those unprotected boys."

"That was off the top of your head?"

She doesn't sound the least bit embarrassed when she replies, "I workshopped it during fourth period. Also, let's just say I didn't win the sixth-grade talent show for nothing. I went the middle school version of triple platinum."

"I want that footage."

"Pfft. You wish. Luckily for me, my dad had the lens cap on the camcorder the whole time."

There's a break in conversation and my thoughts tiptoe

right back to her vibrator. I want to know if she was telling the truth.

"How long have you had *Ian*?"

"Why do you care?"

"Call it boredom."

"If you're so bored, I have some papers you can grade for me."

"Okay then, call it curiosity."

Silence follows. Her footsteps echo through the phone. I wonder if she's in her room now. A door closes and then she sighs. "A few years."

"So he's probably in need of replacing?"

"I don't use him all that often."

"Poor little Ian."

"Don't you worry about him, he's doing just fine."

"What about you? Are *you* doing just fine?"

"Ian..." she chides.

"Sam..." I taunt.

I swear I hear her open and close a drawer on her bedside table.

I smirk and imagine her slipping out of her pajama shorts and panties.

Now I want to say, *Poor little Sam. Using a vibrator in lieu of the real thing? She deserves better.*

"Where are you?" I ask.

She sounds nervous when she replies, "In my apartment."

"Obviously. Where in your apartment?"

"Does it matter?"

"You're on your bed, aren't you?"

"You know I don't have any other comfortable seating in

this place. When your furniture is all from Craigslist, you end up just lounging a lot."

"You're living in delusion, Hot Lips."

"Don't call me that."

She sounds pissed—pissed and turned on.

Sheets rustle on her end of the line.

I want to FaceTime her. In fact, I don't question the urge. I do it.

"Why are you trying to FaceTime me?!" She sounds extremely distraught.

"Why aren't you answering?"

"I'm not decent!"

"Just like I thought," I gloat. "We're best friends, which I thought meant we don't hide anything from each other. Answer it."

"No."

"Then it's a pretty easy guess for what you're doing. Tell Ian hi for me."

The FaceTime connects immediately and her frazzled appearance hits my phone's screen. She's sitting up against her headboard. Her cheeks are pink and her mouth is so soft and feminine I have a sudden overwhelming urge to feel it wrapped around me.

She's wearing a tight cotton tank top, no bra. She's holding the phone so I can only see the top half of her: her creamy shoulders and chest. Her nipples are pebbled and I want to take each one into my mouth. I'd be gentle, *giving*. I'd trace my finger beneath her collarbone and make her blush everywhere. Poor little Sam is right—she'd crumble for me.

"See?" she says with a got-you smirk. "You're not decent either."

She's referring to the fact that I don't have my shirt on. I didn't bother after my shower.

"Yes, but unlike you, I'm wearing pants."

It's a guess, but when her eyes go wide and her blush blazes even harder, I know I'm right.

"Yeah…well…" She clears her throat and averts her gaze to something off-screen. "It's really hot in here—stuffy."

"Well yeah, I imagine things heat up when little Ian is on the prowl."

"That's *not* why I'm hot. I just worked out."

Who the hell does she think she's fooling?

"You're such a bad liar."

"So what?!" She's exasperated by this conversation. "I'm a liar and you're clearly horny as hell. Why don't you call one of the Freshman Four? I'm sure they could help you out—y'know, give you a refresher course before tomorrow morning. You clearly need it."

"You're right, I do."

She swallows slowly. The phone wobbles in her hand.

"Do *you*?" I ask.

She rolls her eyes toward the ceiling. "Why do you think I'm on those dating apps? It's not to meet friends. Now are you going to suggest you can 'help me out' like this is a low-budget porno?"

"You've clearly never had phone sex. You're pretty bad at it."

Her blue eyes hit mine. "*What*?"

"This isn't how it usually starts. I ask you what you're

wearing and you tell me, but I already know: white tank top, panties, nothing else."

"Ian."

My name is a warning, a buoy telling swimmers to turn back now, but I'm sick of warnings, so I head out to open waters. It's time to test a theory.

"Want to ask me what I'm wearing?"

"I bet I can guess: black workout shorts, Calvin Klein boxer briefs."

Interesting. Maybe Sam *does* watch me when I change.

"And...I *have* had phone sex before. Don't think you can intimidate me with this weird game you're playing."

One of her hands disappears from the screen and I know she wants to touch herself. Maybe her hand is on her thigh. Maybe she's barely spreading her legs, trying to convince herself she's only adjusting her underwear. I bet soon, her fingers will skim along the hem of her panties, brushing the silky material against her wetness. She can't take them off or I'll notice. No, she'll just have to tug them to the side if she wants to feel skin on skin.

"But I think I should hang up the phone now," she says, breathy.

"Or you could let me finish what I've started."

"I don't know what you're talking about."

Her innocent act is poorly constructed. I bet she's barely touching herself and trying to talk herself out of it, but it's too late. I know it's been at least a few months for her. I know deep down, she's as starved as I am.

"You want to pretend? Let's pretend. We can call this research for tomorrow."

"What?"

"Me making you come right now."

"*Jesus* Ian."

I could say the same thing to her. She thinks I'm the only one seducing here? She's a walking seduction. Even now, she's biting down on that full bottom lip and I'm seconds away from wrapping my hand around my dick. Her white tank top is paper thin. The hints of her I can see beneath it are driving me to the brink of madness.

"Tell me what you're doing with your hand, Sam."

"Flipping you off."

"Be honest."

"Ian, this is—"

"A fantasy, remember?"

For a long moment, our eyes lock on screen and I'm watching the cogs spin in her head. She wants this and at the same time, she doesn't. I think I have her but I know at any moment, she could press that little red circle on her screen and deny us both.

I don't say a word as I wait for her to make a decision.

I won't coerce her any more than I already have.

Finally, her velvety voice spills through the phone. "Okay, you want to play? I'll play. I'm...touching myself."

"How? Over your panties?"

"Yes."

"Pull them aside."

Her eyes pinch closed.

"Sam," I say, reaching down to adjust myself. My dick is begging for attention, but I want to concentrate on her. "Pull them to the side and tell me how wet you are."

We've probably spoken hundreds of thousands of words to each other throughout our friendship, but right now our sentences sound like they're being spoken by strangers.

Her head tips back and her gaze hits the ceiling. She's exposing her neck. If I were there, I'd drag my teeth along her pulse line.

I hear a little rustling and then her eyes flutter closed.

"Very."

I grin. There, I just proved my point from earlier.

"I'll have a courier bring over a bottle of Gatorade after this."

Her eyes flick open. "*Ian*!"

I wish I could wipe away my expression, but I can't. This is too good, too many years in the making.

"Brush your finger up and down. It's not your touch, it's mine, and if it were me, I'd be thorough. I'd take my time and sink my fingers into you so slowly, and in return, you'd sink your teeth into my shoulder to keep from moaning my name."

I know she's listening to my commands because her breaths get shorter and shorter. I see nothing from her waist down, and yet I feel like I have a front-row seat. My imagination runs wild. I've been in that room. I know her sheets are white. I know her panties are usually lacy and thin. She likes wearing color. Her skin does too. She's flushed from head to toe, no doubt.

"I want you to slide your middle finger inside and imagine it's me."

She shakes her head, but I know she's listening to me. I know she's doing it.

"If I were there, I'd tug those panties off and press your open thighs against the bed."

She chuckles. "I'm not that flexible."

I smirk. "I know for a fact you are."

In the next instant, she drops the phone and the screen goes black. For a second, I think she's gone, but I can still hear her breathing hard, sheets rustling, fabric slipping down her legs.

Fucking hell. She's stripping off those panties.

"How long has it been since someone tasted you? And I don't mean some rushed foreplay, the two obligatory licks, Sam. I mean face buried between your legs, tongue plunging deep over and over again."

"Ian...please..."

"I want to *taste* you."

She's panting.

So close.

Her breaths are shorter and shorter.

Her legs are trembling.

I'm imagining her on that bed, pink and wet and so very good at listening.

"I'm so close, Ian."

"Imagine how well we'll fit, Sam. Imagine how easily I'll fill you up."

"*Ian*...I'm—"

The rest of the sentence dissolves and so does she.

She's fisting her sheets, about to come undone just from the sound of my voice.

"I'll be so gentle at first, but you know what? I've been lonely way too long and I need to fuck—hard."

I know she's seconds away from letting me hear her come and then—suddenly the line goes dead.

She hung up on me.

Damn.

I smirk.

Another man might feel deprived, but I don't.

This is just the beginning, and she should know that.

I text her a few minutes later when I know she's lying on her bed, the residual waves sending shivers down her body. She's flushed and panting, trying to reclaim her breath. I know she's freaking out over what just happened, but I'm not.

Ian: *Next time we'll do that in person.*

Chapter Seven

Sam

It's the morning after THE PHONE CALL and I've developed some kind of PTSD. I don't answer Ian's wake-up call, mainly because I don't need to. I'm already awake and in my kitchen, scrambling eggs. On my counter, there's bacon, fresh blueberry muffins, sliced fruit, coffee, and orange juice. I look like a mom on a sitcom. Any minute now a teenage boy will stroll in with bedhead. I'll tell him to sit down for breakfast and he'll say, *Mom, UGH, I'm late for school!* I'll throw a granola bar at the back of his head as he walks out the door.

I have all this food because I woke up and decided I

needed a hearty breakfast. I need to get my strength up for the day ahead. No low blood sugar for me, not if I intend to be a strong counterpoint for this new version of Ian. Ian 2.0: sexy devil, husky phone-sex operator.

Last night I let him lure me into some weird scenario in which we weren't Ian and Sam, best friends. We were just playing a role: Ian and Sam, horny teenagers. *Plausible deniability.*

I wish I could call in and take a personal day, but they don't exactly give teachers a million days off. I refuse to waste one because I'm scared to face Ian. I doubt he's scared to face me. No, not after that text message he sent last night. It's clear he's the one holding the cards.

I pull the text up again, just to confirm I wasn't dreaming. Yup, there it is.

I shiver, lock my screen, and go back to shoveling food into my mouth.

My outfit is picked out strategically. When I stroll into school an hour later, I'm wearing a dress that could easily be worn in a historical reenactment at Plymouth Rock. The black garment goes down to my lower calves and buttons all the way to my neck. The frilly white lapel adds a nice, colonial touch. It's actually my funeral garb, which is appropriate because last night, my old way of life with Ian died.

Teachers stop me in the hall and ask if we're supposed to be wearing costumes today. *"Shit, it's not Dress Like a Literary Character day, is it?"* They're not even pulling my leg; they're genuinely confused. I decide I can unbutton the top a little. My cleavage is still completely concealed, but the circulation in my neck is able to return.

I turn the corner into my classroom and spot Ian waiting for me. He's sitting in my chair, feet propped up on my desk. I jump a mile in the air. My Tupperware falls to the ground and the lid pops off. Muffins spill out.

"Jesus, Ian!"

He's calm and bored when he replies, "Funny, you said the same thing last night."

My eyes go wide and I whip my head back and forth down the hall.

"You can't say things like that! Are you crazy?!"

I fall to my knees and start shoveling muffins back into the Tupperware. Ian doesn't bother helping, just watches me with an amused little smile.

When I stand back up, he tilts his chin in my direction. "What a dress. Did you wear it for me?"

"Are you asking if I've thought about you since our phone call? Because no, I haven't. I forgot you existed."

"You look like an American Girl Doll named Chastity."

"And you look like you're trespassing. Why are you in my classroom?"

He stands and saunters over, reaching around me to shut the door.

Alarm bells ring, both from the fact that he has me cornered against the door and because he felt the need to close it in the first place. I reach back and twist the door handle, but his hand hits the wood beside my head, not hard, but he exerts enough pressure to keep me from opening it.

Slowly, I glance up into a pair of familiar blue eyes that are currently doing wholly unfamiliar things to my body. My stomach is clenched. My fists are clenched. My jaw is clenched. Everything is rigid and coiled tight like a spring. I'm liable to strain my spleen or something if I keep this up.

I think he's going to try to pick right up where we ended last night. My suspicions ping louder when he steps closer. Our bodies barely brush.

God, he really is tall and foreboding. There's a reason I've never dated a guy as big as he is. He's the horse and I'm the jockey—except jockeys get helmets and whips. I have nothing to defend myself from him, just muffins.

He raises his hands, and my eyes pinch shut.

I'm being completely irrational. I know that, but like I said, his size is intimidating. I should have opted for some kind of platform heel this morning, maybe stilts. Even a pogo stick would allow me to be at his eye level for milliseconds at a time.

Something hits my chest, and it could be a bomb for all I know. Seconds tick down and we could both explode. I relish the idea—I'd love to be put out of my misery.

"Open your eyes, Sam."

His tone is teasing and light. It's the way Ian 1.0 used to sound, so I pry one eye open and then the other. I glance down.

He's pressing a blue Gatorade bottle against my chest.

An innocent little sports drink.

"Relax."

"You're not going to kiss me?"

"Do you want me to?"

My eyes stay glued to the bottle. "I don't know. I can't feel my feet and first period is going to start soon."

He steps back and shakes his head. "Drink up. You look thirsty. And did you forget? No first period today. We have to go teach that sex-ed course."

Every single junior and senior fills the bleachers in the gymnasium. Ian and I are standing to the side, waiting for the principal to introduce us. This is going to be an absolute shitshow. On their way in, the students were supposed to drop an anonymous question pertaining to sexual education into a shoe box. I'm holding it in my arms and it's hefty. These teenagers are curious little bastards.

"Do you have the penis?" Ian asks.

I hold the banana up. It's a week old and speckled, rather sickly-looking, actually. Maybe I'll also use it to demonstrate the dangers of STDs.

"Do you have the condom?"

He tugs it out of his back pocket. The words MAGNUM and RIBBED FOR HER PLEASURE leap out at me like a blinking neon sign.

"You're kidding."

He seems confused.

"You just brought that over from your stash?" I ask, sounding like a mouth breather.

"That's what you said to do."

I don't have time to question him because our names are announced over the microphone and then we walk onto the basketball court to a lot of applause and conversation. It takes minutes to shut everyone up and grab their attention.

The first half of the course is by the book. Principal Pruitt asked us to outline the most common STDs and transmission pathways while an accompanying slideshow plays on a projector behind us. Every new image brings a chorus of groans and covered eyes. One kid passes out and has to be carted to the nurse's office.

"Icky!" a girl shouts from the front row.

"Yes," I respond solemnly. "Neurosyphilis *is* icky, and deadly. Now, that brings us to the next part of the course: a demonstration of proper condom application techniques. Ian, the prophylactic, if you please."

He smiles and shakes his head, tearing open the rubber while I hold the banana outstretched in front of me. I let him explain the best way to unroll it as he's obviously more experienced than I am, a fact I try not to dwell on. After that, Principal Pruitt takes the banana and parades it around the gymnasium so everyone can see it. He's Vanna White's forgotten stepsister.

Next, we start on the shoe box questions. Ian dips his hand in, grabs a folded slip of paper, and hands it to me, and then I read each one aloud.

I was hoping for deeply mature questions, and I don't get a single one.

"What is the average penis size?" I read aloud, provoking snickers from the audience. "Oh, well, yeah…why don't we have Ian answer this one?"

He isn't even a little embarrassed as he replies confidently, "Guys, don't be so preoccupied with that sort of thing. Most women aren't. It's made out to be a big deal in pop culture, but the vast, vast majority of you will fall somewhere around 6 inches by the end of puberty."

He turns back to me and my eyes say, *What about you, Mr. Magnum?*

He sighs and reaches in for another question.

I make a critical error when I read it aloud before first reading it to myself. "Mrs. A is hot and…" My voice fades out as I crumple it up. "Okay. Very funny. Ian, next."

He passes me another question quickly while shooting the boys in the audience a menacing glare.

"Is it possible for a woman to have more than one orgasm during a round of sex?" I read aloud. This question feels deeply personal and I hate that I'm blushing as I reply, "Off the top of my head, the answer is yes."

The question gets discarded quickly and I shoot my hand out for another one, refusing to meet Ian's bold gaze.

"Can you get pregnant from dry-humping through your Nike shorts?" My face scrunches and I turn to Ian. "I don't think…actually, they're sort of porous, aren't they?"

Ian groans and yanks the slip of paper out of my hand. Then he leans over and speaks into the mic, "No. No, you cannot. Still, wear a condom—problem solved."

Three-fourths of the way through the questions, I look up and spot a boy in the front row of the bleachers looking shell-shocked. His eyes take up half his face.

"Oh shoot," I curse under my breath. "Hey, Johnny, can you go sit out in the hall? Your mom didn't sign your release form for this."

Principal Pruitt rushes forward to usher him out. "Just forget everything you saw today, buddy."

There's no doubt we've created lasting scars, for the kids and for ourselves.

After another thirty minutes of prolonged torture in which I do a poor job of answering questions, we're done, and Ian walks me back to my classroom.

There's nothing to say, so we stay perfectly silent.

We're alone in the hall. I'm hugging the shoebox full of leftover questions against my chest.

I have no clue what we used to talk about. Did we ever have things in common or was I delusional? I can't think of a single thing to say to him that doesn't include the Gatorade or our phone call from last night. *Oh, duh!*

"What a nice spring day it is," I say wistfully.

We pass a window and it's pouring outside. Tree limbs fly this way and that. A small tornado tosses screaming livestock here and there.

"Yep. Nice," Ian says with a knowing smile.

"All right, fine, let's just go back to not talking at all. That's easier."

"I'm giving you time to calm down."

"Calm down!? *CALM DOWN*?!"

His eyes slice over to mine and he raises a brow. *Right.* If we passed by a mirror, I'm sure my reflection would horrify me. My hair is probably standing on end, light-socket chic. My eyes are shadowed and wide. I'm minutes away from getting stuffed into a padded room.

"Last night was probably hard for you," he continues.

Yes, phone sex was such a trying experience. I'm fatigued just thinking about it.

"And I know you want to pretend like it didn't happen so

we can go back to normal…"

Yes, yes. I cross my fingers and toes hoping he's about to say what I think he is.

"As friends."

Right.

As Chandler would say, *That would be perfection.*

"But—"

"Samantha! Hey Sam! Wait up!"

We both turn in sync to find Logan jogging down the hall in our direction.

"Hey," he says, coming to a stop and propping his hands on his hips when he reaches us. He's not even breathing hard. If I tried to jog down the hall, I'd have a cramp in my side.

"Oh, hey Logan. What's up?"

"Not much. Sup Ian."

Ian's grunt is aggressive. I frown and try to catch his eye, but Logan speaks up first.

"I was wondering if you'd had the chance to read my little…poem yet?"

My face scrunches in confusion. "Poem?"

He grins, and he's not the ogre I thought he was. He has nice arms, a kind smile, hair that's been trimmed recently. "Yeah, I included it with a teddy bear…for the choir fundraiser thing?"

I've only received a couple red roses, no bears. Ian has the monopoly on those.

"Sorry Logan, I didn't get any poem."

"Sam, we should get going," Ian interjects. "We'll be late for next period."

Logan shrugs good-naturedly. "It probably got lost with all the others. You've got quite a few admirers this year from what I hear."

What in the world is he talking about?

"Oh...um, huh."

Does he realize I'm spending tomorrow alone? Chaperoning a high school dance? I'd win a *Most Likely to Cry Herself to Sleep on Valentine's Day* contest handily.

"I won't let that deter me though." He grins. "Did you do something different with your hair today? Looks great."

I reach up and touch the loose, wavy strands, taken aback by the sweet compliment.

"Don't you have somewhere to be Logan?"

He laughs, clearly mistaking Ian's question for politeness. "This is my off period. Anyway, Sam, if you're free—"

His voice trails off as he meets Ian's eyes. Something there warns him to quit while he's ahead.

"Free?" I push.

"Tomorrow."

"She's not," Ian says sharply.

I grimace. "I'm supposed to volunteer at the carnival in the morning and then I have to chaperone the school dance."

He rocks back on his heels. "Oh, gotcha."

My heart is crumbling for him. He had the courage to ask me out in front of Ian and I don't want to turn him down outright. "But maybe on Sund—"

Ian wraps his arm around my shoulders and redirects me down the hall. "Say goodbye now, Logan."

"Oh. Uh...bye. Wait!" Ian doesn't wait. "Okay! I'll talk

to you later, Sam. Maybe we can try to work something out another time?!"

I'm not given a chance to reply because Ian turns a corner and takes me with him.

When we're out of earshot from Logan, I wiggle out of Ian's hold.

"What the hell was that?"

He shakes his head and directs me into my classroom. For the second time today, he closes the door behind him. We're alone and he's pacing like a caged lion. I feel the need to flee. I want to crack a window and stick my head out and heave in gulps of air. The rain would pelt my face, but it'd be worth it.

Instead, I walk to my desk, uncap my Gatorade, and take a long swig. When I swallow, I remember something.

"Do you think he really sent a bear and it just got lost in transit?"

Silence.

"Ian?"

"Possibly. You know how those choir kids are."

No, actually I don't. Is he suggesting they're criminals? They spend their time binge-watching *Glee* and singing acapella versions of Taylor Swift. They're harmless.

"It seems all of *your* bears arrived on time," I point out.

"Huh."

He hasn't stopped pacing.

"You're being weird. What do you know that you're not telling me?"

He turns in my direction and props his hands on his hips. I wish he wouldn't do that. It's his Superman pose, and today, in his pressed white shirt rolled to his elbows and his black slacks, he could easily pass for Mr. Kent.

"It doesn't matter. You'll laugh when I tell you."

That means I definitely won't.

"Tell me what?"

His eyes narrow, focused out the window behind my head. His features have taken on a stern edge as he replies, "I paid off one of the choir kids to intercept your gifts and deliver them to me instead of you."

What. The. Hell.

"*Why*?"

Maybe I didn't take his supposed bear fetish seriously enough. How certain am I that he donated those bags to the children's hospital? They could be tucked away in his closet, a tiny plush pleasure shrine.

"Why not?" He shrugs, unbothered by my anger. "Maybe I didn't think you should be subjected to Logan's terrible penmanship."

"Real answer."

"That is the real answer. His poem was shit and his handwriting was even worse—scribbles, really."

"Don't try to be cute now." I'm angry—*pissed*. "I can't believe you did that. I've spent the last two weeks feeling like shit because you were getting piles of gifts and I was getting diddly squat. I felt like a lonely loser."

"Sam—"

He tries to step closer and I hold up my hands to block him. I know it's a useless endeavor. If he wanted to reach me, my arms would bend like spaghetti noodles.

"Sam...Samwich...Sam and cheese." Each of my

nicknames feels like he's plucking my heartstrings. He bends so we're face to face. "I did it because it's time you and I stop dancing around the obvious, this *thing* we have between us."

"You're not making sense."

"You're right. I'll make myself clear."

His blue eyes are smoldering and a jolt of fear sparks down my spine.

"Err...or you could just shake my hand, turn, and call it a day?"

He frowns. "What are you scared of?"

I wave off his question. "Oh, lots of things, really. The usual: spiders, roaches, ghosts. Also, losing my best friend because he thinks we should rock the boat."

"It's not like that."

His calm demeanor has me incensed. "What would you call our phone call last night?! Idle chitchat?"

"The exact opposite, in fact. Listen, we're not going to do the friends-with-benefits thing. We aren't going to just have sex and keep things casual."

"Of course. Why would we? That sounds much too easy."

"When you're ready, I'm going to ask you out on a date."

"A date?! I don't even want to hang out with you as a friend right now! You stole my bears, and my flowers!"

"No. *Remember*?" He finally sounds exasperated. "I gave you the flowers."

True, but they burned me up with jealousy so much I tossed them. Now I'm even more angry with him.

I poke his chest and his hard muscle sends a fissure down my finger bone. Great, I've probably broken something.

"Don't try to slip out of this through a technicality, you jerk."

His hand wraps around mine so I can't pull it away, and we might as well be in the 1800s because him touching my hand feels inappropriate and intimate and are there nerves in your hand that connect to your groin?

"I'll buy you a million bears if that's what you want."

Good, let's focus on the real issue. He lied to me and betrayed me, but it's the conspicuous lack of dime-store bears I'm truly angry about.

"No! Nothing you do can make up for this...this *deceit*!"

The very edge of his mouth tips up. "You're being dramatic."

"Unhand me."

He steps back and pinches the brim of his nose like he's trying not to laugh—or scream.

"Clearly you need some time. Do you want to bike together to the carnival in the morning?"

"Absolutely not."

He steps back and heads for the door. "Then I guess I'll just see you there."

Yes! YES YOU WILL!

Chapter Eight

Ian

For the record, I didn't volunteer to sit in the dunking booth at the Valentine's Day Carnival. Someone (take a guess) wrote my name in bold on the sign-up form. Conveniently enough, she opted to operate said dunking booth, meaning she'll get to watch me get drenched dozens of times in between taking tickets and resetting the dunk mechanism.

The carnival officially starts at 10:00 AM. I was hoping the storm from yesterday would preclude the outdoor activities, but probably due to Sam's voodoo magic, the sky cleared up and the rain gave way to a warm front from the south. It's sunny and there's not a cloud in the sky. I'm up on the platform, waiting to be dunked, and Sam is down on the ground chatting with Logan. He brought her coffee this morning. How charming. Oh, and there's a small teddy bear too. Sam hugs that bear against her chest like she's never wanted anything more in her entire life. The show is for me.

"Let's get this party started!" someone shouts near the back of the line.

Yes, there's a line.

There are so many people lined up to dunk me I'm sure the astronauts can see the queue formation from the space station.

"Kyle, come dunk Coach!"

"Steven! Mr. Fletcher is in the dunking booth!"

Bianca is first up. She's wearing a teasing little grin, and every time I accidentally look her way, she waves excitedly.

Sam cuts in front of her and holds out a palm impatiently. "Tickets."

Her bear is forgotten somewhere and Logan is gone.

"How many?"

"Five. Read the sign. Next."

"Here!" Bianca says impatiently, shoving a pile of tickets at Sam. "Just take them all."

Sam feeds the tickets into an empty coffee can then hands Bianca three balls.

She's about to let one loose when Sam cuts in again. "Hey! Scoot back! You're supposed to stay *behind* the white line."

Bianca misses every one of her throws. Her balls land with soft thuds in the grass and when Sam turns to pick them up, she's wearing a big ol' smile. Our gazes lock when she comes near the booth to pick up a particularly bad toss, and that smile fades.

"What?"

"You've got your work cut out for you," I say, tilting my chin toward the line.

Her eyes narrow into slits. "You know they just want to see you in a wet t-shirt."

"Funny, that's the same reason I wanted to sign you up for the dunking booth."

"NEXT!" she shouts.

The Freshman Four each take a turn, and not one of them hits the target. The crowd is starting to grow anxious. Like a medieval mob, they want action. They're out for blood. Sam picks up another round of balls and turns to take them to the next contestant, but then she hesitates, spins on her heel, and studies that target. Her head tilts and I can see her mind at work. "Maybe the people just need a little tutorial."

She takes one hesitant step toward it.

"You wouldn't dare."

"I have no clue what you're talking about."

Another step.

"Samantha Grace Abrams," I warn.

It's no use. She takes one more step then proceeds to feign a huge, slow-motion tumble in which she trips forward and has to break her fall with one thing: the target.

The platform disappears out from underneath me with a quick *whoosh* and then I drop into the water.

Fucking hell. Warm front or not, it's still February. The water is cold.

When I surface, Sam's standing just on the other side of

the tank. We're at eye level. She's sweet and innocent, a baby lamb.

"Oops."

"If you step any closer, I'm bringing you in here with me."

Her eyes widen and she scurries back to the line of contestants.

The dunkings are sparse throughout the rest of the morning, until the Freshman Four subcontract the throwing work out to a few sharpshooting baseball players they were able to find. "Just helping raise money for the education foundation!" they explain, fanning themselves while I clamber back onto the platform. "It's all for...for the kids."

Additionally, Sam dunks me at least a dozen times by herself. Any time I grow courageous and toss out a barb or a flirtatious comment, I go under. By the end of my shift, my t-shirt is plastered to my skin. My hair is slicked back. I feel invigorated and refreshed. By contrast, Sam is sweating. Her eyes stick to my wet shirt and then she peels them away slowly. A moment later, they slingshot right back to where they were.

"How you feelin' down there, champ?"

"Hush up, you."

A replacement arrives to relieve me of my post: Mr. Jones, the potbellied basketball coach. As soon as we swap places, the platform creaks and the line disperses. People scatter and flee the scene.

"Aw c'mon now!" Mr. Jones teases. "Just 'cause I don't have washboard abs like Mr. Chemistry Man over there?"

When I reach Sam, she hands me my towel and keeps her focus on the sky.

"Here, cover yourself. You're indecent."

"I'm wearing a bathing suit and a t-shirt."

"Yes, and women have been going into shock all morning at the sight. I've heard the first aid tent has run out of beds, so just do us all a favor."

"*Us?*"

"Shut up. C'mon, you're going to treat me to lunch for subjecting me to the last two hours of torture."

"Hold on, I have a dry t-shirt I want to change into."

I lead us into the deserted field house behind the carnival. Sam crosses her arms and watches as I shake out my hair and tug my shirt off overhead.

"WHOA! Warn a girl, will you?"

I shake my head and bend down to riffle through my bag for my dry shirt. I take an obscene amount of time. Sam fidgets and groans, and eventually she bends down and yanks the bag out of my hold.

"Here, just let me."

We're so close, and I realize now that Sam's not completely dry either. She's been standing next to the booth all morning getting splashed. Her white T-shirt clings to her body the same way mine did. I can see the outline of her pale pink bra, the curve of her breasts.

"You're dripping on me," she says, though her voice has lost all of its edge.

"Sam—"

"Hold on, I'm going to find it."

She thinks my gruff tone is from annoyance, but she's wrong. I'm seconds away from peeling that shirt off over her head. Any other time, I'd do it, but there are students just outside. The timing isn't right.

"Ah, here it is!"

She stands and holds the shirt out to me with a proud smile. I force my gaze north of her neck.

"That one's for you. I knew you'd get wet, so I brought two."

She's perplexed. Her head tilts to the left and her soft mouth is so fucking close to mine.

She's hesitating, so I pinch the hem of her shirt and shoot her a look: *May I?* For a few moments, she doesn't move. She's calculating her next move, playing out every possibility in her mind. I know she's envisioning me taking her right here. I resist the urge to bite my lip. Eventually, she raises her arms slowly, and I peel the material off fluidly over her head. For a few brief seconds, she's standing there in pale, pink lace and shorts. I can see everything from her neck to her navel. Her bra conceals nothing. Her creamy skin is damp. Her stomach is quivering. She's cold. Goose bumps bloom across her shoulders. My hand reaches out for her waist and my fingers grip her, hard. A war is waging within me. I want to push her up against the concrete wall. I want to dip my fingers beneath the waistband of those shorts and press her cold skin against mine. I could warm her up so easily, *fill* her up so easily.

But, I don't want to be friends with benefits. I want more. Before my resolve cracks, I tug the dry shirt down to replace hers. She's suddenly covered from neck to thighs. Her arms are hidden underneath. She looks like one big black armless blob. *Good.*

"Cute. Now let's go get you some lunch."

f I think I'm going to get any chance to discuss things with Sam during the carnival, I'm sorely mistaken. We're surrounded by teachers and students the rest of the morning and early afternoon. Sam insists on eating a barbecue plate and then a funnel cake and then, while wiping powdered sugar from her lips, she asks if I think it's a good idea for her to get a deep-fried Snickers.

"I think you're getting dangerously close to the competitive eating zone."

She shakes her head. "That's not dangerous, just means I'm getting to my sweet spot. Pun intended."

It's true, she can eat a lot of sugar, but I think she's using carnival food to bury the mix of emotions swirling inside her. My suspicions are confirmed when she is suddenly way too interested in playing all the carnival games. She aims a water gun and throws darts at balloons and tries to land hoops around bottlenecks. She loses at everything and whisks right on to the next activity. I know she's doing it on purpose. She knows we have to eventually address the elephant in the room.

I want us to be more than friends.

Sam wants to continue living in delusion.

By the end of the afternoon, we bike back to her apartment and she's quick to tell me she needs to nap and shower and get ready for the dance. Sugar is crystalized on her bottom lip. Her eyes are wild. If I wrapped my hand around her wrist, I'd feel her pulse pumping a mile a minute.

"Sam, you can slow down. Nothing has changed."

She's already squeezing herself through her half-opened door, pushing it closed behind her.

"Yeah, yeah, I know that. Okay, well bye then! See you at the dance!"

Then the door is slammed shut in my face.

I'd completely forgotten about the dance, to be honest. Back when I signed us up, it was my way of ensuring I'd spend Valentine's Day with Sam even if I wasn't technically *with* her. Pathetic, I know.

I work out and shower, but there are still a few hours to kill. I decide to FaceTime my parents, which I immediately regret because they only care to talk about one thing.

"TELL US ALL ABOUT YOU AND SAMMIE WAMMIE!"

"She doesn't like that nickname," I remind them.

My mom rolls her eyes, pushes my dad out of the frame, and gets so close to the camera that I can see up her nose. "Did you take her out to the Olive Garden yet?"

Why is it that all parents eventually start adding "the" before every single business name? It's just *Olive Garden*.

"No."

"Well you'll bring her home for Sunday dinner soon right?"

"We don't do Sunday dinner," I remind her. "Also, you guys live four hours away."

"Well I'm thinking of implementing it, especially if you start dating Sam!"

"There's a good chance she just wants to stay friends," I say, breaking the news to them and myself all at once.

My dad grunts, steals the phone from my mom, and then I'm treated to a close-up of his ear canal. I'm not sure he realizes this is a video call. "Listen here, son, if you need some tips and tricks, you need to listen to your old man, not your mom."

I wipe my hand down my face. Calling them was a mistake. I'm going to start being one of those kids who only talks to his parents at holidays and funerals—weddings too, if I'm feeling generous.

"I gotta go, guys. Bad connection."

"We can hear you just fine, sweetie!" my mom insists.

I hang up and toss my phone across the couch.

This is a complete disaster. I've thought a lot about how I would transition my relationship with Sam from friends to... more. I was going to do it slowly, carefully. She's like a rabbit, timid and jumpy and mostly wants to be left alone so she can eat in peace. She'll talk herself out of anything if you give her long enough to think about it, and above all, she fears change. Last year, they swapped her classroom and she cried about it for a week. Then, for the next month, she kept accidentally going to her old classroom instead of her new one.

"I'll never learn! This is ridiculous! They can't just move me three rooms down!"

She even typed up a multipage essay outlining why it was important for her to get the use of her old classroom. She printed it out and had me read it aloud over dinner. I made it halfway through then proceeded to rip it up over the trashcan and tell her she was crazy.

We didn't talk for two days.

Eventually, she realized she was being unreasonable.

Another time, I tried to convince her we should move *West Wing* Wednesdays to Tuesdays because I wanted to check out this new trivia night at a bar down the street.

"But it's an alliteration, Ian. West Wing Wednesday— get it? Without the Wednesday, it's anarchy. I won't abide lawlessness."

Some people might think I've wasted good years being "just friends" with Sam when I actually wanted something more, but really, it's provided me vital information I can use to my advantage. I know her favorite things (citrus-flavored candy, especially if it's sour) and I know what she hates (strangers who breeze by without a thank you when you hold the door open for them). I know what kind of guy she needs (me) and what kind of guy is all wrong for her (Logan).

In other circumstances, I would have taken my time during this transition. Phone sex would have happened weeks into dating, after I'd planned and discussed it with Sam ad nauseum. I'd have provided her with diagrams and flow charts. But, Sam ruined that the day she told the school we weren't dating. Sharks prowl in the water now, and I'll be damned if I step aside and let Logan woo her with coffee and cheap teddy bears.

It's time to break out the big guns: Signor Armani.

Chapter Nine

Sam

I can't stop looking at Ian. We aren't even talking. He's across the cafeteria, stationed at the punch bowl, and I'm on the other side of the room, wishing for a pair of binoculars so I can inspect every delicious inch of him.

"Ms. Abrams, you look *radiant* tonight." It's my student Nicholas. He's trying to get my attention. "You know, like Wilbur in *Charlotte's Web*—not that I'm saying you look like a pig, it's just…never mind. Hey, would it be too forward of me to ask for your company during the next dance?"

I shove him a few inches to the right so I can still see Ian over his shoulder. "Yeah, yeah, Nicholas. That's great."

He shrieks. "Are you serious?!"

Oh no. I jerk my gaze toward him and see his eyes welling with tears. What have I done?

"Nicholas, god no. Sorry, I was distracted. Obviously I can't dance with you. I'm a teacher. Principal Pruitt wouldn't allow it."

He fists his hands with determination and spins on his heels. I think I'm done with him for the remainder of the evening but then I catch sight of him over by Principal Pruitt. They both turn in my direction. Nicholas clasps his hands together in front of his chest in prayer. Principal Pruitt laughs and pats him on the shoulder then looks my way so he can throw me a thumbs-up. Oh goody, *permission*—just what I wanted.

Nicholas finds me at the end of the next song. I now notice he's wearing a bowtie and a fancy pair of glasses he must keep tucked away for special occasions. They're horn-rimmed. He's also wearing a boutonnière on the lapel of his tuxedo. Most other students are just wearing jeans. I like the effort and tell him so as we go out onto the dance floor.

"You look so...smart tonight, Nicholas."

"You really think so?"

"Of course."

"Because I was thinking...I know you're ten years older than me, but maybe after—"

"No."

"I graduate, we could—"

"Nicholas."

"Date."

I sigh heavily. "Nicholas, this is just a dance. I'm your

teacher, and while my job is trying at times, you know what's worse than dealing with checked-out seniors who don't care about English? *Prison*. Prison is worse."

There's no deterring him. "That's fine. I hear you loud and clear. We'll revisit the topic when I'm legal."

I sigh and give in to the moment. I'm not hurting anyone, and Nicholas is so damn happy to be out on the dance floor with me. So what if he weighs 95 pounds and is seventeen years old? He likes me! He asked me to dance, which is more than I can say for Ian—who, by the way, is still over there chatting with a few other chaperones, not bothering to look my way.

We haven't spoken all night.

We drove separately.

Principal Pruitt assigned me to the left side of the cafeteria when I arrived earlier. Ian was already stationed on the opposite side. I stashed my cell phone and purse in my classroom and didn't think to bring walkie-talkies, so there's been no communication thus far. I'm not sure he even realizes I'm here. I know this because I've had my eyes on him for 99% of the evening. I can't help it. Tonight, he looks magnificent in a black suit. He's taken the time to style his chocolate-brown hair in some kind of debonair sexy way I've never seen him do before. Usually, the short, slightly wavy strands are free to do what they will. It's cute like that, bedhead chic, the stuff wet dreams are made of. Tonight, he's decided he hasn't taunted us enough already. He wants to make it worse with the suit and the hair and the smoldering gaze. Oh yes, he's stepped it up all right. No doubt his blue eyes are gleaming like sapphires beneath his dark brows. His sharp cheekbones could probably take out an eye.

I shouldn't get too close, not if I know what's good for me. If I'm not careful, I'll sustain lasting damage.

Still...

"Nicholas, hey, twirl me in the direction of the punch bowl."

"Twirl? Uhhh, I didn't make it that far in the instructional dance video..."

I lead us, taking control and basically dragging poor Nicholas across the cafeteria. He trips and tumbles into me. I try to play it off like we're having so much fun and can hardly contain our laughter.

"Laugh, Nicholas," I say sternly.

"You're scaring me."

We're only feet away from Ian now, and I produce a cackle verging on insanity. "Nicholas stop, *stop*. You're killing me."

"Oh my god, am I stepping on your toes or something?"

As a matter of fact, he is, but I ignore the shooting pain and aim a pleasant little smile in Ian's direction. Finally, I catch his blue gaze and he inclines his head with a sexy lift of his brow. The expression says, *Samantha, please. You're fooling no one.*

He wins that round.

My poor feet do not.

Later, as I'm sitting down, icing my toes, I watch as the Freshman Four descend on Ian across the room. They weren't even supposed to be chaperoning the dance and yet here they are, wearing bright dresses in Starburst shades with enough sequins to rival a disco ball. Their seduction strategy boils down to squirrel psychology: to be attractive is to be bright and shiny. Their attack on Ian is coordinated. They each take a cardinal direction so he's surrounded. I watch with glee while he tries to break away from them. If only he wasn't ignoring me, I could go over and help the poor man. He's really done it now. Oh yes, he's going to get it.

Except, a minute later, he holds out his hand and I watch with a gaping mouth as he leads BIANCA out onto the dance floor. BIANCA, the wicked witch of Oak Hill High! She's never looked more smug.

I catch a hint of their conversation and my eyes narrow to slits.

"Bianca *stop, stop*. You're killing me."

Oh, okay, funny man.

They dance dangerously close to where I'm sitting with my ice pack, except Ian knows how to dance, and he also knows how to make Bianca toss her head back with riotous laughter. *Oh please, Bianca. Your sense of humor is limited to the first half of knock-knock jokes. You don't even remember the punchlines.*

When they twirl even closer to me, Ian catches my eye. He tips his head and smiles, so self-serving and congratulatory. I stand up, wince at the pain, and march away as swiftly as seven shattered toes will allow.

I'm not even sure what game we're playing or what the rules are, but I know he upped the stakes with that stupid, magnificent black suit.

I retaliated with a misguided dance with Nicholas, and now he's delivering a backhanded blow with Bianca on his arm. By my count, he's up two to zero. If someone were to ask what the point of all this is, I'd tell them there is a perfectly good explanation but that it's none of their business. In reality, there is no point. I don't know where my motives lie because I don't take a single second to think about them. I'm too busy reacting, strategizing. There's not an eligible bachelor in the room aside from Ian. Principal Pruitt is not only ancient, he's also happily married. Even now, he's out on the dance floor with his wife. They're smooshed together under the disco ball and their love makes me want to spew chunks.

I could have had a date tonight. Apparently, I could have even had *dates* tonight! A veritable reverse harem if only Ian hadn't bribed children to steal from me. I wonder how many bears he intercepted—tens, hundreds, *thousands*? There's no telling. I could have been buried alive in stuffing and fake fur and tiny choking-hazard eyeballs. What a dream.

Even worse, I spent time on my appearance tonight in an effort to make Ian swallow his tongue. I booked appointments for hair and makeup at a local salon and I suffered in a chair with poor lumbar support all afternoon. They did things to my eyebrows. My long hair was twirled, teased, curled, brushed out, and then sprayed in place. Usually, I don't wear much makeup, and right now I feel like I'm about to step on stage at a beauty pageant.

And that's not even mentioning the dress.

It's short and blue and flirty, not so short that students are liable to catch a peek at my privates, but short enough that my legs are "killing it, baby," as the sales clerk noted. I wish I'd just worn a velour tracksuit. I feel ridiculous now that I've gone to all this trouble and Ian hasn't even come over to talk to me.

I hover in the shadows until he's finished dancing with Bianca, and when he's out of sight, I reluctantly retake my post.

It's 8:00 PM. Surely this thing will wrap up soon. Don't these kids have to be in bed by like 8:30 PM?

As if in response to my thoughts, the DJ suddenly switches the music from slow jams to techno, the overhead lights cut off, and flickering strobe lights take their place. The students go wild. The DJ (who, by the way, is just a dorky PTA dad) is jumping in the air, holding his headphones to his ear with one hand, and pumping the other one as hard as he can. He's close to herniating a disk and he doesn't care. For him, this is the final night of Coachella.

"How're your toes?" Ian's voice to my left makes me jump out of my skin and shout an incomprehensible syllable in surprise.

I recover quickly. "Were you just lurking there in the shadows, you creep?"

Technically, now that the lights have been cut, the entire room is shadowed.

The strobe lights are doing tricky things to my sight. Every other second is stolen from view so life looks like a stop-motion movie, and my brain's reaction time is delayed as Ian reaches out to tug on one of my waves. I stand absolutely still, letting it happen and watching in wonder.

"What was it Logan said yesterday?" He has to lean in close so I can hear him over the techno. "Did you do something different with your hair? It looks great."

"Then why have you been ignoring me all night?"

He stuffs his hands in his pockets, and I think it's an

effort to keep from touching me. "I could ask you the same thing."

"You wore a suit."

"You wore a dress."

"We both look like we're going to prom."

"Did you enjoy your prom?"

He looks serious now and I have to look away.

"No. I had to do the thing where I went with friends because no one asked me, but by the end of the night everyone ditched me for boys. It sucked."

"I wish I could have taken you."

The idea is preposterous. I've seen young Ian in framed pictures at his house. There were no awkward teen years for him. You know how in Hollywood they cast 30-year-olds to play high schoolers? That was Ian, tall and strapping even at seventeen. Meanwhile I was teased mercilessly about anything and everything: wild red hair, elf-like stature, bony knees. How's that for fair?

"I could make it up to you now," he suggests, holding out his hand.

My heart tap dances against my rib cage.

"I don't think that's a good idea."

"Why?"

Why?!

"Because I'm like that silly mouse from the children's story. If you give a Sam a dance, she's bound to ask for a kiss. If you give her a kiss, she's going to want…"

My gaze locks with his and my heart plummets. There needs to be caution tape wrapped around his head because his eyes are heated and tempting and I definitely shouldn't get any closer. My body goes haywire. At first, I'm panting and fanning my face. Then my mouth goes completely dry and goose bumps bloom across my skin.

"What?" he persists, stepping closer. "Tell me."

"More." The word rushes out on an exhalation. "I'd want *more*."

Chapter Ten

Sam

Ian isn't touching me, which means he's not technically forcing me, but he's calling the shots all the same. We're walking quietly down the hall. My admission drags behind us like a third wheel. Our gigs as chaperones have ended. A new round of teachers relieved us and now it's time to go home. I need to retrieve my purse, though, and Ian has insisted on accompanying me to my classroom.

His suit jacket is hanging on my shoulders. He offered it to me a few minutes ago when I was rubbing my hands up and down my arms to warm myself up. My little trick worked perfectly. I'm cloaked in *eau de Ian*, an intoxicating blend of spiced cologne and body wash. I tilt my head to the side and sniff as inconspicuously as possible. He still catches me.

"You're weird."

He says it like a compliment, and I don't deny it.

He holds my classroom door open for me and I think he's going to flip the light on, but he doesn't. Moonlight filters in from the half-closed blinds. Just like in the cafeteria, the lighting is playing tricks on my brain. This setting is romantic and mysterious, full of tantalizing possibilities. I need to get out of here immediately.

"Oookay, so I'll just grab my purse and then we can go. Here is my purse, and look, here are my keys."

I think I'm gaining control of the situation by narrating my actions aloud, but Ian has his own plan.

He finds the latest edition of the Oak Hill Gazette sitting on my desk and turns it to face him.

"Oh! That's nothing. Let's go."

It's too late. He's staring down at the front-page story and the accompanying photographs. It's Phoebe's piece, and that photo she snapped of me during the soccer game is front and center. The caption is something innocuous about me watching the game, but it doesn't matter because the picture says a thousand words. At the bottom of the frame, the Freshman Four are tittering over Ian. The rest of the shot is taken up by me, scowling with jealousy. She focused on me rather excellently. It's a great photo, and I'll be forced to give her an A on the assignment.

"Were you not enjoying the game?" Ian asks innocently.

He's fishing.

"Can't remember. C'mon, let's go."

"It's just that you look pretty upset, which is odd considering we had the lead through most of the game."

He's a dog with a bone. I have no choice but to lean over and inspect the picture, pretending to think back on it.

"Oh, yes." I tap my finger against the page. "Now I remember—a grasshopper had just flown into the back of my throat. Nasty thing, really. Where did you park?"

He turns to me slowly and reaches up to touch my cheek. My thighs press together on instinct.

"You're running out of reasons, Sam...reasons why we shouldn't do this."

"Is that supposed to be a riddle or something?"

Our eyes catch and a delicious sense of promise hangs in the air between us. I deflect, poorly.

"Bianca sure seemed happy to be in your arms earlier—think you'll ask her out?"

He stands back to his full height, putting some distance between us. "You gave me no choice but to dance with her. You were ignoring me. I wanted to further test a theory."

"And what was that?"

"Does Samantha Abrams have a crush on me?" His brow quirks. "Does she feel envy?"

"And what'd you discover?"

He steps closer so the tips of our shoes touch. His hands catch the lapels of his jacket where it sits on my shoulders and he tugs me toward him.

"My hypothesis was true. This picture confirms it."

Our chests touch and the warmth of his skin sears me through our clothes. I tilt my head back, back, back until I'm looking right up at him. His thumb reaches up to drag along my bottom lip, and I have to tamp down the urge to draw it into my mouth. I need to know the answer to that age-old question: what does Ian Fletcher taste like?

His head tips forward another inch and I can feel his breath on my lips. It's minty fresh. We're going to kiss. This is going to be a moment I tell my grandchildren about. I will etch the details in stone and send it to the Smithsonian.

Instead, he smiles. "Let's play a game."

My hands, which I'd completely forgotten about, are gripping his hips. I've been pulling him flush against me for the last…oh, several thousand seconds. What little hussies my hands are.

"Fine."

"The game is truth or kiss."

I smirk. "Don't you mean truth or dare? Are you that out of touch?"

"I'm rewriting the rules. I'll ask you a question and if you don't want to answer it…well, you can probably guess what you'll have to do."

Between the two of us, he's the one in charge, the one dressed in black. Me? I'm suddenly sweating under this coat made for giants.

"Seems like a game I'd rather not play."

In a flash, he releases me and steps back. Cold air conditioning replaces his warmth. It's like he's just plunged me in that dunking booth.

"Fine! Okay!" I relent quickly, hoping he'll immediately step close to me again, but he doesn't. He leans back against my desk and crosses his feet at the ankles. The sight throws me into a vivid memory of an old fantasy of mine: the two of us having sex against that desk. I have to look away so fantasy and reality don't start to merge.

"We'll start small. Are you attracted to me?"

"In a general sense?" I wave my hand in circles. "Are bees attracted to flowers? Yes."

My pithy response falls flat. I drag my gaze back to him and find he's crossed his arms. He looks angry, like he wants to punish me, preferably with a ruler. Oh, wait, no—that's the fantasy talking.

"If you're not going to answer honestly, let's not play."

"Yes…I'm attracted to you." I say it like I'm admitting to picking my nose.

It's a terrible habit I really need to work on—being attracted to him, I mean.

He nods, seemingly pleased with the answer. "Even though I'm nothing like the guys you usually date?"

I release a puff of air that sounds like PAH. "Of course you're nothing like the guys I date."

"What does that mean?"

"Is this part of the game?"

The very tip of his mouth curves up. "Yes."

Meaning if I don't answer, we'll have to kiss. Am I prepared for that? His lips on mine?

I shiver at the thought and look down at my newly painted nails so I don't have to watch his reaction while I offer him the truth. "Because you're out of my league, Fletcher, literally and figuratively. You've never dated a woman under six feet. They've all been sturdy and tall. Growth-hormone milk drinkers, if you will."

"Milk drinkers?"

"My mother used to tell me if I didn't drink my milk, I wouldn't grow big and strong. I preferred orange juice, and well, now who's laughing?"

He finds that little insight very amusing indeed. "Adorable."

I want to wrap my hands around his neck and prove to him just how *un*-adorable I can be when provoked. Scrappy is an adjective that comes to mind when people try to describe me. I'm quick in a fight. I can sneak under arms and karate chop you in the kidneys—at least I can in my head.

Ian is looking at me like he doesn't realize my full potential. I sneer.

"You know what? Is this game two-sided? By my estimation, you owe me like fifty honest answers."

"Or…the alternative, if I don't want to answer."

My eyes go wide.

Fifty kisses?! My lips would swell, bruise, fall right off.

His blue eyes promise me if I challenge him, I won't like the results.

I sigh, kick off my heels, and scooch my butt up onto the small desk behind me. "Fine. Keep asking me questions then."

"When did you first realize you were attracted to me?"

Ha.

"Day one. Next."

His brows rise in shock.

"Have you ever been close to telling me the truth?"

"Of course."

"When?"

I shrug. "Maybe three months in, when you'd just broken it off with that dermatologist…but then a guy I sort of liked for a while came back into the picture so I wanted to give it a shot with him."

"Mason," he says confidently. A dark glint shadows his gaze. If we were in a cheesy movie, he'd have said his name while pounding his fist into his palm.

"Yeah, him. Anyway, then you hooked up with that lawyer, the woman who insisted on calling me Samantha and then made it worse by over-pronouncing each syllable. *Sah-mahn-thah*. It's like she had phlegm in her throat or something."

"Karissa. Yeah, she sucked."

"I know."

His eyes narrow. "Why didn't you tell me after I broke things off with her? That was the first time we were single at the same time."

The fact that he knows that is pretty illuminating. If this game were going both ways, I'd interrupt and ask him if he was attracted to me back then too. My pitiful heart can barely handle the possibility that he was—or rather, *is*.

"Sam?"

I stare at a patch of drywall beside his head. "I don't know. We'd settled into a friend routine. It worked and I didn't want to rock the boat."

"And now?"

"Now, I still don't."

It's why I'm playing this stupid game and answering his questions instead of letting him kiss me. *Of course* I want that kiss. Are you kidding me?! Has he looked in a mirror? He's so hot tonight I bet he'd be half tempted to lean forward and lay one on his own reflection, fog up the glass.

"Explain, Sam."

I twist my fingers together and pick at my nail polish. I usually never wear nail polish because picking it off is too fun, like now. What a waste of $30. "It's very simple, really: we have a bird in the hand. You and I make an excellent duo. You're my best friend. Really, actually, now that I think about it, you're my only friend. Everyone we used to hang out with has either moved away or had kids, but not us. We've never grown up or settled down. We still have time for *West Wing* Wednesdays and trivia nights and that one month when I wanted to take up rollerblading and I made you walk beside me and hold my hand."

He suppresses a laugh at the memory.

"Yeah, people thought I was your little sister. Women tried to hit on you because they thought you were a doting big brother, teaching me how to rollerblade like that. Anyway, my point is: I think we've established that this is a super great scenario, and if we decide to start dating, there's a 99% chance it won't work out, and then what? I lose a boyfriend and a best friend in one fell swoop. No bird in the hand, and no birds in the bush. No. I'm not doing it."

"You sound like you've put a lot of thought into this."

"I have. I've even done research. I can recall every sitcom that touches on this topic from the late 1990s until now."

"What about Chandler and Monica?"

"They were just lucky."

"Jim and Pam?"

"Well…it took 'em a while."

"Leslie and Ben?"

"It was rocky there for a bit."

He laughs and pushes off the desk to stand. "I get it now."

He stalks forward like a panther and then he's right there, looming over me. He tips down so his hands rest on the desk on either side of my hips. We're eye level, blue gaze to blue gaze. My knees brush against the front of his suit pants. *Holy shit.* He's big. My eyes grow wide. He lets out a deep breath then glances down. His growl is barely contained to the back of his throat. The bottom of my dress has ridden up to the top of my thighs, and I wish I'd thought to button his coat around me. I need that extra layer if I intend to leave this classroom as put together as when I entered.

I try to slide off the desk, but he doesn't let me. He steps forward and my knees are forced apart.

Now we're wedged together and my thighs are gripping his hips like a pole I'm about to slide down. Firewoman Sam, at your service.

"Is this still part of the game?" I ask, sounding like someone has their hands wrapped around my throat. I'm dying.

"No." One of his hands traces along my jaw. "No more games."

His touch is feather light and I'm embarrassed to find myself leaning into it. I'm a cat, angling for pets.

"The fact is," he says solemnly, "I'm ready to try this out, but you don't seem to be."

He's looking at my lips, studying them like he's going to have to recreate them from memory later.

"So?"

Does that mean he'll take what he wants anyway? Because truthfully, I love that idea—all pleasure and no consequences. He can run his hand up under my dress and touch me like he wanted to touch me on the phone the other night while I pretend like I kept my wits about me. I'll have the moral high road while he explores each of my immoral low roads. Win-win.

"So I'm going to let you slide off this desk and we're going to walk to the parking lot like we always do, as friends."

Is he kidding? I thought this was leading somewhere. My panties are wet because my *entire body* thought this was leading somewhere.

He tries to step back, but my fingers clench the front of his tuxedo shirt in a vice grip and I drag him closer. "Ask me another question."

"No."

"Fine, I'll ask. *Sam, do you want me to kiss you right now?*"

Then I tilt my head and press my lips lightly to his.

Chapter Eleven

Sam

He's so shocked, and for a second, neither of us closes our eyes. We're just two friends with our mouths pressed together. I could be resuscitating him for all anybody knows. But, from this angle, I can see his eyes are eclipsing. For three long seconds, we don't move a muscle. I fall into the Ian ocean, letting those blue eyes completely drown me. We're frozen in time, and I realize we still haven't moved.

He's going to make me do the heavy lifting. That's okay. Years of dating poor kissers have ensured my mastery of the one-sided smooch. One hand skates up over his chest (nice), collarbone (nicer), broad shoulder (nicest), and then it loops around the corded muscle at his neck. My nails drag along the base of his hair and he relaxes against me. I resist a smirk. Step one is complete.

Step two is harder because I have to break the kiss. It's like opening the airlock in space; either the outside door is sealed and we survive intact, or all the air gets sucked out of the moment and I die. For a moment, I keep our foreheads pressed together, but our lips aren't touching. We're oh-so-close and I'm building the suspense by threading my fingers in his hair and wetting my bottom lip. When his hands tighten on my waist, I know I have him, but I have to be sure. The uppercut is when I take his full bottom lip between my teeth. He groans. *Yes, Ian, you'll want to take off that nice suit because I play dirty.*

What the hell are you doing to me? he asks silently.

Beating you at your own game, I mentally reply with a smirk, and then I kiss him again. This time there's no stoicism on his part. He hauls me up against his chest and slants his mouth against mine. It hits me like a ton of bricks that we're kissing. IAN FLETCHER AND I ARE KISSING. I would exclaim this out loud if my mouth weren't currently occupied with something much more important.

Here's the thing: Ian might have been frozen a few moments ago, but he's not anymore. His hands dip under his coat and he pushes it off my shoulders. His palms burn across my neck and then lower, skating the outer edges of my breasts. My nipples tighten. His touch sears. I have no doubt my dress is charred and moments from disintegrating into a pile of ash at my feet.

We're best friends, kissing the exact same way we do

everything else: we take liberties, we go too far, we blur and redraw the borders of our comfort zones.

His hands tighten around my waist and he rocks his hips against me, *grinding*. My fingers curl against his skin and the same adjective from earlier comes to mind: BIG. There's a new one, too: HARD. Full sentences will come later when my brain isn't going haywire.

He rocks his hips again and the gesture says, *Feel this, Sam? That's for you.*

I make a sound in the back of my throat that I've never heard before (a guttural moan mixed with the word "please") and he delivers, gently coaxing my lips apart and touching the tip of his tongue to mine. *Oh yes.* Our PG kiss has turned X-rated. I'm glad to see he's retaliating with vigor.

Don't stop, don't stop.

I've been deprived of this kiss for so long, and now that it's happening, I'd like it to last for at least one to two decades. We'll barricade the windows and door. We'll tear the pages from the English textbooks stacked against the back wall and make a cozy sex nest. We'll survive by taking little nibbles of each other every now and then, like little love cannibals. I'm aware it isn't the most well-adjusted thing to think about during a passionate kiss, but it's just the kind of joke Ian and I would crack up about for hours. It fits.

In an attempt to bring my body completely flush with his, I nearly fall off the desk. He grins against my mouth and I growl in warning. He must be thinking funny thoughts in his head too, which suddenly irks me. I won't share this newfound lust with the old Sam and Ian—they have plenty of things to sustain them, but this red-hot fire is the only thing keeping this moment going.

To prove my point, my hand hits the top of his suit pants. His smile disappears in a millisecond and our kiss ratchets up another few degrees. As a reward for his superb skills, I think I'll let him peel me out of this slip of a dress so we can fulfill every fantasy I've ever had. What a genius idea. Let's get to it.

I slide my hand farther into his pants just as a loud shrieking bell blares overhead, piercing the walls of my quiet classroom. We leap apart so fast I have to reach out to stabilize myself in order to not tip backward off the desk.

Principal Pruitt's voice sounds over the PA system next. "Those were some excellent dance skills, Oak Hill students! I wish we could party all night, but it's time to head home. Please proceed to the carpool lane if you have a parent or friend picking you up. No loitering!"

Then his voice cuts off. *Ugh*. Imagine if your boss had the ability to pipe in his stupid voice while you were in the middle of life-changing sex. Mood officially killed.

Ian and I stare silently at one another.

I'm breathing like I just climbed Everest. I think my heart is palpitating.

I want to pick up right where we left off, but I'm frozen.

Ian looks perfectly relaxed. His breathing isn't even labored. You'd never know I just assaulted him except for the fact that his hair is adorably tousled and his shirt is extra wrinkled thanks to my greedy little pincers.

When I push off the desk and try to stand, my knees decide to function less like bones and more like jelly. I play it off by acting like I wanted to crumple to the floor anyway. I *do* need to put my heels back on.

He steps forward and helps me to stand. Then he grabs his suit jacket and rights it on my shoulders with gentle care.

"Come on. If we don't hurry, they'll lock us in here overnight."

He makes it sound like that'd be a bad thing.

"We have snacks, right? I think I still have one of your Clif Bars under my chair..." I trail off.

He shakes his head and turns to walk out into the hall. I have no choice but to follow.

We barely make it a few steps before a security guard aims an accusing flashlight at us. The hallway isn't even dark. It's a little overkill. "Hey! You kids were supposed to stay in the cafeteria."

"We're teachers," Ian says smoothly.

The security guard purses his lips in disbelief and grumbles under his breath as we pass, "I'll be the judge of that."

"I think we're going to get detention," Ian jokes.

I don't laugh. My sanity is crumbling.

He glances over at me, and whatever he sees makes him shake his head with annoyance. *What? Do I look that bad?*

"Just remember when you go home and freak out, you did this to yourself."

"What?"

"You're spiraling."

I laugh like a shrill lunatic. "No, I'm not!"

I am. A soft breeze could topple me. I don't let him touch me when we get to my car. I'm scared I'll latch onto him again, which would be terrible because we aren't alone anymore. There are other people out in the parking lot—teachers, chaperones, Principal Pruitt. He waves at us as he and his wife head to their car. Ian and I smile and wave like plastic figurines. Our body language says, *No kissing here! None at all! Just two well-behaved employees!*

"I thought you two left after you finished your chaperoning duties?" he shouts from a few cars over.

"We were going to, but then Ian got sick." The lie sails off my tongue effortlessly. I want to pat myself on the back.

"Oh no." Principal Pruitt frowns. "What do you have, son?"

"Food poisoning," I supply for him. "You know how it goes—out both ends, pretty bad. I had to unlock the supply closet to get more toilet paper for him."

"Yup. Sam had it too, even worse than I did. Never heard anything like it before in my life."

I resist the urge to stomp on his foot.

Principal Pruitt looks deeply concerned. "Now that you mention it, you both look like you've been through the wringer. Did you guys share food or something?"

We swapped some saliva—does that count?

We're given orders to rest and hydrate and take it easy tomorrow.

When they're gone, Ian opens my car door and folds me down inside. "Food poisoning? Really?"

"It was the only way to explain our ragged appearance."

He reaches over me and starts my car.

"Can you drive?"

"I don't know. What if I get pulled over? I'm not drunk, but I sure as shit can't walk a straight line right now. Did you drug me?"

He's covering the door and leaning down, filling the entire

doorframe. "I hate the way your brain works sometimes."

The dig cuts deep. I can't change who I am no matter how hard I try.

I stare straight ahead, out the front window.

"Why can't you just let this happen without sabotaging it?"

"I'm not sabotaging it," I insist, offended.

"Okay, then let's go out on a date tomorrow night."

"I can't."

He shakes his head, pissed. "Good night Sam."

NO! Doesn't he get it? Doesn't he understand that I want to preserve what we have? That people fight their entire lives to find a friend like we have in each other? We're soulmates who shouldn't risk mating. Soul buds. Soul pals?

"Wait!" I wrap my hand around his forearm. It's so muscled and sexy, I lose track of what I was about to say. When my gaze drags back up to his angry scowl, I remember. "Don't be mad at me."

He's never been mad at me. I didn't realize it was my worst fear until this moment.

"I'm not. Sam—" He cuts himself off and heaves in a deep sigh. Then he steps back and grabs the door. "Go home."

And I do. I go home and I lie awake in my bed and I try to ignore the terrible feeling that my friendship with Ian will never be the same after tonight, that I've already started to lose him. The thought shreds my heart.

Ian and I don't talk at all on Sunday. It's the worst day I've had in a long time. I mope around the apartment and stay in my pajamas. I grab for my phone every time I hear a phantom ring. I watch a PBS special about jellyfish and remember the time I got stung at the beach and Ian swooped me up in his arms and carried me out of the water like a hero.

Monday morning, my wake-up call never comes. I sleep straight past first period; that's how much I've come to rely on Ian. Fortunately, Principal Pruitt assumes I'm still recovering from food poisoning, so there's no need to explain my tardiness or the fact that they had to pull in a sub to cover for me. During lunch, Ian avoids the teachers' lounge and I'm forced to converse with other people. It's so annoying. I have to complete my sentences and everything or they get confused. Ashley asks me how the Valentine's Day dance went and I'm so paranoid, I snap my gaze to her and ask her what she means.

Her face scrunches in confusion. "Just, like, was it a total bore or what?"

Oh.

I tell her it was fine, eat the rest of my lunch in two bites, and then scurry right back to my classroom. It's not exactly a smart move. After all, it's the scene of the crime. The desk we made out on should be removed from rotation and enshrined. Students have sat at it all morning, oblivious to the fact that Ian rocked my world in that exact spot not 48 hours ago.

I've thought about him a lot since our kiss, obsessed over him. As proof, my mind can warp any topic right back to him. While my students take a test, I look out the window of my classroom at the cloudless blue sky...Ian blue. After class, I overhear my students dissecting last night's *Game of Thrones* episode and wonder if Ian watched it without me. I scroll past a funny meme on Reddit and resist the urge to text it to him.

I never wanted to tell Ian how I felt because I was scared of our friendship crumbling. I didn't want to have to experience life without Ian, and it turns out my fears were valid because this fucking sucks.

One of my students comes up to me after sixth period, after most everyone has filed out. Her name's Jade. She's sweet and she takes my class seriously. I like her.

"Ms. Abrams, could I get your advice about something?"

I'm in no state to be doling out advice, but her eyes are hopeful and I'd feel terrible turning her down. "Sure thing. What's up?"

"Well, I was wondering…I have this best friend, Truman. He's in your fourth period. Anyway, we've been best friends since like sixth grade, but I think I want it to be something *more*."

I blink at her question.

Is this a joke?

"What are you talking about? Did someone put you up to this?"

I can tell from the trembling of her lower lip that she has no clue what I'm talking about. "Sorry. I can talk to someone else—"

"No. Sorry, ignore that. What's going on?"

She tells me the facts quickly and it's like I'm talking to a younger version of myself. The conversation feels like a weird therapy technique. I wonder if it was her note that was confiscated and read aloud in the teachers' lounge the other day.

"Do you think I should go for it?" she asks. "Y'know, tell him how I feel?"

I don't hesitate before confidently replying, "Do not, under any circumstances, tell him how you feel. Take your feelings to the grave."

"The grave?!" Her mouth drops.

Too morbid?

"Okay, just take them to college. You don't want to ruin that friendship."

"It's just—we were reading that Tennyson poem in your class the other day, the one that ends with 'Tis better to have loved and lost than never to have loved at all.'"

"Oh, Tennyson? He's a quack."

"But you said they made him a lord because of the strength of his poetry."

"Did I say that? Well, the point is, why would you risk what you have right now?"

"I think it could be something even more."

"More?!" I want to shake her. "Why do you need *more*? Isn't your friendship great as is? Isn't spending time with him your favorite part of life? Why would you want to go and screw that up?"

There are fat drops of water collecting in the corners of her eyes. I realize I've been shouting.

She turns and runs from the room, backpack nearly taking her down as she swoops around the corner.

Well, my work here is done.

Except, the next day, I see her and Truman holding hands in the hall. Truman leads her over to her locker and then cages her against it for a kiss. If I had a foghorn, I'd blow it in their ears.

Fortunately, Ian is on hallway duty and he breaks up their display of young love before I can.

He tells them to save it for after school, or better yet, for when they turn 25, and then he turns and our eyes catch. It's the first time I've seen him in two days. There's emotion clouding his usually friendly gaze. His trademark easy smile is gone. His dark brows are furrowed into a line.

It's all my fault.

I have to suppress the urge to run and fling myself into his arms.

Be my friend again, please! I want to shout.

His smoldering gaze warns me away. Even more, it says, *That could be us. I could pin you to a locker like that if only you'd let me.*

At least I think that's what it says. I don't have much time to translate it because he passes me by quickly, without a word. My breath whooshes out of me and it feels like I've been shot.

"Ian!" I shout after him impulsively.

He shakes his head and keeps walking. "I have to get back to my classroom."

I'm so emotionally frustrated—and so sexually frustrated—I could scream. In fact, I do. A tiny freshman boy runs past my classroom door, probably trying to get to his class on time, and I don't hesitate to shout, "No running in the halls!"

His face crumples in fear. I slam my classroom door closed and listen as a snarky senior laughs. "Sheesh, Ms. A clearly needs to get laid."

Finally, somebody gets me!

Chapter Twelve

Ian

It's Wednesday…*West Wing* Wednesday. Four days since the kiss, and four days since I've talked to Sam. I don't have a plan. I'm not trying to punish her; I'm just trying to regain some semblance of control. If she wants to stay just friends, that's going to be hard for me. We've crossed a line. I can't erase that kiss or that phone call, and if she wants me to try, I'm going to need some distance. It gets lonely standing out on a limb all by yourself.

Still, I know I'm being a jerk. Her face was the saddest thing when I brushed her off in the hall yesterday, but what does she expect? I'm not a saint. I'm a guy who's in love with his best friend, a woman who seems to eat her cake but also keep it in a hermetically sealed cryopreservation tank for all eternity.

Life continues on in the four days since we last spoke, albeit way shittier. I take my anger out on my soccer players. They think I'm an asshole for making them run so many laps at practice all week, but I run with them, insisting that if I can do it, so can they—except I have a secret weapon they don't: heartache. I think I could run from here to Alaska if I had to, Forrest Gump style.

I step into the shower after practice and crank the temperature until it's scalding. I stick my head under the water and close my eyes, thinking of Sam. She's not going to come to *West Wing* Wednesday. She isn't going to show her face. There are Blue Apron dinners in the fridge going to waste because I'm not going to cook meals meant for two people and eat them by all myself like a caricature of a lovelorn schmuck.

I think I hear a noise out in my living room. I pause and tilt my ear in that direction.

Suddenly, my shower door is yanked open. I think I'm about to be stabbed like I'm in a Hitchcock film.

"FUCK!" I shout, nearly punching Sam in the face before I realize it's her. "Can you not?"

She ignores me and steps into the shower fully clothed. I blink, trying to determine if I'm having a hallucination. *How many laps did I run today? Can a person succumb to heat stroke without realizing it?*

"I know this is a bad idea," she says, holding up her hands to block the spray from the showerhead. It's futile. She's soaked within seconds. "I almost didn't come. I sat outside your house for like thirty minutes, trying to cool down and debating whether or not I'd come inside. Your neighbors think I'm a juvenile delinquent casing the neighborhood. Move over."

"What the hell?"

She pokes my chest so I have no choice but to forfeit some of the hot water.

"I said scooch."

"You're still wearing your shoes."

She kicks off her tennis shoes aggressively, yanks off her socks, and tosses them out of the shower. Then she looks back up at me. "Better?"

I'm completely nude, obviously, and she's standing there in a soaked cotton t-shirt and jeans. "What the hell are you doing?"

She pushes my chest. "Looking for a fight. I'm pissed…I think."

"Want to wait until I'm finished here?" I'm having a hard time defending myself while holding a hand over my dick.

"Obviously not."

"Why are you pissed?"

I think if I had a shirt, she'd grab me by the scruff. As it is, she goes on her tiptoes and wraps her hands around my shoulders. My muscles flex instinctively beneath her touch. It's a warning of sorts: she might be the one doing the touching now, but only because I'm allowing it.

"Because you've broken me in half."

That's when I see the sadness in her expression, her downturned mouth, her huge worried eyes. She sounds deeply troubled and I'm intrigued by her sudden bout of honesty. It's why I'm not pushing her out of the shower…or up against the tile.

"How so?"

"I made two kids cry at school today. I'm an angry fireball. I can't stop thinking about you kissing me." Her hands dig into my shoulders with each word she speaks.

"Are all those things related?"

She sidles up closer and her chest hits mine. Her jeans brush my legs. My hand stays firmly planted in front of my groin. "Listen up, you, I've had enough of this. No more silent treatment. No more pretending like we aren't friends." She's wiping her wet hair out of her face. We're both drenched— drenched and angry. "If there's no going back, I need you to bang me against this tile so we can figure this out once and for all. C'mon, let's go."

"That's probably not a good idea."

My refusal works her up even more. "Oh yeah? You keep pushing and poking and finally I'm giving in, whether you like it or not." She steps back and tries to pry her t-shirt off over her head, but it's stuck to her like a second skin. "Dammit. Hold on."

She has to work at it for a few seconds. It's up covering her eyes now, and she's a toddler trying to dress herself for the first time. She jerks this way and that, knocking my bottles of shampoo and conditioner to the ground and nearly wiping out when she trips on one of them. I reach out and steady her hips. With a heavy sigh, she finally gets it off and flings it over the top of the shower door. I smirk at her newly disheveled appearance. Her hair is a tangled mess. Water droplets collect on the ends of her dark lashes. Her bra is creamy blue and see-through thanks to the steady stream of water hitting her.

"Come on, Ian! Man up! Just kiss me!"

She's got herself so worked up, her skin is flushed everywhere.

"No. Get out of my shower."

I turn my back to her and dip my head under the water. That really pisses her off. Her angry fists pound into my back.

"I'm telling you I want you and suddenly you're no longer interested?!"

She doesn't know what she's asking for, so I decide to show her. I turn back around and my hand drops. I step forward and push right up against her body, tipping my head down to meet her eyes. She wasn't kidding—she's a fuming little ball of molten lava. I think she wants to destroy me for doing this to us, for changing our friendship forever.

My hands grip her biceps, which are like two popsicle sticks. My hardness digs into her stomach and her mouth goes wide with wonder.

"Still want to have this conversation right now, Hot Lips?"

She doesn't answer me. She's in a daze. I've hypnotized her.

"Still think this is a good idea?"

"Everyone at school wants you," she whispers, eyes wide. "You're mine and you don't even know it. I've never told you."

Her admission fucks with my self-control. I want to hitch her legs around my waist so I can burrow myself deep inside her. I'm going to write on her forehead with a Sharpie while she's sleeping: *Property of Mr. Fletcher. Hands off.*

"I don't like the version of Ian you've been the last few days," she says quietly before nibbling on the edge of her bottom lip. She's refusing to meet my gaze. Instead, she's roving the contours of my chest.

"What version is that?"

The edge of her mouth tips up. "The nice guy—or rather, the not-so-nice guy. You walked right by me in the hallway yesterday. You skipped out on lunch in the teachers' lounge. You know I overslept on Monday because you didn't call me?"

I can't resist a small smile. "They make these devices called alarm clocks. Great invention, think they had them back in the Stone Ages."

"I already have one of those and he goes by Ian. Not to be confused with…"

I don't laugh. Not even a little.

"You see, there's our problem: I don't want to be your alarm clock anymore."

Her face falls and she stops charting a course across my chest.

"Oh."

"Yeah, call me crazy, but I'm standing here completely nude and we're chatting—not exactly my idea of a good time. I want to take a shower with you and…"

I shake my head. There's no point in finishing that thought. Instead, I release her and step back so she has enough space to leave. She's going to tug on the glass door and walk away. There will be sad puddles of water left in her wake. I'll probably slip on one and eat shit on my way out of the shower.

She's not moving though.

Her blue eyes are cartoonishly large as she stares up at me. There are so many thoughts flickering through her brain at once, I think she's going to overheat.

"Sam?"

"Just be quiet for a second," she snaps.

Slowly, painfully, her gaze drips down my face, across my neck and chest and abs, and then...lower. It's the first time she's really taken me in and, *Jesus*, I swear her jaw drops. Those rosy cheeks make me even harder, and now I think I'm scaring the poor girl.

I chuckle under my breath and reach over to open the glass door, giving her an easy out.

She yanks it closed again.

"I said be quiet!"

I haven't said a word.

"What are you—"

I begin to ask a question I already know the answer to, but Sam is bending down on her knees in front of me. The glass fogs up. Steam rises. She sits back on her heels and I know the tile is probably digging into her knees, but she doesn't care. In this new position, I block the shower spray from pelting her. She's drenched and beautiful and licking her goddamn lips.

"I want to..." she begins in a whisper.

Now I'm the one overheating.

We've talked about blowjobs before and I know they aren't usually Sam's thing, but she's looking at my dick like it's an ice cream cone melting before her eyes.

"Step closer," she begs.

I obey. Her hands hit my thighs immediately. Her fingers grip hard.

"God, you have the best legs."

She's staring straight at my penis and that's what she says.

"Thanks? Is that what you needed a closer look for?"

"I mean obviously your...*that* is good too. I mean, it's way bigger than I remember it being that one time I got a good peek, but I've always put your legs and your butt on a pedestal. That's why I went comatose at the gym the other day."

For emphasis, she reaches around with both hands and grabs my butt cheeks.

I chuckle and shake my head. "You're the only woman I know who could turn a blowjob into a weird physical exam."

She squeezes my butt twice like she's honking a bicycle horn. "What do you mean? You're not getting a blowjob. I'm just going to squeeze your butt for a while."

"Hilarious."

Her gaze settles back on the end goal and she wets her bottom lip again. A groan dies on my tongue. I don't want to scare her.

"It's been a while since I've done this."

I laugh. "Yeah, you can save the awkwardness. I don't care. It's just us, Sam. Me and you."

"Right." She nods, growing confident enough to drag one of her hands back around to the front of my hip. Then she slowly reaches over and circles her palm around my dick. She has the softest, surest grip. My eyes roll back in my head. My hips jerk forward on instinct. "Sam," I warn.

"I'm barely touching it!" she says defensively.

Yeah, I know. It's been a fucking while since I've slept with someone, and also this fantasy has been building for, oh, I don't know...a millennium. I won't last for shit.

"Just don't drag it out. Our entire time as friends has been a tease, foreplay. It's been like five-play or six-play."

She leans forward and presses a closed-mouth kiss to the

tip. It's adorable and I'm ascending to nirvana. I press my hand to the tiled wall behind her and she gets the hint. Her hand starts sliding up and down my length slowly. Water hits my shoulders and drags down my body, making her strokes wet and warm. She picks up the pace and she's looking up at me. Her eyes are so open and earnest, it's almost hard to meet them.

I've never had a handjob that felt this good. I don't know if it's her technique or how badly I've wanted it, like how on some days the diner burger you've eaten dozens of times tastes like five-star cuisine.

Eventually, when I've all but converted to Samanthaism, she leans forward and wraps her mouth around the tip. I'd throw my hands up in a hallelujah, but I'm in danger of collapsing on top of her. I have to keep ahold of the tile wall as she takes me in and out. It's everything, the alpha and the omega: the sight of her full lips wrapped around my length, the feel of her warm mouth and the back of her throat. My stomach clenches and she takes me deeper.

Drops of water slide down her chin and neck and the top of her chest. I can see her breasts through her bra, two pink tips beneath blue lace. I reach down with one hand and circle my thumb there. Her eyes close and she moans. I feel the vibration in her throat and there's no sensation better. I do it again and she speeds up, sucking me off with short, tight strokes. I don't think I have blood circulating anywhere else in my body. It's all headed south, as if every one of my trillions of red blood cells wants to be a part of this moment. I try to stave off an orgasm for as long as possible, which is a perfect microcosm of my relationship with Sam, a high-stakes battle between denial and submission.

Her hand clenches at the base of my dick, holding me steady as she pumps me in and out of her mouth even faster. Tingles start at the base of my spine. I'm seconds away from coming and I try to tell her so.

"Sam...I'm..."

Communication isn't working for me. I tap on her head like I'm trying to turn off a blaring alarm clock.

She smiles, shakes her head, and keeps going.

I take my foot off the brakes after that. I lean down and wrap my hand around her neck and I fuck her mouth like I will one day fuck her. She holds still and opens up and takes everything like a good little Sam. I can hear her starting to struggle for breath, and I'm not trying to kill her, but in my head it's suddenly a matter of life and death. I watch her eyes, knowing she'd tell me if she wanted to tap out, but there's no fear there. She's loving this as much as I am, and it's that thought that finally sends me over the edge.

I close my eyes and groan as shocks of pleasure rack through my body. I pump into her mouth and her fingers dig into my lower back as she swallows and swallows some more.

It's a slow descent back to reality. I think I must stand there in a haze for an hour or two. I've used up all the water on Earth before I think to turn back and cut the shower.

Sam pushes up to stand and wipes her mouth with the back of her hand like a goddamn champ. She's smirking, proud of herself.

"Still with me?"

"Yes."

"Aren't going to freak out and run?"

"I don't think I have the energy."

"Well then, c'mon," I say, stepping out and reaching for two towels. "Let's go get you some ice for those knees."

"Oh thank god. That tile hurts! That's the last time I try to be sexy on a shower floor. From now on it's a soft mattress or nothing, unless I can find those rollerblading kneepads."

Chapter Thirteen

Sam

I've decided to take a newfangled approach to life in which I don't think ten steps into the future and instead live in the moment. I endured four days without Ian and it sucked completely, so if I have to give him a blowjob in his shower to keep him around, so be it.

I want him. It's obvious. What could possibly go wrong?

After our shower, I cook dinner in some clothes Ian loans me—an oversized T-shirt and baseball socks that stretch to my knees—and then we sit on his couch and watch *The West Wing*. The show holds 5% of my attention, the other 95% focused on Ian's lips.

He's aware of this because midway through the episode, he pauses it and turns to me. "We aren't going to do anything else tonight."

This is news to me. I was hoping we'd both at least make it to third base. I shaved my legs before coming over for a reason.

"Why's that? Y'know, in Western society, the BJ is typically a quid pro quo sorta thing."

He shakes his head and stands to collect our dinner plates from the coffee table. Ian is a cleaner. His house is always immaculate, and he hates how messy I am when I cook. He thinks I use every pot and pan and cutting board he has just to spite him. Little does he know, that's only half the reason I use them.

"It's not that—believe me, I am looking very much forward to...returning the favor, but don't you think if we continue at this pace you might...I dunno, spook?"

"Pfft. Whatever. How about we just do a nice slow-jam make-out while R&B plays in the background?" I ask. "Spotify has playlists for every occasion."

"No."

"Okay, what about a light massage, oil optional, with an accompanying cool jazz playlist? I have one of those too."

"Not happening."

"We could just hold hands in silence? Does Spotify have a silence song?"

At that, he pauses the dishes and props his hands on the counter. I think he's either laughing or trying to calm himself down. I can't see his whole face, but his eyes are definitely pinched closed. Poor guy.

"I'll make it easy for you: I'll just get naked and you can

come graze, nibble, take what you'd like. I'm like a reasonably priced Chinese buffet."

His head whips around as if to confirm whether or not I'm stripping on his couch.

I'm not. I'm smiling fiendishly.

"Sam, we aren't friends with benefits. I want to make that perfectly clear. If we're doing this, we're doing it right."

I laugh. "Well I hate to break it to you, bucko, but we've already screwed up. Phone sex and a blowjob before our first date? As Shakespeare said, Shit's fucked, yo. No point in trying to correct it now."

He turns back around, straightens his shoulders, and now suddenly, I know the discussion is closed. "Not happening, Sam."

Fine. I push off the couch and stomp to his freezer where I know I'll find a pint of his favorite ice cream: Rocky Road. I'm going to eat it all just to spite him. That'll teach him to turn me down.

I also reach for a bag of peas for my knees as an afterthought.

True to his word, Ian doesn't touch me all night.

I have to go home and touch myself to memories of him in that shower like a horny teenager.

I think our next kiss is imminent. It has to be. The next day, I moisten my lips with ChapStick every fifteen minutes. I make sure my breath is fresh and minty. I check for food in my teeth incessantly. Nicholas tells me I look different during first period. "Glowing" is his exact word. The kid is too observant.

At lunch, I wait for Ian in the teachers' lounge with my food laid out in front of me on the table. He walks in, talking to another teacher, and my lungs collapse. I'm gasping for breath like a lifelong smoker.

Today he's wearing a pale blue shirt that matches his eyes. His navy slacks are new and they fit his ass too well. His hair is coffee brown and thick. These are the details causing my asthmatic symptoms.

I'm not alone.

Ashley is sitting beside me, staring at Ian like he's a juicy lamb chop.

"*God*, I love when he wears blue," she says on a soft exhale.

If I had a weapon within reach, she'd be dead and I'd be facing life in prison, but no worries—I'd hire NPR to do a podcast about me. They'd unveil my passionate love for Ian and the audience would feel bad that he didn't go down on me last night. They'd deem the murder a crime of passion and demand a retrial. The judge would overturn the conviction on an arcane cunnilingus law and I'd end up walking free in no time. Sorry Ash.

I watch as Ian curves around the room to make it to our table. Has he always been such a strapping lad? Have I always been in love with him?

I sit up straight and stare down at my food, hyperaware that Ian and I have some splanin' to do if anyone catches me staring at him with hearts in my eyes. I don't know if it's against the rules for teachers to date. It's probably just frowned upon, but still, I don't want everyone to know our business. Gossip spreads like wildfire in this school, especially if it's as juicy as this.

"Hey there, Ian!" Ashley exclaims as soon as he pulls out the chair across from me.

He nods in her direction as he takes a seat. Our knees bump and he might as well have just put his hand down my panties from the way I blush.

"Do anything fun last night?" she asks him. "I got sucked into a *Real Housewives* marathon. Ugh, I just can't resist those catfights!"

"Oh, uh, yeah, my night was fine. Nothing memorable."

"Not a single thing?" I snap before I can think better of it.

He wipes away a smile, busying himself with emptying his lunch onto the table. "Now that I think about it, it was just one of those nights that really *sucked*, y'know?"

I grunt out a sound somewhere between a laugh and a cry.

Ashley is confused and staring back and forth between us. "Well I'm sorry to hear that. You're always welcome to come binge Bravo with me!"

"I don't know what that means." He turns to me. "Sam, I brought the leftovers from yesterday. It's a lot. Want some?"

"Yeah. Here, I don't want my peanut butter and jelly sandwich. You can eat it for a snack before soccer practice."

"Leftovers? So you guys were hanging out last night?" Ashley asks Ian. "What were you up to?"

"Does it have raspberry jelly?" he asks skeptically. "I thought you ran out."

I roll my eyes and shove the sandwich toward him. "I picked some up on the way home last night because every time I use grape you groan about it for four days straight."

"Guys," Ashley says, tired of being ignored.

"What?" I ask impatiently.

"What were you doing?"

I shrug. "Watching *West Wing*."

Ian is wearing a secretive smile and Ashley notices.

"Well that doesn't sound too bad. What sucked about that?"

My eyes go wide with fear. Since when are we under her microscope? Oh right, since she decided to have a crush on Ian.

"Just wasn't a good episode," he backtracks into a lie. Any true fan knows there is no such thing. "And I stubbed my toe."

He's trying to help, but he's only making it worse.

"Oh...okay. Well I hope Sam here gave you a foot rub or something..."

She knows. *She knows!*

I act fast.

"Do you like pretzels, Ashley?" I ask genially.

She perks up. "Love them."

I toss the bag her way and she drops it into her purse.

Then I watch as she realizes the power she suddenly wields.

"Y'know, I like chocolate too," she says with a smile that's too polite. Her point is perfectly clear: give me the chocolate or I tell everyone you two were fooling around. I slap my dessert pudding cup in her hand and she gloats. "'Preciate it." Then she turns to Ian. "Anyway, Ian, I was wondering what your plans are for this Saturday? I want to check out this new nature path near my house and you seem outdoorsy." She wags her eyebrows. "Could be fun."

Wait. *What?*

"As friends," she clarifies, testing the waters. "I'm inspired by how *friendly* everyone is around here."

Ian tells her he's busy this weekend and then Ashley blabs about something else I don't care about. I'm too busy watching her spoon my goddamn pudding into her mouth. She dribbles a little bit on her lip. I chew on my fingernails. She licks the spoon and I resist the urge to slap the container out of her hand. Then—THEN—she doesn't even finish all of it.

"Ugh, I'm so full."

My fingernails dig into my palm so hard, I draw blood.

Ian is smart enough to buy me a chocolate bar from the vending machine on the way back to our classrooms. He slaps it into my hand and tells me to eat it all.

"And calm down. No one cares about what we're doing. You're being paranoid."

He's right, I am being paranoid, but it doesn't matter. Soon, my life implodes on itself anyway.

Chapter fourteen
Sam

The INCIDENT is largely Ian's fault. I will blame him because it feels better to deflect, and really, it *is* his fault. The day after our shower fight/love sesh, I think Ian's going to kiss me. When he doesn't, I grow restless. I try to get creative. After his soccer practice, I show up at his house in a trench coat. I'm wearing clothes underneath, but he doesn't know that. I think he's going to fall to his knees and beg for it, but he doesn't. In fact, he completely turns the tables on me because when I arrive, he's just out of the shower, shirtless and wet and tan and how does someone have such clearly defined muscles?

I reach for them like a toddler reaching for candy. *Gimme.* He shakes his head and locks his arms on my shoulders, holding me at a distance like I'm contaminated waste. He deposits me carefully on the couch and then goes to put a shirt on. When he's finished, he drags me out for pizza.

It's intentional on his part.

"Did we leave your house so nothing could happen?" I ask in between bites of pepperoni. "Because I don't have any qualms about doing it in the bathroom at a sleazy pizza joint."

He swallows his bite and stares at me like I'm from Mars.

"You have sauce on your chin, and on your shirt, and there's a little on your cheek too."

Point taken—I'm not at my sexual peak while shoving stuffed crust down my throat. Next time, I'll order a salad.

After pizza, Ian drives us back to his house and leads me straight to my bike. He hoists me onto the seat and leans down. I brace for it. THE KISS. I'm going to rock his world. I'm going to do things with my tongue he's only ever read about on the dark web.

Then I realize he's buckling my helmet for me and making sure it's secure.

"Go home, Sam. This weekend, we'll go out on our first date. Saturday morning, I'll pick you up and take you to breakfast and I'll ask you about your hobbies."

"I don't have any hobbies."

"After, we'll hold hands and stroll around the park."

"Will this park have dark corners for doing dark deeds?"

"It's going to be 85 and sunny. Children will be flying kites."

"It better not be the park where I learned how to

rollerblade. I still get funny looks."

"It'll be any park you want it to be."

"And then after?" I ask, urging him on.

"After, we'll go back to my house and I'll kiss you for as long as you want to be kissed, and maybe we'll see about getting to second base."

"Can't we just start at home plate? The batter starts there anyway. That way you don't have to bother running around those pesky bases."

"Sam, I swear…"

He pinches his eyes closed and I poke his chest.

"I'm kidding." Kind of.

Anyway, that's how we leave that night, and to his credit, Saturday is great. It's one for the books. We meet at our favorite breakfast spot in the morning. I'm there early, sitting in a booth and chewing my fingernails down to nubs. At 9:30 on the dot, Ian strolls in, and I reach for my coffee so I appear calm and casual rather than deranged and lovesick. He spots me and smiles. Dimples flare and my stomach flips and I hold up a hand to wave at him—*wave*, like I'm on a parade float.

"Morning," he says as he slides into the opposite side of the booth.

"Hello."

"That your first cup of coffee?"

It's my third.

"Yup." I shrug coolly. "I just got here a few minutes ago."

Our well-meaning waiter blows my cover. "Oh, look! Here's your friend. I was beginning to wonder if you'd been stood up."

Ian smiles like he's just discovered some deep, dark secret of mine.

I tell him I think our waiter is on something.

After breakfast, Ian fulfills his promise to take me to a park, except we never make it out of his car. It's too hot to take a walk and I've been a good girl, sitting across from him all morning long, completing full sentences when what I really wanted to do was toss my scrambled eggs and bacon at the wall and leap over the table at him.

Now, we're in the parking lot at the park and Ian is about to open his door, but I reach over and grip his forearm. It's solid, strong…more tantalizing than a simple body part should be.

"Don't."

He pauses and turns to face me, brow arched with interest.

"I don't want to take a walk."

"What do you want to do?"

A slow, devious smile spreads across my lips.

We make out in his car for what feels like hours. I straddle his lap and my elbow hits the horn so a roving group of kids turn and stare at us. A minivan pulls into the spot beside us and a family of five scrambles out. I fold my body down, trying to hide, but one of the kids presses his face right up to the window.

"Mommy, come look! She's sitting on his lap! Is he Santa Claus?"

Ian hauls ass out of there before the police get called.

Unfortunately, come Monday, we've still only done a lot of kissing. The kissing is great, but I'm ready for more. So, being the impatient idiot that I am, I decide to tease Ian a little.

He emails me a recipe that morning before school, asking if I can grab a few things from the store on the way to his house. They're innocuous items: oregano and olive oil.

I email back: *Sure, but what's for dessert? ;)*

Ian: *Have any ideas?*

After a stroke of genius, I email back a photo of myself shooting whipped cream into my mouth. It's cheeky and hot. There's a teensy bit on my nose too. Below it, I type, *I'm all out of chocolate chips. We'll have to get creative*. It's not really meant to be sexy. It's meant to make him laugh, but, I mean, if it turns him on then all the better. Bonus: I got to have whipped cream for breakfast.

I don't think twice about it until I'm sitting in my classroom before first period and the teacher one classroom over, Mrs. Orin, dips her head past the doorframe.

"Hey, Sam. I think it's really brave of you to show up today. Most people wouldn't have the guts."

Then she holds up a fist for solidarity.

Okay, well, that was the weirdest experience of my life.

Ten minutes later, Logan comes by. For some reason, he can't meet my gaze. "Hey, sorry, I would have never asked you out if I knew you and Ian were together. Friends still?"

All of the blood drains from my face. *What the HELL is going on?*

When he leaves, I scramble for my phone and check my email only to find that the worst possible thing in the history of the world has happened to me: I didn't send the whipped cream photo to FletcherIan@OakHillHigh. I send it, along with the rest of our conversation, to FullStaff@OakHillHigh.

NO.

NOOOOOO.

NoOoOooOOoOoOoOoOoOoO.

I clutch my chest. I can't catch my breath. I look around for some kind of defibrillator, but there's only a fire extinguisher. It won't help in this situation unless I hit myself in the head really hard and give myself brain damage. Actually...that's a pretty great idea.

Here's exactly how this happened:

I thought I hit *reply*, but I must have hit *forward*.

I hit F and Gmail autofilled the wrong email address.

I was too distracted at the time to check who I was sending the emails to and now I'm going to go hit my skull with a fire extinguisher and hope I go into a month-long coma.

This sort of thing has happened to other teachers before. Last year, our nurse accidentally emailed the entire school a copy of her W-2, letting everyone know how much money she makes. She was mortified. The year before, one of the volleyball coaches sent us all a gym selfie that was meant for his wife. We teased him mercilessly. Those don't hold a candle to this.

THIS IS MUCH WORSE.

Teachers started replying to the email right away, making jokes and trying to lighten the mood. I can't read a single one of them. My hands are shaking. I fight down the urge to vomit all over the lesson plans on my desk.

Ian calls my cell phone twice and I ignore it.

I put my head between my knees and practice breathing exercises.

Students are starting to filter into my classroom for first

period. I'm supposed to teach, but I'm on the verge of a nervous breakdown. I want to pretend like this isn't happening, but that won't work. Instead, I decide the best course of action is to nip it in the bud. I shoot out an email quickly, trying for honesty: "Well, this is extremely embarrassing. Please disregard my last email. It was a bad joke made in poor taste." I decide to not even address the fact that I was openly flirting with Ian. I'm hoping if I don't draw attention to it, no one will notice. I'm wrong.

Emails continue flying in.

HillBianca@OakHillHigh: *Not dating, huh?*

MillerGretchen@OakHillHigh: *Yeah, is this even allowed?*

If I could afford to replace it, I'd fling my phone into the nearest volcano.

I'm crying now and students are looking at me like I'm weird. One of them speculates loudly about my Aunt Flo visiting. Another posits that I'm too old to still get my period. HOW OLD DO THEY THINK I AM?!

"Ms. Abrams, are you okay? Should we call the nurse?" one gentle, sweet student asks, and I stand, shake my head, and walk out of the classroom, mumbling at them to start reading chapter 11.

I make it to the women's bathroom before the waterworks really start. I crash into a stall, tell the lingering students to scram, sit on a toilet, and cry. I cry and cry and resist the urge to bang my head against the stall door. This is a complete disaster. I'm going to lose my job. I'm going to have to move to another city. There's no way I can show my face at another staff meeting. I'm completely mortified.

My phone vibrates in my hand and it's Ian again. I press ignore and try to figure out what I need to do. Right now, I want to flee. I have to get out of this school.

Yes. YES. I'm leaving. It's completely inappropriate to bail in the middle of the school day, but there's a protocol in place in case an emergency arises. Valid emergencies include: you're sick, or your kid is sick, or you accidentally sext all your coworkers and you need to get the hell out of Dodge.

I email our admin and ask him to pull in a sub ASAP, get Mrs. Orin to cover my first class, and then haul ass out of school. GOODBYE OAK HILL. HELLO AZERBAIJAN.

My first destination is a bridge about a mile away from school. I don't think I'm suicidal, but this seems like a nice place to contemplate it. I park my bike, walk to the very center, and look down. I guess I thought the bridge was a lot taller—there's no canyon underneath and there's definitely no rushing river. It's a trickling creek at best. If I jump, I'll be lucky to twist an ankle. So much for a dramatic gesture. Instead, I keep riding to the froyo place down the street.

"Welcome to Fro-yo-yoyo!" the middle-aged pot-bellied man sing-songs as I walk in the door. His enthusiasm is worrying. The place is empty. It's nine o'clock on a Monday morning.

"Do you allow samples?" I ask, dropping my purse on a table without pause and heading straight for the machines. If they don't, I'll just stick my mouth under one of the nozzles and hold on until they drag me out.

"Oh sure. Here ya go!"

He hands me a thimble-sized paper cup, and just as I begin to fill it my brain reminds me that dessert was what started this mess. My vision goes black as I replay the email over and over in my head. *Sure, but what's for dessert? Sure, but what's for dessert?*

"Lady, you're getting it everywhere."

When I snap back to the present, my hand is cold. I look down to see thick ropes of frozen yogurt piling onto the overfilled cup, my hand, and my shoes.

How long was I out?

After a quick apology and cleanup, I opt for the largest to-go tub they offer and start to fill it. When that's done, I get another. I wonder how many mini M&Ms I'd have to force into my stomach before a doctor would determine my body is made up of more chocolate than water. I'd rather be remembered for that than be Email Girl for the rest of my life.

After I pay, I take my tub to a lonely table while Mr. Fro-yo-yo watches me like a hawk from behind the counter. He's scared I'm going to cause another mess. As I eat in silence, Ian keeps calling me, but my phone is on silent and halfway across the table. There's nothing he can say that will make this situation any better.

He did this to us. *Yes.* Oooh, that feels good. *Deflect. Put the blame on him.* He decided we should explore this simmering need churning within us instead of leaving well enough alone. I was doing just fine! I had my dirty dreams and my fantasies and I could have used those to sustain me for another 1000 years.

This entire situation is exactly what I was afraid of. EVERYONE KNOWS. Everything is changing and I can't go back to school without everyone staring and gossiping behind my back. The other teachers will make lewd jokes about whipped cream and I won't have the strength to laugh it off—and oh god, the students are going to find out and we'll never hear the end of it. This thing is so new—a baby bird of a relationship—there's no way we'll survive. This is the beginning of the end.

My phone lights up again and my gaze snaps to the screen. If it's Ian, I'm going to have to answer and tell him to stop calling, but it's not.

It's an incoming email from Principal Pruitt.

I read it while holding my breath.

He wants to set up a meeting with Ian and me to discuss the "situation" and the "potential consequences".

I slam my froyo tub on the table and dart to the bathroom, throwing up every sugary morsel I just stuffed down my throat. More tears spill out.

I can't believe it. I'm in trouble. I don't get in trouble! Back when I was in high school, I never served time in detention, and I never brought home a grade below an A-!

"Lady, are you doing what I think you're doing in there?"

Froyo man pounds on the door, clearly sick of my shit.

"I'll be—blughhh—I'll be out in a minute!" I shout between heaves.

"Gah, and I just put the mop up."

I stumble weakly to the bathroom door, yank it open, and sear him with my eyes. "My life is over."

He doesn't look very sympathetic. "Well can you take it somewhere else? And for the record, I've never seen someone so little eat so much frozen yogurt."

If this were any other day, I'd take that as a compliment.

I have no clue where I'm going when I hop on my bike a few minutes later. I'm saddled with a metric ton of frozen yogurt. My breath smells like a wrestler's perineum. My eyes are swollen and red. It's only 9:35 AM. I have an entire day of despair ahead of me, and I need to pace myself. All I want to do is call Ian, but I can't. Usually, if something like this were to happen to me, I'd run straight to him. He'd distract me with a horribly embarrassing story of his own, but that won't work this time.

My friend Ian is gone.

I take off on my bike and my froyo slips out of my hand immediately after I make my first turn. My M&Ms scatter across the pavement.

Even the candy gods have forsaken me.

I've never felt more alone in my life.

Chapter Fifteen
Ian

've called Sam 34 times. When I try for 35, my phone rolls its eyes and gives me an alert that just says, *Dude, it's not going to happen.* This day has been one of the worst on record, especially in comparison to the days that came before it. Taking Sam to breakfast, making out in my car, flirting over email—life was going according to plan and then she had to accidentally send that photo to the entire school. *Fuck.* I wish it'd been me. Sam tries to act strong and resilient, but she's made of marshmallow fluff. She won't be able to laugh this off and move on. To her, it's mortifying, and she proves that fact by bailing during first period. I went to her classroom to force her to talk to me and there was an elderly woman sitting at her desk. My first thought was, *Wow, stress really does age you*. Then I realized it was Mrs. Orin, standing in until Sam's sub arrived.

I'm pissed at Sam for ignoring my phone calls and shutting me out. I want to help share the burden. She's not the only one going through this.

But then, I get it. There's a double standard. If she'd stayed, she would have been ridiculed and mocked mercilessly. Meanwhile, all day at school, male teachers and coaches bump into me in the hallway and offer congratulations. I sidestep countless high fives, fist bumps, and shoulder claps. The next guy who grunts or winks in my direction or tries to make a joke about Sam and whipped cream will have to get their shattered jaw wired shut.

At the end of soccer practice, I skip a shower and head straight for Sam's apartment. I knock on her door for so long, her neighbor shouts at me to go away.

I ask him if he's seen Sam and he says, "Never heard of him."

Right—we're each other's only friends.

When I get back to my car, I try to call her again and it goes straight to voicemail. I have no choice but to drive around town to all the destinations where I could possibly find her. I check the bakery where she likes to get cupcakes, the other bakery where she likes to get cookies, the third bakery where she likes to get banana pudding. No one has seen her. I check out the ice cream shop, the popsicle shop, and then finally, the frozen yogurt shop.

The man there shakes his head angrily.

"Petite thing? Red hair? Yeah, she was here—almost had to kick her out. She was high on drugs, came in and made a mess of the place."

What the fuck?

"Did you see where she went when she left?"

"Probably to get more horse tranquilizers."

I go back outside and try to think like Sherlock Holmes. I look for clues in the parking lot, try to put myself in her shoes, but even in my head, they're so small they don't fit.

I'm fresh out of ideas and then I decide it can't hurt to check her parents' house, even though she's not that close with them. They're snobby and judgmental and I doubt she'd turn to them on a day like this, but sure enough, her bike is lying in their driveway.

I park and head for the front door, but my first few knocks go unanswered.

The downstairs is dark and the shades are drawn, but I hear voices inside. Someone's definitely home. I jiggle the door handle and it opens. It was unlocked the whole time.

I step inside and call out, but no one answers. The voices I could hear outside are coming from a radio in the kitchen. Creepy.

Her parents clearly aren't home, but I know Sam's here. I've only been here a handful of times, but I remember her room is the first one on the right upstairs.

Sure enough, that's where I find her, splayed out on her bed, staring up at the ceiling.

I pause in the doorway as a slow smile spreads. It feels good to have found her, to know she's okay...sort of. I mean, she's lying there wearing her dorky band uniform from high school. The stiff red and black material completely drowns her. On her head, she's wearing the band hat with red plumage. It makes her look like a rooster. Her parents' cat is toying with it like it's a mouse.

Her eyes are red, her cheeks are flushed. I wonder how much she's cried today.

I take a hesitant step inside and her gaze stays rooted above, like she's gone comatose.

"Where are your parents?"

"On an Alaskan cruise." Her voice is calm.

Makes sense.

"They leave NPR on while they're gone?"

"They want to make sure burglars are informed on current world events while they're burgling."

My smile widens.

I want to kiss her, but I get that it's not the right time.

Instead, I take a seat at her desk—or at least I try to. Her chair is very small and my hips barely clear the armrests. I manage eventually, and we sit in silence for a while as I take in her room. I've never had the chance to really inspect it before today. She was too shy to let me poke around the last time we were here, but now I get my fill of teenage Sam. Her walls are painted lime green. CDs line an entire bookshelf. There are band trophies and UIL journalism awards arranged on top of her dresser. Where other girls would have a framed picture of a boy band, she has a photograph of Jean-Luc Picard on her nightstand.

I love her.

She makes a sound like an animal caught in a bear trap and I jerk my gaze to meet hers. She tries to readjust her position on the bed, but the stiff material of her band uniform makes it hard for her to move.

"What's with the getup?"

She looks down as if just now remembering she has it on. "Oh, yeah. I'm going back to a point in time before I sent that school-wide email. I think in the psychiatric world, they call this regression."

I tip my head to the side and wait for her to meet my eyes, but she won't.

"I totally get not wanting to be at school today, but just so you know, this is not a big deal. There's no rule against sending funny pictures."

When she speaks next, her words drip with sarcasm. "Oh, goodie. I'm so glad there's no rule against public humiliation— but wait, if there's no rule against it, why did we get called to the principal's office?"

"You're not 'called to principal's office' as an adult. You're summoned for a meeting."

"Either way, we're fucked."

She picks her arms up and then lets them flop back down dramatically. Her flute cartwheels to the ground.

"He just wants to meet to talk about the email."

"And tell us we're fired."

"He'll probably just have us sign some kind of HR disclosure concerning the relationship."

"Relationship? I'm 15-year-old Sam. I haven't met you yet. Now, please leave so I can go back to watching *TRL*. *MTV Cribs* comes on after and I don't want to miss it."

All right, I'll let her do this. She's had a rough day.

I turn and start snooping around her desk. I want to

look in every drawer, flip open every book. In her desk I find a purple Game Boy, a blink-182 CD, and a handwritten list of her Myspace Top 8. Names are scratched out and new ones have been added below. I wonder where I would have fallen.

"What are you looking at?"

"Nothing."

She groans and moves off the bed, too curious. My ploy worked. She comes to stand right beside me, trying to close the drawer. I don't let her. Instead, I pull out a worn paperback that has its cover torn off.

"What's this?"

"NOTHING! IAN LET ME HAVE THAT!"

Her over-the-top reaction ensures I won't give it back to her any time soon. I stiff-arm her so she can't reach me and then I read the spine.

"*Pirate's Hidden Treasure.*"

Oh, this is too good.

"Did teenage Sam like to read romance novels?"

"Ian, c'mon."

"Let me just read one page."

With a growl, she sneaks under my arm, wrenches the paperback out of my hand, and flings it across the room. It splats against the wall then crumples to the ground.

My jaw is slack. Sam's breathing is hard. After a moment, she rights her hat and tugs down her uniform top. Then she admits coolly, "My mom wouldn't let me read anything but *Chicken Soup for the Teenage Soul*. I had to steal that book from my friend just to...y'know, see what it was all about."

I act like I believe her. "Oh, so you only had it for curiosity's sake? 'Cause that spine looked pretty worn."

She groans. "Listen, yes, I read that book incessantly. Teenagers these days have Kindles and high-speed internet and I had *PIRATE'S HIDDEN TREASURE*, so leave me alone."

I reach out for her hips and tug her onto my lap. Her ancient wooden desk chair groans in protest. At any moment, our combined weight will prove too much and we'll go crashing to the ground.

Sam tries to wriggle free, but I have too good of a hold on her. When she finally gives in and settles on top of me, I reach up and yank off her hat. It falls to the ground and I smooth my thumb across the angry red line it left on her forehead. Her blue eyes catch mine and it's the first time she's had the courage to hold my gaze. I've never seen her look so dejected.

My brows tug together in a sad, angry furrow.

"I'm sorry about today."

She closes her eyes and her bottom lip juts out. "No. God, I'm the one who messed up. I should be apologizing to you."

Her eyes flick to the ceiling and I see tears collecting within. She tries so hard to keep them from falling as my hands tighten on her waist. My thumb barely slips under her band shirt, and her soft skin feels so good I dip my entire hand beneath the material then slide it around to cradle her back. It's not much contact, but it makes my heart thud in my chest to have her this close.

I watch as a tear finally breaks free and then Sam leans forward and plops her head on my shoulder. Her knees tuck in and now she's a ball in my lap. I pull her even closer. I think if my shirt were stretchier, she'd try to burrow underneath it and hide there forever.

"This is silly. I'm not just crying about what happened today. There's been a lot of change lately, and I'm not equipped to handle it. It's too much."

I already know this. Sam's a creature of habit, which means the last few days have been doubly hard on her.

"How can I help?"

Her head rocks back and forth on my shoulder as she shakes her head. "You can't, but at least you smell good."

I smile and remember something from earlier.

"The froyo guy said you were doing drugs or something."

She chuckles softly but doesn't lift her head. "No, I was throwing up. Don't worry, I brushed my teeth when I got here."

I frown. "Why'd you throw up?"

"I got Pruitt's email, and it made me sick to think of what could happen to us."

Damn.

"Well stop worrying. Everything's going to be fine."

"I don't believe you. I'm going to call in sick tomorrow."

"Well I'm going to the meeting. I understand if you want to stay here and continue doing whatever this is."

"Regressing, remember?"

"You're stronger than this, Sam. The email isn't that bad."

She groans.

"In fact, when you get the chance, you should check the thread. You might be pleasantly surprised by what you find there."

I feel a slight dip in the chair. Wood creaks and trembles. One second, Sam's cuddled on my lap, and the next, we're splayed out on the floor. One of the chair's legs jams itself into my lower back and I wince in pain.

If I were an English nerd instead of a science nerd, I'd realize this tableau is an apt metaphor for our current situation. Sam has to explain it to me: "Welcome to rock bottom."

Chapter Sixteen

Sam

Ian drives me home from my parents' house, walks me inside my apartment, waits for me to shower, and then tucks me in bed.

"Do you want me to stay?" he asks, brushing my hair away from my forehead like I'm four years old and sick, and it feels glorious. I'll have life-altering events happen more often if it means he's going to dote on me like this.

Of course I want him to stay, but if he stays, I'm going to have sex with him, and I don't think we should have sex for the first time on the same day as THE INCIDENT. Knowing me, I'd probably butt-dial the local news in the middle of climax.

"Better not," I say, tilting my head up and offering him my mouth so he can lean down and kiss me goodnight. He keeps it short and chaste and I miss him the second he leaves my apartment.

I think I'm going to cave and call him, demand he come right back here this instant, but then I remember the email thread. He talked about it again on the way home. My nose scrunches just thinking about it, but I know he has my best interests at heart. If people were making fun of me, he would steal my phone and chuck it in a dumpster. If he wants me to read it, I probably should. So, I settle in under my covers and tap the email app on my phone, bracing myself.

Holy cow.

There are 68 new emails since the last one I read. There hasn't been an email thread this popular since that time Mrs. Hill offered up two free tickets to Hamilton. The first 25 emails were desperate and pleading, then the next 25 were booing and hissing when she clarified (stupid autocorrect) the tickets were actually for Oak Hill High's production of Hamlet.

I start from the beginning and breeze past the emails I already read—the ones that make my stomach twist with anxiety—and pause when I come across Ian's email address.

IanFletcher@OakHillHigh: *This is a photo of me from middle school, dressed up as Yoda with full orthodontic headgear. My mom told me I'd be able to laugh at this picture in fifteen years, but honestly, it still hurts.*

IanFletcher@OakHillHigh: *Oh, whoops, sorry everyone. I meant to just send that photo to Sam...*

A tiny, microscopic smile tugs at my lips. He was trying to deflect the attention from me with a ridiculous photo of himself. I immediately save it to my phone and then continue scrolling. Mrs. Orin sends the next email with a photo of herself after she let her granddaughter do her makeup. There is eyeliner etched down her cheeks and red lipstick smeared across her chin. Her caption is the same as Ian's: *"Oh, sorry. Meant to just send that to Sam."*

Next, the art teacher shares a picture of herself after she got her wisdom teeth pulled. She's a puffy chipmunk. "Oops! This was supposed to go to Sam."

After that, Ian's idea catches on like wildfire. Teacher after teacher submits their own most horrifying photo, and by the end, I'm genuinely moved by everyone's kindness. I actually laugh when the oldest teacher in school, Mr. Kelso, sends a sepia-toned photo of himself in hot pants. His caption reads: *"Who am I kidding? I totally meant to send this to everyone. Look at those legs! This was back in the free love 60s!"*

It's all in good fun until one of the part-time administrators ends up taking the gesture of solidarity too far, sending a photo of her doing shots out of a dancer's belly button in Cabo. There is an eye-catching nip slip and the timestamp on the photo is from only two weeks ago. Her caption: *"OMG so embarrassing meant to send this to my AA sponsor!!"*

All of a sudden everyone is sad.

But me, actually—I'm grateful. All the other photos were nice and made me feel like I wasn't quite so alone, but that nipple really took the heat away from me. I couldn't have planted a better diversion if I'd hired a fancy PR team to come in and handle it for me.

As I walk into school the next morning, I expect some sort of fanfare. A few snide comments, crass jokes, *something*. Fortunately, gossip about Pauline has stolen the spotlight. No one's talking about my photo because all anyone cares about is the fact that PAULINE SENT A PICTURE OF HER BOOB TO THE ENTIRE SCHOOL AND SHE NEEDS OUR SUPPORT IN HER BATTLE WITH ALCOHOLISM. It's a big deal. The IT department has to lock down our email server and go in to wipe everything from the thread, including my original whipped cream photo. I'm sure it's still out there circulating somewhere. Just like with Ian's headgear picture, someone certainly screenshotted it before it was too late, but what do I care? I have a picture of Ian with headgear!

I'm going to make it into a quilt and put it on my bed.

Even though Pauline did a solid by diverting the spotlight away from me, Ian and I still have to meet with Principal Pruitt after school. At precisely 3:05 PM, the bell rings, my students filter out of my class in barely contained sprints, and then I look up to find Ian waiting for me at my door. He looks edible in a white button-down with navy slacks. For a moment, I wish Principal Pruitt were gay or that I wasn't so against using my feminine wiles on a married man. We could get ourselves out of this situation lickety-split.

"Ready?" he asks with a small, dimpled smile.

"No. I think you should go ahead, fight on both of our behalves. I'll go get your car and wait for you in the parking lot in case we need to make a quick getaway."

"Charming. Let's go."

I feel like a dead man walking as we head to the main office.

"Although I feel bad for her," Ian says, "I'm glad Pauline sent that picture. No one cares about us anymore."

I nod in agreement. "It's too bad IT couldn't wipe the whole incident from Principal Pruitt's mind too." I reach out to grab his arm. "Wait, should we ask if they can do that?"

He lays his hand over mine and tugs me forward. "Let's just see how this meeting goes first, shall we?"

I'm annoyed by how quickly we arrive at our final destination. I would have appreciated a bit more dillydallying, maybe a pit stop near the vending machines, a quick lap around the band hall, but Ian insists we have to be early.

"What's that?" Ian asks as we wait outside Principal Pruitt's office. He's pointing to the hefty bag at my feet. Guess he didn't notice when I grabbed it from underneath my desk back in my classroom.

"Oh, just baked goods."

His eyes widen in wonder. "Why do you have so many? That bag is overflowing."

"I couldn't remember what Principal Pruitt's favorite dessert was, so I made them all."

"*All*?"

"Brownies, cookies, blondies, lemon bars, and mini pecan pies. When I bribe, I bribe hard."

"Sam, we're going in there for a meeting, not a bake sale."

Oh, Ian. For such a handsome fellow, he can be such a dimwit. When we walk into Principal Pruitt's office a few minutes later, I unveil my creations and our boss starts to salivate. His sausage fingers wriggle with impatience.

"I guess dessert was on your mind, heh-heh. How did you know I can't resist lemon bars?" he says with a full mouth. Crumbs spill out onto his desk, but he doesn't care because he's so overcome with love for my treats.

I turn to Ian with a smug smile and silently say, *See?* Maybe before this he was going to fire us, but now we'll be spared thanks to that flaky graham cracker crust he's licking off his fingers. *You can thank me later.*

We sit patiently as Principal Pruitt munches his way through a second lemon bar, gives an enthusiastic shoulder-shimmying "Mm mm mm", wipes his hands, and leans back, assessing us.

"I really hate to have to call you two in here for something so silly. Really, that picture was pretty funny, especially considering what came after it—well, except for..."

He doesn't have to say it; we all know he's talking about Pauline.

"Yeah," he continues, frowning. "I had to put her on leave today. Not something we can tolerate here at Oak Hill."

Oh god, he's already fired one person? Maybe he got a taste for it and he's ready to keep dropping the axe. Thinking quickly, I reach down and unzip the small cooler at my feet. "Cold milk to wash down those lemon bars?"

His eyes widen. "Is that two percent?"

"Good eye. Here, you can take the whole thing."

He gulps it down, and when he speaks again, he has a

frothy milk mustache decorating his upper lip. At least if we're about to be fired, I'll have this memory to take with me to the unemployment office.

"Anyway, listen—with everything else going on, I wouldn't have called you in here at all, but the head of the PTA, Mrs. O'Doyle, caught wind of the whole ordeal. She got a few of the parents worked up and the only way I could get them to calm down was if I promised to see that the proper steps were taken. That's why you two are here today."

"What does she seem to think is the problem? We're both adults," Ian points out.

"That you are, but unfortunately"—he leans down to retrieve something from his desk drawer...two somethings, in fact—"the employee contract you signed during your orientation stated that neither of you could participate in a relationship with another staff member. You both agreed to the stipulation."

He pushes the contracts our way and I'm dismayed to find he's taken the liberty of tabbing the section in question with a neon yellow sticky note. My John Hancock is right there. Dried black ink glistens under fluorescent light. I don't even think I read through the contract properly before I signed it. I was too focused on Ian. We'd only just met, and I was still 95% convinced he was a mirage.

Still, who cares about a signature? There's a little tool I like to call Wite-Out—I even have some back in my classroom. Ian can run (he's faster) and retrieve it in no time.

I smile extra sweet and lean forward. "Yes. Okay, I see that we signed, but can't this all be solved now if we disclose that we're dating and practice discretion?"

I wink-wink like *c'mon, help a sister out*. We're buds, friends—*lemon bar buddies*.

His face hardens.

"Was that email your version of discretion?" he asks.

Oh okay. It's going to be like this. We're playing hardball.

I sit back in my chair and fold my hands over my lap dutifully, wishing I could go back in time and retrieve that wink.

"What about Karen and Neal?" Ian asks. "They both teach here and they're in a relationship."

"They're married. It's different."

We all sit silent for a few seconds then Principal Pruitt sighs and pushes one last piece of paper in our direction. It's a copy of the email Mrs. O'Doyle has been circulating among the other PTA parents. My embarrassing photo is enlarged up top, and below, it reads, IS THIS WHO WE WANT TEACHING OUR CHILDREN?

She acts like I'm holding a penis next to my mouth instead of an innocent can of whipped cream.

"I feel like I'm partly to blame for this," Principal Pruitt says with a heavy frown. "She might have left well enough alone, but she also got word that you two ran the sex-ed course the other week, and if you remember that one student who had opted out but ended up catching the first half…that was her son." Ian and I both audibly groan. "Exactly. Not only did we accidentally—and I quote—'offend the goodliness and godliness of her little boy', she also thinks you two were in there teaching sex tips from the Kamasutra or something."

Her email's not good. This lady is out for blood. She demands our jobs, declaring that she won't stop until we resign, move, change our names.

I glance over at Ian, expecting to see him sitting there looking as hopeless as I do, but his eyes are narrowed on me. He looks determined—excited, even. He's got ideas churning under that thick head of hair. I sigh in relief. He's going to get us out of this mess. I know it.

After the meeting, Ian doesn't ask, just drives me straight to Sonic. He pulls up to the drive-through, orders a Blast with extra Oreos for me and a plain vanilla milkshake for himself. We sit in the car and eat in silence. I'm trying to give him space to finish formulating his master plan. Meanwhile, my brain goes wild with possibilities: we kidnap Mrs. O'Doyle, or we hack into her computer and send a follow-up email full of praise about Ian and me, or we break into Principal Pruitt's office after hours and insert devious loopholes into the contracts. I think I have a black ski mask in my apartment somewhere. It'd be useful for all three options.

I slurp down my ice cream, and by the time my blood sugar hovers in the pre-diabetic range, I'm not even a little bit worried.

I turn to Ian and smile.

"So what's the plan? I mean, I'll be honest, during that meeting, I was convinced one of us would have to move to another school or something, or we'd have to go back to being just friends and pen some bizarre-o apology letter to the entire school." I sigh dramatically. "Ugh, please tell me we aren't going to have to do that."

He swallows the last of his milkshake, sets the cup down, and turns to me. He dabs his mouth with a napkin and smiles. He looks thoughtful and adorable. His brown hair is mussed up and the setting sun is shining in, brightening his blue eyes.

"There's only one option, and I thought you would have figured it out by now."

I breathe in deeply and nod with a steady seriousness. "Yes." I exhale. "We kidnap her."

"What? No," he says, nonchalantly reaching out the window and pushing the order button again.

"Yes, may I take your order," crackles the speaker.

"Small order of onion rings for the road, please."

When he's done paying, I demand answers.

"If we're not going to kidnap that crazy lady, what's your big plan?"

"Why do you think I ordered those rings, Hot Lips?" He smirks. "We're going to have to get married."

Chapter Seventeen

Sam

I sit perfectly frozen, almost as if he just turned me to stone. Day turns to night turns to day turns to night and I'm still staring at him, unblinking. Years pass. My hair turns gray and my hands are wrinkled and feeble when I finally realize he's kidding.

I bark out a laugh and bat his arm. "Oh my god, Ian, I thought you were serious there for a second!"

So much silence fills his car, the windshield splinters down the middle, trying to alleviate some of the pressure. My smile fades slowly.

He's not kidding.

He tips his head to the side and studies me.

Slow as molasses, his mouth spreads into a smile and my stomach drops.

"You're not serious!" I insist. "C'mon, we need to focus. What are we actually going to do? Hack Mrs. O'Doyle into little pieces and ship her to different corners of the United States?"

"We can do that, too, but first let's get married. They might send us to the same prison."

He's not dropping this joke. It's getting old.

I roll my eyes. "Right, okay. We'll get *married*. Ha. Married," I sing-song. "Glad that's settled."

His smile fades and he turns to glance out the window. If I didn't know better, I'd say I offended him.

I frown and reach over, taking his bicep in my palm. I squeeze it twice, trying to get him to meet my eyes. He won't.

"Are you kidding?"

His brows furrow deeper. He looks so angry and so beautiful. "Nope."

"Not even a little bit?"

"No."

That answer hits me like a ton of bricks.

If he's not kidding, then he's on crack.

IAN IS ON CRACK! Somebody warn the anti-drug froyo guy.

My soothing, gentle voice is gone. In its place is a shrill, exasperated shout. "MARRIED?! Ian, YOU'RE CRAZY! I just gave in to dating you like a day ago, and now you want to propose marriage?!"

This makes no sense. Between the two of us, Ian is the

logical one. He's thoughtful about everything. I don't think he's been spontaneous even once in his life. He plans vacations two years in advance. He keeps the owner's manual for every appliance he's ever purchased, down to his can opener. Last year, when he helped me put together my new IKEA dresser, I ripped open every package, flinging parts across my living room. Meanwhile, Ian read the entire instruction booklet cover to cover (in English and in Swedish).

I open my mouth to argue some more, to throw reason at him, but I'm too dumbstruck to form words. I bob my mouth open and closed like a fish.

"Realistically, what would change?" he says, still staring ahead. "We already share a meal service subscription and a Netflix account. In fact, if you won't marry me, I'm going to change my password."

Well, he does have me there…

NO!

"We can't get married!" I cry, tossing my hands in the air dramatically. "We haven't even had sex!"

"Yeah, well, we can fix that," he says, unveiling a hint of a smirk. "These windows are pretty tinted."

Damn this delicious Sonic treat. Their ice cream is so thick I can't even dump it out on his head.

He finally turns to face me and I'm hit with cobalt and powder blue and something else: LOVE. He reaches out for my hands and cradles them over the center console. This can't be happening. I'm shaking. This feels like a real proposal… except the car next to ours is blaring rap music so loudly their bass is shaking our windows. Behind Ian, there's a rusted dumpster and some tasteful graffiti telling me to $uk d!k.

There's not a single rose petal or lit candle in sight.

"Honestly though, is that your only reason against it?" he asks, brushing his thumb across my knuckles. My heart hammers in my chest. I feel like I could start sobbing uncontrollably at any second.

"I don't know." I shake my head and try to pull my hands back, but he doesn't let go. "I haven't had time to have a real freak-out."

He shakes his head, determined. "I'm not going to give you time. Don't think. Oreos or M&Ms?"

"Oreos!"

"Summer or fall?!"

"Fall!"

"Tator tots or French fries?!"

"Both!"

"Do you want to marry me, yes or no?"

"YES!"

Then I jump across the car and kiss him so hard he falls back and crashes against the window. The kids in the rap car holler at us to get a room.

Chapter Eighteen

Sam

An hour later, we walk into the county clerk's office wearing plastic rings we traded two quarters for at the grocery store across the street from Sonic. I expect quite the hullabaloo once we're inside—balloons, streamers, white drapery—but it feels a lot like we're in line at the DMV when a no-nonsense broad by the name of Ethel calls our number.

We sit down in her cubicle and I'm hopped up on sugar and love. Ethel, on the other hand, clearly missed her afternoon cup of joe. She checks her watch twice before finally acknowledging us.

"State your names for the record."

"Hi! Hello! I'm Sam—Samantha Abrams. This is my fiancé, Ian Fletcher. OH MY GOD MY LAST NAME IS GOING TO BE FLETCHER! I'M NOT GOING TO BE FIRST IN ROLL CALL ANYMORE!"

Everything is hitting me all at once.

I'M GETTING MARRIED!

I AM GOING TO BE IAN'S WIFE!

I'm jittery and smiling so hard my cheeks ache. Ian laughs and takes my hand in his. He's not shaking like I am, much closer to Ethel's energy level than mine.

"A-b-r-a-m-s?" Ethel asks, aiming her coke-bottle glasses at her computer screen.

I lean forward and nearly shout, "Yes!"

Everything I say is capped with a smile and an explanation mark. She could ask me if my great-grandparents are dead and I'd grin from ear to ear and exclaim, YOU BETCHA, DEAD AS A DOORNAIL!

"F-l-e-t-c-h-e-r?"

Ian nods. "Yes ma'am."

Ma'am! My fiancé is so respectful!

I stare at him with misty eyes and he squeezes my hand.

Ethel keeps on typing, pounding keys like she's banging on drums. She doesn't seem very enthusiastic. Can she tell we only got engaged an hour ago? Is it obvious that this is spontaneous and stupid?

What if she asks us questions to verify we're in love and we say different answers?

Ian, does Sam prefer man on top or woman on top during coitus?

HE DOESN'T KNOW!

Suddenly, I feel hot and sweaty. I'm panicking like this is a green card wedding.

In reality, Ethel only asks questions about whether or not we're in any way related or if either of us is overdue on child support payments, but that doesn't stop me from telling her lies about our relationship, just in case.

"He did this huge, over-the-top proposal, helicopters and everything. Bill Murray was there!"

She grunts as she continues to type.

"We've actually been dating three years today," I brag. "That's why I'm so emotional."

Ethel looks at me over the rims of her glasses. "Congrats." She doesn't sound congratulatory. "Are either of you already married?"

I blink, confused. "I just told you we've been dating for three years."

She sighs and glances at her watch for a third time. "I have to ask every question on the prompt. Yes or no?"

"No," we answer in unison.

So much for romance. Ethel prints forms, slaps stamps, and pushes us out the door as quickly as possible. We have a manila-colored marriage license in hand and strict orders to wait 72 hours before tying the knot.

This is news to me. I sort of thought we'd get the license, hop over to the courthouse, and have this all finished by dinner time.

72 hours feels like a lifetime—certainly enough time for this sugar high to wear off and for us to realize how utterly irrational this all is. I don't want to think. I want to keep playing Ian's game. I want to be married right now!

I think Ian can sense this because he stays quiet as we head back to his car. He opens my door, and once we're both seated, I reach for his hand again. He has a hard time navigating out of the parking lot and back onto the road while I have ahold of him, but I can't let go. It's the only thing keeping me on earth.

"Should we drive to Vegas? There's no waiting period."

"It would take us 72 hours to get there and back. Let's just wait here."

"But I feel like we have to keep moving! Is this actually happening?"

He nods and turns right at the light.

"This isn't some elaborate prank on your part? Because really, you could do much better than me."

"Don't talk like that. You're beautiful and funny."

"WHAT?!"

It's one thing to propose marriage and another thing entirely to call me *beautiful and funny*. I'm not sure which one is more important.

"Ian Fletcher thinks I'm beautiful," I say to no one in particular. "Wowee."

"Uh huh. Try not to look so stunned. Do you want me to drop back by Oak Hill so we can grab your bike?"

"Yes please."

"What should we do for dinner? Want Chinese to celebrate?"

"Yes! Sesame chicken. Wait, shit—I have to go over to my parents' house. They got back from their cruise this morning, and I promised I'd eat dinner with them so they could show me pictures." Dang it. "I could cancel?"

"No. You hardly see them."

Such an understanding hubs.

"Why don't you come and we can share the news with them together?" I ask, hopeful that he won't leave me to fend for myself.

He shrugs. "I guess that's not a bad idea. How do you think they'll take it?"

"If the past few days have taught me anything, it's that it is completely useless trying to predict the future. Let's just roll with it."

I was intentionally ignoring the obvious outcome. My parents, Genine and Thomas, are deeply boring and old-fashioned. My mom didn't let me cut my hair until I was 7. I couldn't wear makeup until I was old enough to buy it for myself. They don't drink alcohol. They're judgmental, and I generally try to avoid them while at the same time not cutting them out of my life completely.

When I show up for dinner with Ian unexpectedly in tow, they act deeply put out.

"It's just that I only set the table for three," my mother says, as if they only keep three plates in the entire house.

"And I only bought three steaks," my father grumbles.

"If we all cut off one quarter, everyone will have ¾ of a steak!" I point out cheerfully.

"I like all my quarters," continues the grumbler.

"Oh-*kay*, you can have all of mine."

I'm too nervous to have any real appetite. Also, that milkshake was huge.

"I suppose that's fine," my mom says with a sneer.

After they've made it abundantly clear that he isn't welcome, I expect Ian to make some kind of strained excuse (He left the oven on? Has to wash his hair?) and then exit stage left. But, no, he stays right by my side, accepting of the fact that I still have a death grip on his hand. By now, our skin is fused. He'll have to go in for surgery if he wants to remove me.

As if reading my thoughts, my mom glances down at our hands and her expression makes me look down as well. She looks so horrified I briefly think, *Oh no, are we accidentally having sex or something?*

No, just holding hands like the loose, immoral people we are.

"Samantha, would you like to use my bathroom to freshen up before dinner?" my mom asks, continuing her perusal of me and clearly finding my appearance lacking. "I think I have another dress you can put on if you'd like."

I'm still wearing my blue dress from school. It's fine. In fact, I felt kind of pretty in it before she said something.

Ian meets my gaze, narrows his eyes, and shakes his head. "You look great," he says loudly enough for both of my parents to hear.

Right. My mom turns to continue prepping dinner with pursed lips. For a few minutes, there's no conversation while my dad fusses with the steaks at the stove and my mom hurries to add a fourth place setting at the table.

She mumbles under her breath the whole time, pleasantries like, "Would it have been too much to call ahead of time?"

I don't engage her. If she's this upset about an extra dinner guest, how is she going to take an extra member of the family?

When my dad declares the steaks ready to eat, my mom directs us to the table and tells us to take a seat. I begrudgingly let go of Ian's hand.

"Can I help with anything? Get drinks?" he asks.

She shakes her head. "No, no, we have everything taken care of. Would you like still or sparkling water?"

What I wouldn't give for a whole trough of wine.

"Still is fine. Thank you," Ian replies, and I agree.

Then, the dinner from hell begins. My father sits at the head of the table. My mom sits across from him, and Ian and I are smashed in the middle. It's not that the table is that small, but their judgement takes up a lot of space.

"So how long have you two been an item?" my mom asks with a snippy tone.

"Oh, um, just for a little while," I say, sidestepping the truth with a generality.

"I wasn't aware things had progressed. Weren't you just friends before this?"

I nod and offer as few details as possible. "It's new."

"Ian, what is it that you do for work again?" my father asks, staring over at him from beneath his thick scraggly eyebrows.

"I teach at Oak Hill with Sam."

"Oh yes." He nods. "I remember now. And do you make good money there?"

My eyes bulge out of my head.

"Dad."

Ian doesn't care about the intrusion. "The pay is okay, but money has never been my motivation."

"Oh, don't tell me you're one of those hippies who thinks

money isn't important. Hate to break it to you, but peace and love don't keep you warm in the winter."

Ian keeps a straight face as he replies, "You're right. Luckily, I worked in pharma for a while after college, saved up quite a bit, and I've invested it well over the years. It's enough to keep the gas on, anyway."

My dad's brows rise in shock, mainly because Ian had the audacity to call him on his bullshit.

"But as a side note, peace and love get you pretty far in life. Sam and I don't need much to be happy." His gaze catches mine and I smile.

My dad grunts, and it's clear he thinks Ian has a lot of growing up to do.

"Just wait until you have a family to feed. It's expensive raising kids."

KIDS.

Heat travels up my neck. We haven't gotten that far. Ian might not even want kids. I look down at my 3/4 steak and know I won't be able to force down even one bite.

"We'll manage, I'm sure," Ian replies with an amused tone. He hates this. He doesn't understand why I bother with my parents at all. "I'm thinking if we have 9 or 10 kids we can put them to work as chimney sweeps—"

"*Oh*, have you two already discussed the future?" my mom interrupts with a high-pitched lilt.

Ian and I lock gazes again and his brows rise. His point is clear: *Take the opportunity. It's now or never.*

I set down my fork, take a deep breath, and then proclaim simply, "Ian and I are engaged."

Cutlery falls to the table dramatically. I glance over

and my mom has her hand pressed over her heart in shock. "*Engaged*?!"

She exclaims the word as if she's performing for a packed Broadway theatre.

I smile, easy and simple. "Yes. We're getting married in 72 hours."

"72? *Hours*?! What—"

My dad's question gets cut off by an errant sob from my mom.

"Samantha Grace, what are you talking about? 72 hours?! This is nonsense." She stands and slams her linen napkin down on the table. "Is this a joke?"

Ian and I both shake our heads.

"We've put a lot of thought into this." All of twenty minutes.

"This is extremely sudden," she says, pacing and pressing the back of her hand to her forehead. "You two weren't even dating the last time I checked!"

"Your mother's right," my father's voice booms. "You two need to slow down. We have premarital counseling at the church. It's a six-week course."

They're confused. "We don't want to wait. We want your support."

"Well you don't have it. Please, be *rational*."

What she means to say is, *Please, do it the exact way your father and I did it. Come in for premarital counseling, don a poofy white dress, and walk down the aisle not too slow but not too fast, all so I can prove to all of our family and friends that I've raised a classy young woman, not a heathen who elopes.*

"We've already made up our minds," Ian insists with a

strong, no-nonsense tone. "We're going to elope, and we'd love for you two to be there if you'd like. Once we know the time and place, we'll pass it along."

"The time and place?!" Her lips tremble. Her hands are shaking. My mom is having a mental breakdown before our very eyes. "You don't even know that yet?! *Good heavens*."

She storms off and starts weeping near the extra salad on the island in the kitchen. My father hurries over to comfort her. I honestly think they're taking it worse than if I'd told them I had cancer.

"Look what you're doing to your mother, Samantha," my dad chides.

All of a sudden, I've had enough. They're being ridiculous. I understand needing a few minutes to adjust, but this is taking it to a whole new level. I jerk to stand, causing my chair to tip back and crash to the floor.

"Ian, let's go. Grab your plate. Yes, take it—and your glass! Here, I'll help you."

My arms are loaded up with stolen cutlery and dinnerware as we bolt from the house. My parents are crying as if they've lost me forever.

"Sam, are you sure you don't want to go back in there?" Ian asks after we've buckled up.

I shake my head and utter one word.

"Drive."

Our stolen dinner sits untouched on my coffee table. Ian sits beside me on the couch, and the aftermath of our afternoon and evening has struck us both silent. I was riding a high, running from Principal Pruitt's office to Sonic to the grocery store to the county clerk's office. It was the most exciting few hours of my life. I couldn't wipe the smile off my face, and then my parents had to ruin it.

Are they right?

Are we being irrational?

I shift my gaze to Ian and see him staring at the ceiling with his brows furrowed. I think he's having the same second thoughts I am. Any moment, he's going to turn, look me square in the eyes, and tell me he doesn't want to marry me after all. The thought sends a worried tear down my cheek. I swipe it away quickly.

"Do you want kids, Ian?"

He frowns. "You know I do."

"Do you want them with me?"

"Sam."

I shake my head and nibble on my bottom lip. "Maybe my parents are right. Maybe this is crazy. I've put more thought into the placement of a tattoo I'll never get than this marriage. This is the rest of our lives we're talking about."

"Just because it's spontaneous doesn't mean it's wrong." He sounds confident. "What would make you feel better?"

"Let's have sex."

"Sam, you're crying."

"Then overload my brain with your mouth."

"No. Not tonight."

He sounds mad.

I sit up and turn to him. "Why?"

His hand finds mine on the couch and he squeezes. "It feels old-fashioned to wait until after we elope. I like it. Also, no offense, but I'm not exactly in the mood. It feels like I'd be taking advantage of you."

"Great." I toss up my hands. "I'm marrying a prude."

"Shove over and hand me the remote. I know what will make you feel better."

"I don't want to watch HBO porn."

He pulls up season 2 episode 12 of *The Office*, the one where Michael grills his foot on his George Foreman Grill. This episode has pulled me out of an end-of-summer funk, a bad-relationship-turned-into-bad-breakup slump, and that one time I got strep throat right after the flu. Ian was there for all of that and he's here now, watching the episode beside me on my couch. My future husband. Mr. Samantha Abrams.

I'll find his short brown hair on my pillow. On Saturdays, he'll insist on making a big breakfast and I'll eat it even though I really just want a slice of peanut butter toast.

Michael Scott wraps his foot in bubble wrap on screen and I start to remove the bubble wrap around my heart. I've kept it there from the beginning of my friendship with Ian. No girl befriends a guy as handsome and charming as him without some kind of safeguard. My heart beats faster as if it's aware of its newfound freedom. I've been holding it back, but now it's beating at its full potential, thumping and demanding the love I've deprived it of. He's beautiful and he's going to be mine. I can hardly believe it. I want to lift my hand and feel the contours of his face, his nose, his chin, just to prove to myself he really exists. This isn't just another dream.

"Are you watching?" Ian asks, aware of my gaze on his profile.

"No."

"You're missing your favorite part."

It's when Michael asks Pam to rub Country Crock on his foot to help it heal.

"How do you think we'll watch TV when we're married?"

"Probably like this."

"Oh."

"Except we'll obviously be nude."

My jaw drops. He sighs and turns my way, reaching out to close my open trap.

"I'm kidding, Sam. Stop thinking. You'll spin yourself out of control."

"I can't turn my brain off. That dinner was intense. My parents are going to disown me. They're probably spending my dowry on replacement dinnerware."

He feigns disappointment. "Really? That was the only reason I proposed."

"You can back out if you want. There's still time."

His gaze falls to my mouth and he reaches out to yank my lip free from my teeth. I didn't realize I was nibbling on it.

"I should be saying the same thing to you. You're the one who's rebelling against her parents. My parents love you. When I call them later to tell them about this, my mom will probably lose her voice from screaming so loud."

I grin. "That's because I'm loveable."

His finger traces my knuckles. His touch is feather-light. "I know."

POP. POP. POP. My bubble wrap keeps deflating.

"What time did we get our marriage license?" he asks, changing the subject like a pro.

"I don't know…4:50? The courthouse closed at five o'clock and we were the last ones in line."

"So then at 4:50 on Friday, we will have waited the required 72 hours."

That's soon—three sleeps soon.

"I think it's a good idea if we don't see each other until then," he continues.

"But tomorrow is *West Wing* Wednesday."

We've never missed one, not even for illness. Once, Ian watched in his bedroom while he had a stomach bug and I watched in the living room. We shouted to each other through the door.

"I know, but I think it's important to give you time to really consider what we're about to do."

"Oh, yeah. Okay." He does have a way of overloading my brain. "Do you need time too?"

"No."

That word was locked and loaded in his chamber. He says it so quickly, without a blink, and it hits me like a bullet.

Ian's in love with me.

POP. POP. POP.

Our gazes lock and my apartment becomes a furnace. My sofa seems even smaller than usual and Ian takes up so much of it. I'd only have to scooch over a little bit to reach his lap. I could crawl on top and hook one knee on either side of his hips. He'd be trapped there, completely at my mercy.

"What on earth are you thinking about?" he asks huskily.

"Taking advantage of you. Remember how we were sitting in your car on Saturday? With me on your lap?"

He groans and pushes off his knees to stand. The episode isn't over yet. Ryan hasn't even crushed up Aspirin into Michael's pudding.

Ian goes to the bathroom and when he walks back out, it looks like he splashed cold water on his face. I think Ian wants to have sex with me and he's trying to convince himself it's a bad idea. Just the thought makes me clench my thighs.

"Where would your dream wedding take place?" he asks, keeping a safe distance from me across the room.

That's easy.

"The star exhibit at the Natural History Museum. You know the room right before you go into the planetarium?" It's domed and lit up with a million stars. "It's where you stepped in gum that one time. Now come back over here and sit down so I can kiss you."

He nods and moves to the door. "Okay. If you still want to marry me, meet me there at 4:50 on Friday."

I jump to my feet. *WHOA*. This is happening. "Do I need to do anything?"

"I'll handle all of it."

"What about my dress?"

"Wear whatever you want. It can be a pantsuit for all I care."

I grin. "I always knew you had a thing for Hillary Clinton."

"Sam." He's staring at me with serious eyes…I-love-you eyes. "Think this over." His hand tugs through his hair. "I don't want to feel like I'm forcing you into anything. Don't come on Friday unless you're sure."

"You're scaring me."

"Maybe we should be scared."

I scurry over and cut him off on his way to the door, blocking his way out. If he wants to leave, he'll have to go through me.

"I'm not going to change my mind."

His gaze is on my lips. That cold water is all gone and his bedroom eyes are heating up. I take full advantage, grabbing ahold of his T-shirt and tugging him toward me. He obliges and takes a step closer. I tilt my head back and his throat is so close to my mouth, I tip onto my toes and kiss him there, right on his pulse line. His hand hits the door beside my head.

"Sam," he warns.

"Kiss me before you leave, just once. I need something to remember you by if I won't see you until Friday."

His fingers trail up my neck, slowly. He's thinking over my request, weighing the pros and cons. I wish I was wearing a teasing little slip. My blue dress is fit for the classroom, not for seduction. My hands are my only weapon, so I trail them up his neck and then I'm cradling his face. His bristly jaw tickles my palms. He swallows and his muscles shift. I've never dated a guy as big as him. In the past, I chose pipsqueaks on purpose, guys I could have shared pantsuits with. An image of Ian trying desperately to shove his leg into a pair of my pants sends a smile to my lips.

He tips his head. "Why are you smiling?"

His words whisper against my mouth and a full-body shiver rolls through me, one he definitely sees. It makes him smile too, and then our lips are finally touching, but we're both still smiling. I laugh into his mouth. His hands

grip my butt as he rocks his hips against mine and my heart
slams against my rib cage. The move reminds me that Ian
can flip the script so easily. One second, he's my best friend,
and the next he's the not-so-nice guy, the man who handles
me like he's barely resisting the urge to devour me whole.
Our smiles fade, he presses closer, and our kiss turns hot.
His hands burn across my skin. A few of the buttons on my
dress are undone. My hand is down his jeans. I've never
undone a zipper so quickly. It's a talent I've largely ignored
up until now, but maybe I should go on tour and show off
my skills. *THE SPECTACULAR SAMANTHA: Look
how quickly I can seduce my fiancé. Don't blink or you'll
miss it!*

My hand sneaks down the front of his boxer briefs. My little
kiss is turning into a little more, and I'm so damn pleased with
myself. I'll get an orgasm if I'm lucky, but Ian is smarter. He
knew my plan all along. He extricates my hand with a heavy
sigh and steps back. I hate him for his superhuman resolve.
Why does it matter when we have sex? Why can't we just bang
it out right here on my welcome mat? Who cares if the letters
on the mat imprint themselves on my ass? Who cares if my
neighbors hear us when they walk down the hall to get their
mail?

*Leonard, grab that package. Wait, do you hear that? I
think an animal is dying in 2A.*

They'll file a noise complaint and I'll tape the yellow
warning slip to my refrigerator with pride.

"Friday," Ian promises before picking me up underneath
my armpits, shuffling me to the side, and walking out my front
door.

Chapter Nineteen

Sam

72 hours is enough time to go up and down a rollercoaster of indecision so many times I feel nauseous. One minute, I'm feeling spontaneous and adventurous and I tell myself things like, *Don't second-guess this. Do it! Live!* The next minute, I start to think of the logistics. We're making a hasty decision. You don't just marry someone on a whim. We know each other so well, but I'm sure there are still hidden sides to Ian. For instance, I've never slept in a bed with him. I don't know what temperature he likes to set the thermostat to at night. He could be an inconsiderate blanket hog.

I sleep very little Tuesday night and on Wednesday

morning, it's time to face the music. All the commotion about the potential elopement means the whipped cream photo took the back burner in my mind.

Technically, Ian and I have been placed on probation until further notice. It's Principle Pruitt's way of saving us from a mandatory leave situation, or worse, termination. Mrs. O'Doyle isn't satisfied, though, and the part of my brain that isn't taken up with thoughts about Ian is waiting for the other shoe to drop with her.

She's not the only person hungry for retribution.

Bianca and Gretchen are waiting for me outside my classroom when I get to school.

Bianca's arms are crossed and she blocks my path so I can't unlock my door. "Was that fun for you both to see us drooling over Ian like that? Why'd you tell us you weren't together if you clearly were?"

I sigh, tired from lack of sleep and a constantly whirring brain. "I wasn't lying that day in the teachers' lounge. At the time, we weren't together."

"Save it. We know you're on probation for dating him. It's against the rules. The parents are upset. You two won't last the rest of the week."

She huffs and sticks her nose in the air then snaps for Gretchen to follow after her.

It's not exactly the way I want to start my day, but then I walk into my classroom and find a thermos full of hot coffee, a granola bar, and a single red rose waiting for me on my desk. Its petals are full and open. I promptly trim it and put it in water right away then proceed to stare at it for most of my day.

Ian stays true to his word and we don't see each other at all on Wednesday or Thursday. He doesn't come to the teachers' lounge during lunch. Ashley sits with the Freshman Four and I'm left all alone, picking at a turkey sandwich and missing Ian. We don't do *West Wing* Wednesday. We don't even chat over text or email, which feels weird, but I think he really wants to give me space. I walk to the bike rack after school on Thursday and catch sight of the soccer field in the distance. Ian is out there running drills with his team. My legs want to carry me in his direction until I'm right there in the thick of it. Soccer players would have to dive out of the way to keep from pummeling me. I'd fling myself onto Ian's back, hook my arms around his neck, and tell him to continue on with practice. I wouldn't get in the way. I just want to smell him, to feel his arms and hands and hair and remind myself that this perfect human wants to marry me and I'd be absolutely insane to turn him down.

Instead, I bike extra fast on the way home.

I'm surprised to find my dad waiting for me at my apartment. He's wearing one of his fancy lawyer suits and looks very uncomfortable out on the curb. His scowl warns me to expect another battle and I steel my shoulders accordingly, but when he sees me ride up, he stands up and waves.

"Hey kiddo."

I drop my weapons. "Hi Dad."

He's only ever been to my apartment a few times. He thinks I should live at home to save money. To him, the chipped linoleum and ugly brown carpet are beneath me.

"I like what you've done with the place," he says after I let us in. He's poking at one of the books on my shelf and reading the spine. I'm grateful it's not *Pirate's Hidden Treasure*.

"Thanks. Did Mom send you?" I ask, bringing him a glass of water.

He accepts it and nods. "She wanted to make sure you were okay after the other night. Also, she wants her plates back."

His teasing smile surprises me and I laugh.

"Right, well, you can have the plates, but if you're going to try to talk me out of marrying Ian, you shouldn't bother."

He sips his water then places it on a coaster on the coffee table. "I'm not."

"Oh," I say hesitantly.

"But I'm going to tell you something, and I want you to listen." He turns to me, his hands on his hips. He suddenly looks like a formidable opponent, and I wonder if this is what he looks like in a court of law. "Marriage is not something you should enter into lightly. Your mom and I were in love when we got married. We've been together for over 30 years now, and there have still been a lot of hard times."

This is news to me—they've always seemed perfect.

"I know it seems exciting right now, but there will be trials down the road, and if you don't start with a solid foundation, it's going to make it ten times harder to weather the storms."

"I've thought about all this."

His brow arches with interest. "And you still think you're making the right decision?"

There's no point in lying, so I sidestep his question. "Has Mom come around to the idea?"

I take a seat on the couch and he joins me.

"Afraid not. She's still crying about the fact that you won't be wearing her grandmother's dress or getting married at the church."

I lean my head back against the cushion and smile, thinking back to the monstrosity hanging in one of the upstairs closets back at the house. "I wouldn't wear that dress even if I was having a traditional wedding."

He leans his head beside mine and we stare up at the ceiling together. "That's what I told her."

"Dad?"

"Yes?"

"I could be making a huge mistake."

"You could be."

"Or I could be making the best decision of my life."

He nods thoughtfully. "Who's to say?"

I glance down and see a folded blue handkerchief in his hand. It's the one I remember him wearing when I was a kid. He'd fold it into a neat square and stuff it into the front pocket of his suits. His initials are embroidered on the bottom corner, and when he notices me staring at it, he opens his palm.

"Something old, borrowed, and blue." He offers it to me. "Best I could do on short notice."

Chapter Twenty

Ian

I found our officiant on Craigslist. He's technically a rabbi, but when I explained our situation, he agreed to marry Sam and me in the museum. Fine by me. I don't really care how we get married. If we somehow get converted to Judaism in the process, so be it. *Shabbat Shalom.*

The last few days have flown by. In between teaching and coaching, I've been putting plans in place for Friday. When I called to tell my parents about the wedding, after my mom stopped crying, she told me she always knew I'd do something like this.

"Once you put your mind to something, you do it! No

questions asked. When you wanted to learn how to ride a bike, you went out on the driveway with a helmet and kneepads and kept right on trying until you were pedaling right past all the other kids in the neighborhood."

They wanted to drive down for the ceremony, but they couldn't get off work on such short notice, so instead, I told them I'd keep my phone on in my shirt pocket so they could hear the whole thing.

They're on the phone now.

I tip my chin down. "Testing, testing. Can you hear me?"

"Loud and clear!" my dad shouts back.

I get an amused look from the rabbi.

It's 4:45 PM. The rabbi and I are at the museum, standing in the antechamber where guests wait for the next star show inside the planetarium. The tall ceiling is domed and lit up like the night sky. Even still, the room is pretty dark and crowded. I'll have a hard time seeing Sam. She really is small.

"Is she there yet?" my mom asks.

"No."

"Describe her to us when you see her!" she insists.

It feels like I've been waiting forever. I really shouldn't have arrived so early, but I wanted to scout out the area and make sure everything was set. After that, I went to the bathroom…found a snack…wandered around the museum.

I've lost track of how long I've stood here, and I don't want to check my phone again. If it's after 4:50 and Sam isn't here, I don't want to know. As it is, I'm still hopeful that she'll come.

Another group of guests funnel into the planetarium and more people take their place. The rabbi shifts on his feet and I think he's annoyed with me for making him wait so long, but then I glance over and he offers me a pitying half-smile.

"Sweetie, is she there yet?" my mom asks.

"You're supposed to be listening, not talking. I'm going to hang up on you guys if you ask me again."

I'm sweating now. I can't believe Sam is going to stand me up on our wedding day. This wasn't supposed to happen. We were supposed to be wild and crazy. I don't want to give her a boring love story. For us, there are a million stars and a rabbi and a room full of screaming kids. It fits us better than any chapel could.

I catch myself pleading in my head, *Please come, Sam. Please come.*

Maybe I should have called her on my way here, just to see where her head was at, but I intentionally gave her distance. I didn't want to influence her decision. I didn't want her to feel bad if she changed her mind about going through with this.

Sam needs space and time to adjust to things. The last 72 hours have probably been terrible for her. I imagine her pacing in that apartment and pulling out her hair. I wouldn't be surprised if she shows up completely bald—*if* she shows up.

Shit.

Now I'm second-guessing myself. This was so stupid. What was I thinking suggesting we get married? We can find new jobs. We can go back to being just friends if it means I get to keep Sam in my life. I'll keep my hands and my thoughts to myself. If she doesn't want to be with me, I can accept that. Losing Sam altogether though? No. There's not a fate worse than that.

A small horde of children scream and run away from their chaperones near the entrance to the antechamber and then right behind them, in walks Sam.

Holy…

The air rushes out of my chest. A wave of goose bumps cascade down my body. I have to resist the urge to clutch my hand over my heart.

"Ian! Why are you breathing hard! Are you having a heart attack or is she there?!"

"Both."

"How does she look?"

"She…her…I think…"

My mom is exasperated with my lack of brain-to-mouth connection. My synapses have all disappeared.

"What is she wearing?!"

Sam and I lock eyes from across the room and she freezes when she sees me. There's worry there—worry and amusement. She presses her lips together to hide her smile. Her head tips to the side and she shrugs like, *Yup, I'm here, even though this is absolutely insane.*

I've cried twice in my adult life. The first was when I fractured my tibia during an intramural soccer game. It was so painful, I passed out. This is the second time. I'm a complete schmuck as I watch her start to walk toward me. She doesn't have a clear path. She has to veer around kids who are running wild and adults who completely miss her. One lady steps back and nearly topples into her before apologizing.

"IAN!" my mom shouts, desperate. "What is she wearing?!"

I scan down her body. "A white dress…lace."

"Poofy?"

"Straight."

I'm not sure how she managed to find it so quickly, but it

looks like it was made just for her. The top of the dress is fitted and the V-neck dips down across her chest, her creamy skin glowing under the night sky. The bottom half flows around her legs as she walks.

"Is her hair up?"

"No. It's down and wavy and long, the brightest thing in the room."

A few kids stop and stare at her as she passes. One girl asks, "Mom, is she a fairy princess?"

I wipe the back of my hand across my cheeks, jerking away the tears in the manliest way possible. It's no use. Sam's crying too, crying and laughing as she nears me. When she gets close, I finally notice she's holding the red rose I left on her desk with a blue handkerchief tied around it.

"Hi," she says shyly.

"Hi."

"I like your tuxedo."

"I love your dress."

Her eyes widen at the compliment, and then she glances down, smoothing her hand over the fabric. "I found it at a consignment shop. $30."

"Nice."

"I bet you look so beautiful, Sam!" my mom shouts.

Sam jerks up and looks around, trying to figure out where the voice came from. I pat the breast pocket of my tuxedo. "My parents wanted to be here too."

She laughs and tips forward until her mouth is aligned with the phone. "Hello Mr. and Mrs. Fletcher!"

"Call us Mom and Dad!" they shout in unison. "If you want!"

The rabbi steps forward and introduces himself to Sam. He and I talked logistics and he knows the drill. We can't loiter here for very long. This can't be a full-length ceremony.

"Rabbi?" Sam mouths to me as he gets started.

I smile and shrug.

"You two might not know," the rabbi says, "but a traditional Jewish wedding ceremony takes place under the *chuppah*, or a canopy, which symbolizes the home the new couple will build together." We must look confused, because he continues. "So, getting married beneath the entire Milky Way might mean the two of you have quite the future ahead of you."

"Even if we aren't Jewish?" Sam asks.

He laughs. "Even then."

I keep one eye trained on the entrance to the room as he continues. If we're careful, we should be able to pull this off. He tells Sam and me to join hands, and I see a security guard lock eyes on us then speak hurriedly into a walkie-talkie on his shoulder. I swear I hear him whisper, "We've got a Code Matrimony, all units please respond."

"Oh god."

Sam follows my gaze. "What?"

"I think we're busted."

"Busted? What do you mean?"

I turn back to the rabbi. "Plan B."

Without a moment's hesitation, he pulls the rings I gave him out of his back pocket and asks us quickly if we take the other person as our lawfully wedded husband and wife. We quickly say yes and Sam's hand is shaking as I fumble to put her ring on. I had to guess the size, but it fits and she's really my wife now. I'll have time to revel in that fact later.

"Ian, what's going on?! Why are we rushing?"

I don't have time to fill her in because the security guard is onto us and we still have to sign the marriage certificate. I hand her the pen and turn around so she can use my back as a desk to scribble her signature just as another security guard joins the first. They start making their way toward us. I sign as fast as I can.

"GO!" the rabbi shouts, yanking the certificate out of my hand. "I'll drop this in the mail for you guys! GO! HURRY!"

I grab Sam's hand and take off toward the exit across the room from the security guards. She trips over the hem of her dress before she reaches down and hoists it up to her knees.

"Why are we running?" she shouts, but I don't slow down. "Ian!"

"Hurry, c'mon. The museum has a strict policy against unsanctioned ceremonies!"

"What?!"

"It's like $20,000 to get married here. We aren't millionaires!"

Security is rushing toward us and calling for backup. I pull Sam to the left, using a group of preschoolers as little human shields as we rush out of the room. The entrance to the museum is in sight, but we still have to make it through the entire front lobby. There's a large fossilized T-Rex standing between us and freedom. I want to run between his legs, but then we'd really be in trouble.

I veer around it.

"Hurry! HURRY! They're coming!"

"HEY! YOU TWO LOVEBIRDS! HALT OR WE'LL CALL THE POLICE!"

Sam screams then breaks out in a fit of laughter. "Oh my god! They're going to lock us in museum jail!"

We break free of the museum and I keep running once we're outside, tugging Sam after me. I didn't necessarily know we'd need a quick getaway when I was planning today, but this arrangement works out nicely. We're across the street and inside the lobby of a swanky hotel before the security guards even make it out of the museum. I turn and glance back just as they dart outside. They jerk their gazes this way and that, scratching their heads like we up and vanished into thin air.

"Are we going in here to throw them off our scent?" Sam asks as we rush through the lobby.

Everyone stops and stares at us, not only because we're running in a fancy hotel but because we're very clearly dressed like we just got married. Sam's still holding her rose.

We're at the elevators and I press the up button incessantly.

"We probably need a room key to use the elevator," Sam says, clutching her chest like she's about to keel over.

It's in my wallet.

The elevator dings and slides open. We step inside and I press the button for floor 4.

Her eyes slice to me and I unfurl a slow smile. "Happy honeymoon, Mrs. Fletcher."

It's the first time we've stopped since I initially saw her in the museum. It's our first moment to breathe.

"No way! Only rich people stay here! Mafia Dons and foreign dignitaries and Beyoncé!"

"If anyone asks, we're from the Russian consulate. Let me hear your accent."

"Iz theez the ótel Zaza?"

"Too French."

"Right. Let's just say I'm the Queen of France."

"Wasn't Marie Antionette the last queen of France?"

Then, her hand flies to her chest and her eyes go wide. "IAN!" Her chest is rising and falling dramatically. She's gulping in air like she hasn't breathed in a decade. "We didn't kiss. We didn't have our first kiss!"

She says it as if it's a deal breaker, as if because there was no kiss, we aren't really married.

The elevator ascends and I only have seconds to make it happen, but it's enough. I cross the elevator and push her up against the handrail. My hand cradles her cheek as I lean down. I can feel her pulse beating wildly. Her tongue wets her bottom lip in anticipation. She sucks in a sharp breath and her hand tightens around my wrist.

"You may now kiss the bride," I whisper before pressing my mouth to hers.

Now she's officially mine.

"Uh, yeah..." my mom says from my tuxedo pocket. "By the way, we're still here."

Chapter Twenty-One

Sam

We're running down the hall to our hotel room and my cheap, poorly fitted shoes are gone. I have no clue when exactly they fell off, but I'm barefoot now and the floor is lava. It's burning our feet and we both know without saying—only the hotel bed will be safe.

"Hold on," Ian says, and before I can ask him what he's doing, he yanks me to the side, crashes us up against the wall, and kisses me, hard. That elevator ride sparked something. We can't get enough of each other. Good thing he hung up on his parents or I'd never be able to make eye contact with them again.

His hips press forward, pinning me in place. His hand curves around my neck and I'm fisting his tuxedo jacket like I'm trying to rip it in two. I've never kissed someone while this worked up. We have to break apart every few seconds to gulp in air or we'll die, but then we go right back to it. He takes my lower lip in his mouth and bites down. Tingles *ZING* down my body until they settle right between my legs. I'm warm and turned on and anxious to make it to our room.

Actually, any room.

"Where do you think they keep the ice machine?"

"Why?"

"I think we should just try to make it there. It should be secluded enough."

"No, we're almost to the room."

He says this while nuzzling my neck and fingering the zipper of my dress. Dear god, I think he's going to strip me down right here.

A door opens down the hall. Voices filter in our direction and we take off running again.

"What's our room number?"

"419. C'mon!"

And we're off. Ian is sixteen times my size and has legs that go on for miles, so he does the running and I am mostly just along for the ride. I'm a small teddy bear flailing in the wind behind him.

There's no danger. The security guards gave up the chase as soon as we left the museum, but I don't think Ian and I are running from danger anymore; we're running toward it.

"412!" he shouts, picking up the pace.

"Agh! I have a cramp! Go on without me!"

He doubles back and hooks his arm under my legs so he can swing me up against his chest. He runs the last few yards carrying me against him, and for the first time all day, we're the stereotypical image of a bride and groom. He's about to carry me over the threshold.

We reach the room and he holds me with one arm as he extracts the key with the other.

"Mrs. Fletcher, would you do the honors?"

The name chokes me up, but I don't let him see my reaction. I focus instead on trying to turn that little red light green. It takes 45 years. I'm too impatient.

"Hold it there for longer," Ian instructs.

"I am!"

Of course I'm not. I tap it, jerk the knob, and curse when we're still locked out.

"Here, gimme."

Ian yanks it out of my hand, opens the door, and sweeps me inside. I don't touch the lava even once. He tosses the key and my rose in the general direction of the desk then hauls me up against the back of the door. My lace wedding dress gets shoved up somewhere near my thighs, not because we're *there* yet, but because it's the only way to wrap my legs around him without tearing the delicate fabric. Still, it tears a little.

"Shit, I'm sorry," Ian says, breaking our kiss to glance down.

"I DON'T CARE—KISS ME!" I jerk his face back to mine and kiss him senseless. His tongue sweeps into my mouth as I tilt my head, and we're kissing like someone's about to grab ahold of each of us and drop us on boats sailing to opposite ends of the world.

"I...I think I need water."

I really do. I'm parched, and if we're going to do this all night (which we are) I need proper hydration. Ian sets me down on the ground very carefully while also taking hold of my hand. He leads me into the bathroom and fills two glasses with water. We drink them while staring at each other in the mirror. We swallow the last of it and drop them to the counter at the same time. Our reflections breathe heavily, eyes locked. The tile in the bathroom matches his eyes. I feel like I'm surrounded by Ian on all sides.

He steps behind me and drops his hands to my shoulders. It's a perfect fit with me nestling snugly under his chin. I meet my own reflection and realize how wild I look. My waves have gone mad. My chest and neck and cheeks are flushed. My eyes are bright, wide, and rimmed with coal black mascara. I wore red lipstick to the museum, but it's been completely kissed away.

"Do you have your cell phone? Mine didn't go with my dress."

He nods and tugs it out of his pocket. I hold it up and capture us just like that, with his hands on my shoulders and our mouths beet red. It's the only photo we'll have of our wedding day—well, other than the grainy museum footage of us they'll show on the local news, and probably *America's Most Wanted*—so I take three more just in case.

"I can't believe we actually went through with it," I say, setting his phone on the counter.

Ian toys with the straps on my dress, brushing his fingers

underneath so his knuckles rub against my skin. I shiver and shift my gaze to his reflection. He's staring down at me, watching his hands at work. He's concentrating hard, brows furrowed deep in thought.

"How do you feel?" he asks. "Any regrets?"

"None."

In a flash, his eyes meet mine and any remaining resolve burns away.

He unzips my lace dress in one quick tug and it pools at my feet. I'm wearing a matching bra and panty set in the palest shade of blue—Ian blue. Like my dress, they're lace. Unlike my dress, they're brand new. I picked them up yesterday at a lingerie shop. I rubbed the silky fabric between my fingers and imagined Ian looking at me while I wore it. Reality is better. His eyes devour my newly revealed skin: my delicate collarbones, the soft swell of my breasts above the lace cups, my quivering stomach. There's a tiny bow at the top of my panties, in the very center, and that's where Ian's eyes stop for a short eternity.

"Sam…" He exhales, sounding pained.

"I'm not Sam—I'm the Queen of France, remember?"

He reaches one arm around my stomach and tugs me back against him. My butt hits the front of his tuxedo pants and I feel his hard length press against me. His fingers dip beneath my panties and my stomach swoops.

Not so fast. I turn and push him away so I have room to turn and hop up on the counter.

"You have to undress too. Bareness is fairness."

"Want to do it for me?"

"No. I want to watch."

He chuckles and rubs the back of his neck. If I had a radio handy, I'd tune it to slow jams, something he can sway his hips to. I want a show.

First, he bends down and picks up my wedding dress so he can hang it on the back of the door. I'm about to call him out for stalling, but it's a sweet gesture, so I let it slide. When that's done, I lean forward and wait. If this were a cartoon, I'd have a cloth napkin tied around my neck and a knife and fork clenched in my fisted hands.

"You sure you don't want to move to the bed?"

"*Ian.*"

He relents, tugs his bowtie loose, tosses it onto the counter beside me. I reach for it and loop it around my neck. Now, I look like I'm all wrapped up, a present just for him. Clearly, he likes the idea, because he pauses and moves forward to kiss me, brushing his hands around the curve of each breast. I tsk and push him back to the task at hand.

"You've got a long way to go, buddy boy."

His shirt goes next, and there is no chest more perfectly toned than Ian's. He takes his workouts very seriously, and I applaud his efforts. Next, he reaches for his pants.

"No, wait. Come closer," I beg.

He steps within reach and my hands feast on his chest and shoulders. I pick a favorite part—his biceps—and then immediately change my mind—his abs.

"Are you flexing?"

"No."

"Did you do pushups in the museum before I got there or something?"

He laughs. "They actually frown on using the place as a gym as well as an illegal wedding chapel."

"So you just look like this...always?"

That can't be the case. We'll never leave the house. I can't be married to someone with this kind of body. People will pass us on the streets and wonder why he settled.

"What about you?" His hands are on my waist and he's tugging me to the edge of the counter. I stay perfectly silent while he touches me, scared of the strange primal noises that could slip out of my mouth if I let them. "Are you this smooth everywhere?" he asks, dipping the tips of his fingers into the waistband of my panties.

My stomach clenches and I dig my fingers into his shoulders.

Dirty questions like that will get him mauled. He really should be careful.

His head tilts down to rest on my shoulder and he sighs. "I'm losing my head here, Sam."

My fingers thread through his hair and I let him hold me for a few seconds before I remember my goal. "You can continue now. I want to see the rest."

"You saw me naked in the shower," he reminds me, stepping back and unbuttoning his pants.

"That was ages ago. I need a refresher."

His tuxedo pants fall to the floor and Ian stands in front of the hotel shower in nothing but a pair of white Calvin Klein boxer briefs. I bite my lip, tilt my gaze to the ceiling, and count to ten.

"What are you doing?"

"Praying."

"It looks like you're about to break off a chunk of that granite counter."

Maybe I am.

"Wait." He steps closer. "We aren't even. You need to catch up now."

I stare back down at him with an arched brow. "What do you mean?"

"Your bra...lose it."

It's Not-So-Nice Ian talking now—demanding, in fact.

I think my face goes slack.

"Or do you need help?" he asks with a wicked gleam in his eyes.

He steps forward and I hold up my hand to stop him. If he touches me, that'll be the end.

I reach back and find the clasp for my bra. "Are you sure?"

He tilts his head and grins. "You're right, leave it on."

I sigh and drop my hand. "Phew. Okay."

In one second, he's on me, reaching around and unhooking that clasp. The lace cups fall away and cool air rushes in. My nipples tighten and I wrap my arms around myself to cover up, but then I remember it's Ian who's standing in front of me, my husband. My breath rushes out of me every time I think that word. I can't be shy around him. He's waiting for me, rubbing his thumb just below my ear, up and down the side of my throat, coaxing. Slowly, I drop my arms, and he releases a shaky breath. I look down to see what he's seeing. My breasts are cream and pink and perky, and they really are decent, not so big that they'll knock someone out, but when Ian reaches for them, they fill his palm, and best of all, they're oh so sensitive. My head tips and hits the mirror behind me as my eyes roll into the back of my skull. He's working his magic, rolling his thumbs in slow circles, and then I hold my breath as he bends down to taste. Slowly, methodically, he takes each breast into his mouth, looking up at me while he does it.

It's such a startling sensation that I nearly pitch forward off the counter, but his hands are on my hips, holding me in place as he licks and teases and blows warm air on skin that is not touched nearly enough. I thought the delicate lace lingerie felt good, but Ian feels better. His tongue laps at the tips of my breasts, his mouth closes around each one, and I've never had an orgasm like this, but that's why they say there's a first time for everything.

He laughs when I tell him that, and then there is no more laughter, because his hand dips into the front of my panties and there's so much wetness there, I'm nearly embarrassed. My cheeks burn. Before, I could have played this whole thing off with a few shrugs and cool smiles, but now there's no lying. My body wants Ian and he knows exactly how much.

"Open for me a little," he begs, and I oblige dutifully.

The outsides of my knees hit the cold counter and he takes the thin blue lace that covers me up and pulls it gently to the side. My hands are on his shoulders, and there's no way I'm letting go now, especially when he emits a sexy groan and drags a teasing finger up and down my wetness. He's taking things slow, staring down at me like he's assessing a newly acquired piece of property. *This is mine, and this is mine*, and then he sinks his middle finger into me and *oh yes, this is mine*.

"Ian," I whimper as he drags his finger out slowly then pumps it right back in.

"Years, Samantha—*years*."

That's all he says, but I get it. *Years for me too, Ian*.

I find his mouth and we kiss again, and there's less frenzy now and more heat. We linger and lick as he pushes a second finger inside me.

He works me up with his hand, pumping and speeding up his seduction until my nails bite into his shoulders. There's no rush, no spot left untouched.

Foreplay turns into a little more.

My thighs are shaking.

I'm holding my breath.

This poor bathroom is so fogged and hot they'll have to demolish it when we're done, but the angle is just right. The counter's height means Ian is in the perfect position after he rolls on a condom. He asks me twice if I'm sure I don't want to move to the bed, and I respond by pushing my knees apart just a teensy bit wider. My butt is right on the edge. My breasts ache to be touched and he doesn't neglect them when he slides into me inch by inch. His mouth is there, sucking, and my mouth is on his neck, kissing and whispering words of encouragement.

I wince just barely as he settles himself deep inside me. I need time to adjust. I knew there would be some... accommodating to do.

"Sam? Are you with me?" he asks, brushing my hair away from my face and tilting me just enough so our lips can meet easily.

I nod and he drags out then slides back in. His hips roll

and I clench to let him know I like it. A smirk unrolls on my lips at how blissfully amazing this feels.

"Hold on," he warns. I grip his neck and suddenly, there's no need for the bathroom sink—I'm barely touching it. He has ahold of my hips and he keeps me stationary as he thrusts in and drags back out, in and out, in and out, nice and slow. He does all the work, which leaves nothing to distract me from my building orgasm. Every time he pumps all the way in, he brushes against me in just the right spot. I tell him and he starts to go a little faster, pumping harder, holding tighter. I'm building, building, building, and this is it.

Yes. Yes. YES.

But then Ian sets me down. A protest forms and dies on my tongue as he turns me to face the mirror.

The mirror.

I'd completely forgotten all about it, but Ian hasn't. He turns us and tells me to press up onto my tiptoes. It's the only way he can align himself with me, and even then, he has to bend his knees. He takes my wrists and props my hands up on the counter without asking. His chest hits my back and I feel enveloped by his warmth right up until he stands back to his full height. I watch him in the mirror and this man isn't the Ian I'm used to. I'm aware now of the details I used to try to ignore: the chiseled jaw, the sharp edge to his gaze. They're parts of him that seemed a little too intimidating. Now they're all I see. When he pumps into me for the first time at this new angle, I collapse forward onto the cold counter. He smiles and picks me back up, holding me more carefully so the next time, I stay standing.

"Is this too much?"

Of course it is. I'm being forced to watch what he's doing to me. I'm looking at my flushed, heated skin; that black bowtie around my neck that smells like him; my wild, tangled hair; the crazed look in my eyes. There's no escaping what he's doing to me and maybe I won't always want it this way, but right now I do.

"Not enough," I beg, and Ian delivers.

He slides into me slowly and he's deeper than before. He stays pressed there and our eyes lock in the mirror.

I've been naked for a while, but in the reflection, I'm stripped bare. Ian has his fist wrapped around my soul.

"I have to be careful with you."

I shake my head then his hand hooks around my waist and he rubs soft, quick circles between my thighs. His other hand toys with my breast and those two combined sensations thrust me to the finish line quicker than I'd like. I want it, and yet, I want this to last forever. The cold granite bites into my hips. Ian's thighs sear the backs of my legs. His hand grips my breast and he thrusts again, harder than ever before, and then again. He speeds up and I clench around him, reaching up to wrap one hand around his neck. His hips are rolling and grinding. He delivers another deep thrust and a swirl of his thumb, and my nails bite into his skin.

"I'm coming. *I'm coming.*"

It's like I'm giving him an offering. *Here, take it.*

And he does. He pumps so hard, and he never stops rubbing circles. The lingering sensations from my first orgasm make me overly sensitive and needy. One moment, I don't think I can take one more whisper of a touch there, and then suddenly I'm falling again. It's harder and quicker than the first time, and Ian finally lets himself tip over the edge too. We come together and he thrusts deep inside of me, almost violently. His teeth bite gently into my shoulder and if there's any broken skin, I hope it scars. It'll be a little memento from our wedding night.

Chapter Twenty-Two

Sam

Ian lets me shower while he orders room service. When I'm done, I wrap myself up in a plush terrycloth robe and step out of the bathroom.

In the ten minutes I stood under that shower stream, I let the images of our lovemaking flash back through my mind. Ian is a fucking catch. Women should be throwing themselves at his feet, and now, somehow, he's my whirlwind husband. I wonder if he regrets having the wedding before the wedding night. I wonder if I was even half as good as him, then I chuckle. I barely had enough brain power to process what he was doing to me, much less think of things to do to him.

I step out of the bathroom and see him sitting on the bed. He has his boxer briefs back on, but nothing else. His hair is disheveled from my hands. He's on the phone finishing up the food order, but his eyes cut to me. I flush and he smiles, curls his finger, and mouths, *Come here.*

My feet carry me closer and he drags me down to sit on his lap with my back pressed against his chest. My head hits his shoulder and his hand trails up the front of my robe. I think he's going to play fair, but then his hand slips beneath the lapel and his palm covers my breast. We just finished having sex and now suddenly I'm right back at the starting line. These are truly uncharted waters.

"Yeah, you can throw in an extra order of fries," Ian says into the phone.

He sounds completely unaffected by what he's doing to me right now. By comparison, I'm basically mewling like a cat.

"Sam, do you want anything for dessert?"

Sam can't come to the phone right now. She's dead.

"Sam?" he asks again, but it's a whisper against the shell of my ear—a taunt.

I turn and take the phone out of his hand. "Chocolate milkshake. Room 419. Thank you."

Then I toss the phone toward its base without looking. It clatters to the floor and I leap onto Ian. He's caught off guard, so for a few seconds, I have the upper hand. It's glorious. He tips back onto the perfectly made bed and I straddle his hips. The tie around my robe comes loose and the two sides start to peel apart.

"Aren't you hungry?" he asks, grinning and cradling my

hips so he can rock up against me.

I see I'm not the only one treating tonight like a marathon.

"They'll have to send paramedics when we're done," I say, stringing kisses down his neck.

He lifts his chin to allow me better access and now I *am* hungry—for knowledge. I'm going to memorize every inch of his body: the small groove beneath his collarbones, the inch-long scar along his left bicep, the exact dimensions of his chest measured by the width of my palms.

He groans and tries to roll over, but I throw my full weight against him. "Hold still, you."

"You're killing me here."

"I just want to know who I married," I say, in a daze, focused on the sharp contours of his abs.

"You know me," he says wistfully.

"I thought I did," I admit. "But that scene in the bathroom? That was some next-level lovemaking. I was not expecting that from you, Fletcher."

He quirks a brow. From this angle, he's so adorable I want to throttle him. "What'd you expect?"

"In my fantasies, it's usually pretty vanilla, gentle and sweet—y'know, nice guy stuff."

"You want gentle and sweet?" he asks while smirking.

I roll my eyes and lean forward to kiss him. His hands grip my ass and he tugs, tugs, tugs my robe up until I'm bare from the waist down. I should have put on some coveralls, or at the very least double-knotted my robe.

"I can be gentle and sweet," he teases as his hand trails up the inside of my leg. His touch is feather-light and soft when he reaches between my thighs. I'm already wet. I groan and my elbows collapse. He uses the opportunity to roll us over. I'm on my back and he shoves me higher on the bed. I'm smack dab in the middle when he stands and pushes those boxer briefs back to the ground.

I have two seconds to prepare myself before he presses my knees apart and dips his head between my thighs. There are levels to the seduction: first his breath hits me, warm and shocking. I buck off the bed but he pins my hips down with his arm. Second, his mouth is there, pressing a kiss to the most intimate part of me. I fist the bedspread and then finally, his tongue laps me up, nice and slow, up and down.

"We don't...the food."

That's not even close to a full sentence, but Ian gets it. The food will be on its way up in no time and they can't just roll it in while we go at it like we're on the Discovery Channel.

"*Yes, would you two like any ketchup? Maybe some flavored lubricant?*"

Ian doesn't start to rush. He takes his sweet time lapping me up. It's a lesson, I think. He's being the gentle and sweet version I wished for, and now I regret opening my stupid mouth because not only should he be rushing because my milkshake is on its way up, but also, I'm THIS close to having another orgasm and he knows it. The smug smile tells me so. He dangles me right in the middle of insanity. I can't come like this. He's going just a teensy bit too slow, dragging his feet and showing me just how tortuous "sweet and gentle" can be. I'm squirmy and needy, begging him to just let me...give me...have some damn mercy on my poor soul!

I'm seconds away from breaking out into tears of frustration, and then he stands up. I pry my eyes open. He's gloating and wearing a panty-melting smirk.

Boy, is he enjoying this.

"Happy?" I ask, eyes narrowed in mock anger.

"I feel...nice. Like a *nice* guy," he replies, repositioning my legs on the bed so he has room to settle himself between my thighs. He picks up my hips, positioning me at the exact right angle, and then he slides into me inch by inch.

I fist the sheets and my eyes pinch closed. My bottom lip is between my teeth so I don't cry out loud enough to disturb our entire floor.

"So, is this how you envisioned it? Sweet and gentle?" he asks, leaning down and taking my hands in his. He drags them up and over my head and presses them into the bed. My eyes blink back open as he leans over me, putting me in his shadow. His hair hangs down on his forehead. His sharp features seem even more intimidating from this perspective. He pulls out and thrusts again and I groan because his full weight on top of me is intense and wonderful.

His face is right over mine. Our gazes are locked up until the moment he bends down and seers me with a sweet, seductive kiss. One hand takes control of both of my wrists and the other snakes down my body, hooking around my hips. He uses that hip as leverage, angling just a little to the left so he can really work himself in and out. He's grinding into me now, keeping up a fast, insanity-inducing pace. His hips roll and I look down and I think I'm going to die.

My arms hook around his neck and I drag him flat against me. Nails press into skin. Words are murmured against his shoulder. His teeth bite down on the soft flesh of my earlobe and I'm shaking against him, forcing him to feel every wave of my orgasm as it shocks through me.

When he's sure I'm finished, he sits back up and turns me over so I'm on my hands and knees. Now, there's no more sweet and gentle. Ian is relentless. Pounding. Thrusting. *Fucking.* I'm slack-jawed, wide-eyed, and any number of other hyphenated adjectives. My arms give out and my cheek hits a pillow, but he holds on to my hips to keep me from collapsing altogether. Never once does he break pace. When I glance back, I see him staring down between us, watching what he's doing to me, and whatever he's seeing must send him over the edge, because he pulls out and grips his hard length and comes just like that, with my name on his lips.

He leans down to kiss me, tells me to lie still, and then comes back a few seconds later with a damp towel to clean me up.

I smirk like a greedy little cat as he does the heavy lifting. Once I'm good as new, he helps me sit up and reaches down to fix my robe.

Then I remember where we are, how fancy this place is. I glance around and yup, there's a minibar filled with delicate nuts and chocolate truffles. The walls are covered in an intricate gold-leafed design.

"Ian, how much do you think this entire bed costs? Frame and all?"

He laughs and shakes his head. "Why on earth are you thinking about that?"

"I'm wondering if we'd be able to afford to..."

"Buy it?"

He really has no idea what I'm hinting at.

"No, no—to replace it if we break it."

His brows ratchet up to his hairline and then there's a knock on the door. "Room service."

YES. My milkshake! I shove Ian out of the way and run for the door. "Oh, and PS, I'm not sharing my dessert."

"Even with your husband?" he asks, dipping into the bathroom to turn on the shower.

HUSBAND! My heart skips a beat. My stomach, however, does not.

"Cute." I smile. "But no."

Chapter Twenty-Three

Sam

Even though I have a few months left on my apartment lease, I move in with Ian that Sunday after we check out of the hotel. We left a large tip for the cleaning staff, but I still feel bad. For 48 hours, we consummated our marriage in that room. If there was a surface on which you can have sex, my butt was on it. Sorry, next occupants.

On the way to my apartment, nerves creep in and I suggest we could keep living separately.

"Why?"

Because I'm a lot to handle and I don't want you to regret marrying me.

That's the truth, but I water it down. "Just…I don't know. In case you want to slow things down."

"I don't."

"In case you get sick of me."

"I won't."

Alrighty then.

Moving doesn't take us long. Most everything I own, Ian has a better version of. My pots and pans are antiques, and not in a good way. My bed creaks and is too small to fit us both comfortably. My bathroom rug is new, but it's pink and floral. Ian gives me the choice whether to take it or leave it, and I smile because deep down, I know he would let me put it in his bathroom, but I spare him.

I bring over my clothes and Ian allots me half the space in his closet and dresser.

"I really don't need that much room."

"Why?"

I don't know exactly how to phrase it, but it feels like I'm coming over for an extended sleepover. I want to make my presence here as negligible as possible, that way he won't get annoyed and divorce me. I keep telling him I don't need much space and I can just leave my toothbrush under the sink, but he puts it in the holder beside his and insists this is my house too now.

"Okay, then I want to sleep on the right side of the bed."

He laughs and walks out of the room. "Not gonna happen."

We'll see about that.

I keep waiting for things to get more complicated, for us to hit the inevitable roadblock. For example, Ian could say, *Oh, by the way, I secretly like to train birds and I keep a dozen foul-mouthed parrots in the garage.* Or he could open the guest bedroom door to a mountain of trash and soiled adult diapers sliding out.

I check every nook and cranny of his house while I move in, looking for secret meth labs or size 11 stilettos, but even his guest room closet is organized and tidy. *How disturbing!* I would have preferred a dead body.

By Sunday night, when we're sitting on his couch, spooning spaghetti into our mouths as fast as we can, I realize my fears might be unfounded.

"This is pretty great. We should have married each other ages ago," I say, mouth full.

His eyes slice to me and I give him a big, toothy, spaghetti grin.

"Wow, gorgeous. I guess the honeymoon period really is over."

I smirk and go back to my food. All that moving worked up my appetite.

"I plugged my phone charger into the outlet on the right side of the bed—y'know, because it's *my side*."

"Huh." He nods. "My is a really strange way to pronounce *your.*"

"*Come on*! Don't you want to be my protector, the one sleeping near the door in case someone breaks in to murder us?"

"Sure, but what if they come through the window?" he asks.

"Good point. I'll take the left side, you take the axe-murderer window."

I beam. *Our first example of healthy conflict resolution as a married couple!*

Normally, after dinner, I head back to my apartment to sleep. I'm so used to the ritual that I load my plate in the dishwasher and head straight for the door. I'm slipping my shoes on when Ian's shadow falls over me.

"What are you doing?"

"Going ho—" I pause and laugh. "Oh my gosh!"

I turn off autopilot and kick off my shoes. Ian leans down and hooks his hands under my arms to lift me back to my feet.

"Leaving me already?" he teases. "We've only been married two days. Who is he, what's his name?"

"Bad Ian."

I spin around and he tugs me into him. My hands hit his chest.

"Sorry, I guess things are happening so fast it's taking my brain a little while to catch up."

"We can slow down if you want."

"How?"

He thinks about it for a second and shrugs. "I'm not sure, actually. I could sleep on the couch if you want?"

I think I give him a perfectly executed look that says, *Are you fucking insane?*

Later that night, I walk into our bedroom after brushing my teeth and find Ian, shirtless, reading in bed.

I hide my smile and scurry to crawl under the blankets beside him.

"Thanks again for being my fleshy axe shield."

He grunts before going back to his book. I follow his lead and pull my Kindle onto my lap, but there's no reading happening. I sit there, studying Ian's bedroom and taking in the newly added details. A candle and delicate jewelry case sit up on the dresser beside his cologne. One of my spring scarves hangs on the doorknob of the closet because I don't want to forget to wear it in the morning. My antique floor lamp in the corner brings a feminine touch to the otherwise masculine space.

Sitting here, I have a giddy, anxious feeling in the pit of my stomach, and I wonder how long it will last. Days? Years?

I glance toward Ian out of the corner of my eye. His gaze is on his book. He's been a source of calm throughout all this, and I wonder if, under all those abs of steel, maybe he feels anxious too? If maybe he's just a little bit better at hiding it?

He doesn't say a word as I study him. He turns a page in his book and I scoot closer until our hips touch. Then I reach over and drag my pillow over so I'm propped up beside him. He has a king bed, so we don't have to be crushed together in the very center, but feeling his skin on mine unknots my stomach. I take the first deep breath of the day.

For three years I've trained myself to ignore my feelings for Ian. I never imagined he could possibly feel the same way I do, and now here we are married, living together, reading in bed.

"You okay?" he asks.

I nod and lean my head against his shoulder. His arm dips around the small of my back so he can grab my hip and drag me even closer. I'm basically sitting on his lap.

He must realize my brain is going a million miles a minute because he asks if I want him to read his book aloud. I nod and close my eyes and listen to his voice, deep and steady as he picks up right where he left off. It doesn't take long for my heart to mimic the rise and fall of his chest so we're breathing in sync.

His voice is so soothing, like the sensation of sinking into a warm bath on a cold winter day.

I'm so close to drifting off when I speak up. My voice sounds drowsy and soft.

"Hey Ian?"

He pauses reading.

"You know I'm in love with you, right?"

His heart thumps against my back and his breathing quickens. There's a long, heavy silence, and I blink one eye open to look up at him. He's staring down, studying my face with intense focus. My words clearly caught him off guard.

"Once again—*years*."

I smile.

"Say it again."

"Which part?"

His mouth tips down and captures mine. His poor book doesn't stand a chance now. We're supposed to be sleeping and resting up for work tomorrow, but instead, Ian strips me out of my pajamas and presses a kiss to every patch of skin he can find. His lips hit the center of my chest and he tells me he loves me too. He moves lower and kisses my naval and tells me again. The words are muffled, but he says them so many times there's no way to miss them.

We fall asleep tangled up in one another, and in the morning, I wake up to "I Got You Babe" by Sonny and Cher. It's Ian, calling me from the kitchen.

I smile and reach over for the phone.

"When did you have the time to change my ringtone?"

"Last night after you drifted off. You were snoring."

I groan and sit up so my feet dangle off the side of the bed.

"Tell me the truth—what's the point of these songs?"

"Haven't you guessed?"

"I think you just like to torture me."

"No. I've been trying to tell you how I feel."

I think back on the last few I can remember. I just thought they were cheesy songs. Now, I realize I should have read between the lines.

"They were all love songs by dynamic duos, just like us."

"Awwwwwww! Ian Fletcher, you big softie!"

He hangs up on me and shouts from the kitchen for me to get my butt out of bed.

He loves me big time.

"This isn't fair. Our honeymoon wasn't nearly long enough."

"Yeah, well, we can't skip school. I checked my email while you were showering and Principal Pruitt wants us to be at the PTA meeting later today. He thinks a public apology would go a long way to settle tensions."

"An apology?" I sound affronted by the idea. "This O'Doyle lady is a terrorist! We can't negotiate with her."

"We're married now, so it shouldn't be a problem anymore, but I'm worried she's gotten everybody so worked up our new wedded status won't matter. Maybe I should look into going back to work for my old company."

"No." I know how much he hated working there after college. "We'll figure it out. If I have to paste on a fake smile, I will. I can do it."

I tell him that, but really, I'm not so sure. I have a lot of pride and I'm not very good at apologizing when I don't feel like I've done anything wrong. So what if Ian and I canoodled? We did it on our own time and away from school premises—well... mostly. There was that Valentine's Day dance chaperoning incident, and that time we nearly made out in the field house... but let's not get bogged down in the details here.

Ian and I stroll into school side by side but not touching. He walks me to my classroom and I can tell he wants to kiss me, but we save it. Instead, I say, "Let me see it."

He wipes away his grin and holds out his hand. His thick gold wedding band sends a shiver of pleasure down my spine.

"I love it."

"And yours? Do you love it too?"

"Are you kidding?"

My ring could do some major damage if I ever decided to partake in a street fight. I glance down and the diamond twinkles up at us.

My students immediately notice it, one in particular: Nicholas.

"Good morning, Ms. Abra—OH MY GOD WHAT IS THAT ON YOUR HAND?!"

"Nicholas, deep breaths."

He fans his face like he's going to pass out.

"It's a wedding ring," I admit calmly.

"Go Ms. Abrams!" another student hoots from the back of the class.

Nicholas sends them a death stare then flings his glare back to me. "How could you do this to me? I was going to wait for you!"

I ease him down to his seat, just in case he's about to lose consciousness on me. "Well, Nicholas, Mr. Fletcher and I—"

"Mr. Fletcher?! So he's the homewrecker!"

For the rest of class, he refuses to meet my eyes. When we go around the room, discussing this week's newspaper assignments, he declares he's going to write an opinion piece on marriage failure rates in America.

"Last I heard, nearly half of all marriages end in divorce," he warns, gaze slicing through me.

"Sounds like an interesting feature. Dig into it."

I don't have the energy to nurse his wounded teenage heart. I need to keep my focus on the PTA meeting coming at the end of the day. I practice apologizing to myself in front of the bathroom mirror in between periods.

"Yes, Mrs. O'Doyle, you may go sit on a pineapple."

Hmm…not quite right.

I stretch my mouth and practice a few jaw exercises before I try again. "Mrs. O'Doyle and members of the Oak Hill PTA, I'm here today to tell you all that I am so…so ready for you all to…move on to the next piece of mindless drama. Also, did y'all know there's a sale on choppy bobs down at the hair salon?"

All right, scratch that. Maybe I'll let Ian do the apologizing and I'll try to look deeply contrite in the background.

By the time lunch arrives, word about our elopement has spread to the entire school. Ian and I knew it would, and we didn't go to any lengths to keep it a secret. There's no point. Being married should help us out of the hot water in which we've found ourselves, and, incidentally, we're both pretty excited about it. I really wasn't sure how the rest of the school would take it, but when I arrive for lunch, Ian is recounting the museum story to the entire lounge. Everyone turns to me as I walk in and explodes into a round of clapping and whistles. Someone's even taken the time to decorate the room with balloons and streamers, and yes, there's a can of whipped cream with a bow on it waiting for me at my chair. I hold it up and laugh.

"Ha ha. Very funny."

Really, it is. I'm going to lick whipped cream off Ian's naked chest later.

Life is grand.

There's even a cake that says, *Happy birthday, Mary!* I don't understand the joke, but hey, cake is cake.

After we cut into it and dole out all the slices, a soft voice chimes in near the back of the crowd, "Aww man, is that my birthday cake?"

The Freshman Four stand scowling in a corner. When I glance over, Gretchen slices a finger across her neck menacingly and Bianca elbows her in the ribs. "Jesus, we aren't going to cut her throat, Gretchen!"

"Oh, that's what that means? I never knew! Sorry Sam!"

We open a card that was very obviously hastily passed around for people to sign just before lunchtime. Half of the signatures wish Mary a happy birthday. There's clearly a lot of confusion about what we're actually celebrating at the moment. Poor Mary. We really stole her thunder.

Just before we head back to our classrooms, one of the teachers demands a kiss, and Ian and I look at each other and laugh. We shouldn't, really. We're on probation. We're supposed to have our tails between our legs, but one kiss won't hurt, right?

So we kiss, just once, and everyone applauds—right up until Principal Pruitt walks in and announces that the party's over. Mary rushes forward and uses her fingers to scrape off the last bit of icing from her re-appropriated birthday cake.

Pruitt asks to see us out in the hallway and we trail after him. The cake settles heavily in my stomach.

"You two really aren't masters of discretion, are you?" he asks, pointing to the balloons filtering out into the hallway.

"We didn't do this!" I say quickly. "Honestly we were going to keep everything low-key, but someone got wind of things and threw us a little reception."

"So it's true then? You two eloped over the weekend?"

I hold up my ringed hand and Ian replies, "Yes, sir. That should clear up the breach in our contract, right?"

He laughs. "Honestly, there were easier ways to do that. You two didn't need to go get hitched. I wasn't going to let Mrs. O'Doyle and her PTA gang actually force you out of the school. I just needed to show her I was taking her concerns seriously."

"So our jobs were never in danger?"

"No."

We all go silent, and then, *duh*, I remember I'm in love with Ian and didn't just marry him for this silly job.

"Not going to go get it annulled, I hope?"

"No!" I'm quick to reply, and when I glance over to Ian, he's grinning down at me.

"Right, then I'll see you both at the PTA meeting after school. Try to wipe those grins off your faces before you get there. I'd like you looking remorseful, even if it's just pretend."

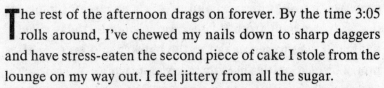

The rest of the afternoon drags on forever. By the time 3:05 rolls around, I've chewed my nails down to sharp daggers and have stress-eaten the second piece of cake I stole from the lounge on my way out. I feel jittery from all the sugar.

Ian and I walk into the PTA meeting with Principal Pruitt by our side. I wish I were wearing a helmet or armor. I have no clue what to expect: angry scowls? Pitchforks? Rotten tomatoes? I swiftly remove my delicate scarf, just in case.

In reality, we walk in to find Mrs. O'Doyle sitting at the front of the classroom with her arms crossed. A self-righteous scowl mars her face—though, from the deep set of those wrinkles, that might just be what she looks like normally. I don't think her smiling-related facial muscles have been utilized since the early 90s.

Meanwhile, all the other PTA parents are hovering around the snack table in the back of the classroom, picking their way through nuts and what looks to be a plethora of homemade cookies, macadamia chocolate chip if my nose doesn't deceive me. If it goes as planned, I'll grab a fistful of them on my way out. If things turn south, I'll take the whole damn tray.

Mrs. O'Doyle's eyes follow me into the room, but she doesn't offer any greeting. Two seats are marked with little reserved signs at the front of the classroom and I realize they're for Ian and me when Principal Pruitt tells us to have a seat. Oh, I get it: this is a trial. Mrs. O'Doyle is the judge, jury, and executioner. Ian and I are destined for the guillotine.

I check for a scythe near her feet, but instead I find bright orange wedges. I did not see that coming. How can someone so pissy enjoy such bright footwear?

"I hereby call this PTA meeting to order!" she says, banging a wooden gavel against the desk. She looks like she's pretty comfortable with that thing. I bet if I looked closely, I'd find that it's engraved and everything. She sleeps with it under her pillow and takes it with her into the shower. "The first order of business is the discussions of last week's Whipped Cream-gate."

That gets everyone's attention. The crowd around the snack table disperses as everyone vies for a good seat.

"Mrs. O'Doyle, this incident is not on the level of Watergate. Let's not make this more tedious than it needs to be," Principal Pruitt demands. "I only brought Mr. and Mrs. Fletcher here so we might clear up a few things and move on."

"Mr. and *Mrs.* Fletcher?" asks a PTA mom beside me, mouth full of cookie. "I thought the whole issue was that they *weren't* married?"

There's a chorus of disgruntlement. These people came for a show and now they feel deprived.

"Yeah! What gives?"

"ORDER! ORDER IN MY COURTROO—I MEAN, CLASSROOM!" Mrs. O'Doyle shouts, banging her gavel so hard I hold my hands up to protect my face in case it splinters. "What do you mean, Mr. and Mrs.?"

Principal Pruitt sighs and turns to us, like, *Well, get on with it.* With glee, I hold up my ringed finger like I'm flipping her off. If I were Matt Damon in *Good Will Hunting*, I'd toss in, *How 'bout them apples?*

"No!" Mrs. O'Doyle's face crumples. "A sham marriage—you can't! Surely there's something in the teacher handbook about this. Principal Pruitt this cannot, must not, will not stand. Teachers can't go around canoodling and then getting married just to escape consequences. I will take this all the way to the highest court in the land—THE SCHOOL BOARD!"

He chuckles. "The board has reviewed the incident as well as the district policies. So far, the only judgement they've handed down is one of congratulations."

"So what about their probation?!" She's red-faced now.

"It's over as of today."

"Because they got hitched?" Angry spittle spews from her mouth. "I feel like I'm taking crazy pills!"

I stifle a laugh. Might be, lady. Check your prescription.

"All right, now that that's cleared up," a parent shouts from the back of the room, "can we move on to the issues with the single-file carpool lane? I shouldn't have to wait in line for nearly forty-five minutes just to pick my kid up."

"Yeah!" a chorus of parents agree.

"Also, what about our end-of-year fundraiser for the softball team?!" another parent demands.

Our trial is over. Principal Pruitt gets our attention with a small wave and tilts his head toward the door. It's time to scram. We did our part by showing up, and I didn't even have to apologize.

"Do you think I can take a cookie?" I ask Ian under my breath as we stand.

He wraps his arm around my shoulder like he's worried

I might give it a go. "I think O'Doyle made them. Better not push our luck."

I sigh like I was afraid he'd say that.

"I'll get you something on the way home. C'mon."

A perky soccer mom with a blonde ponytail and a pearly white smile reaches for my arm, intercepting me before I reach the door. "Hey, I was going to tell you..." Her voice is barely above a whisper. "Between us girls, if you're into whipped cream, you really ought to try some chocolate sauce warmed up just a little—not too hot though." She winces. "Learned my lesson the hard way with that one, ha! Oh, by the way, I think you teach my son—Nicholas?"

Oh JESUS.

I run-walk the hell out of there.

Chapter Twenty-four

Sam

Ian has a soccer game today, and I'm in attendance as always. Things are back to normal. The throngs of young, hot female teachers have moved on to the lacrosse game taking place a few fields over. If I squint, I can see their cleavage and orange slices. Oak Hill High just hired a new lacrosse coach from LA. He's tan, and cute, and allegedly went on three dates with one of the stars from *Vanderpump Rules*. Ian is old news—my old news.

The soccer stands are pretty empty, just me and a few parents. I thought about remaking my GO IAN signs, but instead, I had a shirt printed. It has a large screen-printed picture of Oak Hill's mascot and beneath that, in big, black typeface, it reads COACH'S WIFE. It lacks subtly, but then again, so do I.

Ian laughed when I showed it to him last night.

"I don't have to wear it," I said. I mean, it was kind of a joke.

But he shook his head, smile plastered wide. "No. Wear it."

I had it strategically hidden under my sweater all day. If Nicholas had seen it, he would have spiraled. He still thinks he and I are destined for one another someday.

"I guess I understand that you need someone to bide your time with until I'm old enough."

A shadow falls over me and I glance up to see Ashley making her way down the line of bleachers in my direction. I brace for the worst. After all, she's all but been inducted into the Freshman Four (Five?). Maybe she's here to do their bidding. I check her hands for knives and find them empty. There's a chance I'm being a tad bit dramatic. I don't think murderers coat their nails in baby pink nail polish.

"Hey," she says, gaze falling to my shirt. She smiles. "I like that. Did you make it?"

I look down. "Oh, thanks. I, uh…had it printed."

I wish I still had my sweater on. I feel silly now.

She nods and waves to the expanse of open seating beside me. "Is it okay if I sit here?" Again, I'm confused, but she doesn't wait for me to think of an answer, just takes a seat and props her feet up on the bleacher in front of her. "Listen, I don't care about you and Ian."

My face is a mask of shock. "You don't?"

She laughs. "I just started here. Why would I care who's

dating whom? I just thought he was hot, that's all."

"But you sit with the Freshman Four at lunch…"

"I sit with them because it's better than sitting by myself."

"Oh."

"Yeah, but it's getting kind of old. I'm considering eating lunch in the library by myself from now on. At least then I won't have to listen to Gretchen ask Bianca if mayonnaise has calories."

I laugh.

There's a chance I might have misjudged Ashley. Imagine that.

"So, how's married life?" she asks, continuing the conversation.

I stifle a grin. Still, bliss oozes from my pores. "It's been good." My tone is even and cool.

She can tell I'm restraining myself. "Just good?"

It's like she took a pickaxe to my self-control.

"Okay, it's been really awesome—I mean, better than I thought it could be."

She smiles. "I'm glad. You two are really cute together. And hey, sorry I stole your pudding cup the other day."

Her apology means more than she knows. I was prepared to carry that incident to my grave.

I hold out my hand for her to shake. "Friends?"

She smiles and accepts. "I'd like that."

I decide to go out on a limb. "Have you ever watched *West Wing*, by chance?"

Her face lights up. "I love that show!"

I'm waiting for Ian to finish up at the gym. It's our one-month anniversary. It's a big deal, and I'm going to seduce him when we get home. The Zumba class I just took should help with that. I'm feeling limber.

Ian is doing a set on a bicep machine and I'm standing a few yards away, sweat dripping down my body as I try to keep it together. His arms are so sexy. His face is chiseled perfection. If we weren't already married, I'd demand we march down to the courthouse right now.

Maybe we won't even make it home. Maybe husbands and wives are allowed to find secluded sections of the gym parking lot. Maybe Ian will have his work cut out for him.

His eyes slice over to me and I smile.

"Almost done," he mouths.

No, Ian. Not even close.

Chapter Twenty-five

Ian

Sam tells me our new life still doesn't feel real to her. She's scared she'll wake up one day in her old apartment, on her tiny bed, without me. I get it. For three years, we were best friends who were secretly in love with each other. Three years is a long time to subdue a crush. It became a habit to ignore my feelings for Sam, and that habit became second nature. We're having to rewire our brains slowly.

"Remind me again," she said the other night while we were brushing our teeth side by side. "You *love me* love me? Like not just as a friend?"

There's a newness to our life that makes every mundane

task exciting. Sam is quick to point them out: "We're going grocery shopping for food for OUR house! We're picking out a plant to put in the corner of OUR bedroom! We're planning a vacation we'll take as HUSBAND AND WIFE! IAN, THIS PIECE OF MAIL IS ADDRESSED TO MRS. FLETCHER!" Her enthusiasm is infectious.

Each passing day builds another layer of stability. Those first few newlywed months fly by as the school year wraps up. Her apartment lease ends. We get a joint bank account. We talk about when we want to have kids and how many we'll have.

"Pretty simple to decide," she declares.

"How's that?"

"Well, if we have one baby per year until I turn 45, that makes 18—a nice, round, dozen and a half," she proclaims with a straight face.

"Whoa whoa whoa," I protest. "That's crazy!"

"Why's that?" She maintains the poker face, so I up the ante.

"Because one baby per year means you're giving yourself *three whole wasted months* between pregnancies. I was thinking I could just climb up on top of you in the postpartum room, and that should give us—"

"AOUGHHGH, stop stop stop. I'm kidding. Let's start with one, and if we don't mess it up too badly we'll do it again."

Sam's parents are hosting a dinner party tonight to blend the families. It's going to be a shitshow. It's been almost six months since we eloped, and this dinner is her parents' way of making amends...sort of. Sam's mom still calls every few days and asks her if she'd be willing to partake in a small (300 people) church ceremony. Sam says no, and her mom takes it as a personal insult every time.

"I know it seems callous, but I've given in to her demands my whole life. I'm not doing it anymore. I had the wedding I wanted. Nothing could top it. We ran for our lives!"

"I agree."

"Okay, good," she says as we stroll up the front path to her parents' house. "So when my mom inevitably asks about it again tonight, you have to have my back."

I nod—not that it matters, because her mom won't ask Sam about it tonight. Her mom is all about appearances and she'd never get into a fight with Sam in front of my parents, who, from the sound of it, are already inside. I can hear my mom's laugh from a mile off.

Sam opens the door and there they are: two couples who couldn't be more different. Her parents are small and thin, human birds. They dress in khaki and cream, single-handedly keeping the beige trend alive. My parents are slightly heavier set with big smiles. Like Sam and me, there's a bit of height difference between them. Tonight, my mom's wearing a pink dress and my dad has put on his nicest Hawaiian shirt.

The second we walk in the door, my mom runs over and envelops Sam in a life-ending hug. Sam squeezes my hand as if trying to deliver a message via Morse code: *please STOP help me STOP can't breathe STOP.*

"You look so beautiful! You're glowing!" Her voice drops. "You aren't expecting, are you?"

"Mom," I warn.

She steps back but keeps hold of Sam's outstretched hands. "Sorry, sorry. Wishful thinking!"

Sam's own mom pats her shoulder. "Hello dear."

"Hi Mom."

"I, ummm…" Her mom takes a moment to peruse Sam's appearance. "I like what you've done with your hair tonight."

It pains her to deliver the compliment. Sam's hair is wild and curly. By contrast, her mom's hair has been forced into a tight up-do that yanks her forehead skin so she wears a perpetual look of surprise. She looks like the headmistress of a boarding school where you send troubled youth.

Her dad claps my shoulder and we shake hands. "How are you, Ian?"

"Good, sir. Thanks."

"Taking good care of my daughter?"

His question might seem formal, but his tone isn't. Out of the two of them, her dad is much easier to handle. He just wants Sam to be happy.

The strangest thing happens over that four-course dinner: our parents become friends. Our moms get along exceedingly well. I think it's because my mom could talk to a shoe and call it her friend. She peels back Mrs. Abrams' layers like a highly-skilled psychiatrist.

"So, tell me more about your childhood!"

After dessert, they all want to move into the living room and play board games, but Sam and I have had our fill of family bonding.

We bolt the first opportunity we can get.

"Thanks for dinner, Mom, Dad! Talk soon! Mr. and Mrs. Fletcher, we'll see you in the morning for breakfast before you get on the road!" Sam shouts, quickly dashing around the room to dole out hugs.

After we step outside, she reaches for my hand and tugs me toward my car as fast as her short legs will take us.

"Hurry, hurry! My mom is probably thinking of some way to drag us back inside as we speak."

We hop in and buckle up quickly. We're out of their neighborhood in no time.

"Phew. That went well. I think our moms are in love."

I nod. "Yeah, it went better than I thought it would."

"I wouldn't be surprised if your mom invites my parents to breakfast tomorrow."

"Yeah, we should probably prepare ourselves now."

"Hey, can you stop at that pharmacy up there?" she asks. "I need to run in and pick up a few things."

I get into the right lane so I can turn into the parking lot.

She jostles her legs in the passenger seat like she's hopped up on something. "Don't you want to know what I need?"

"Um, not real—"

"A pregnancy test."

I nearly careen off the road.

I end up taking up 2 ½ parking spots near the back of the lot. Justin Timberlake is singing on the radio and Sam and I sit in the car while my brain catches up.

She jostles my arm. "Ian, you there?"

She waves her hand in front of my face, and reality snaps back into place like a rubber band. I turn to her, dopey smile and all.

"What the hell are we waiting for?!"

She beams and we simultaneously turn to yank on our door handles.

Inside the pharmacy, Sam drags her arm across the shelf

in a dramatic flourish. Our small basket is filled to the brim. We buy one of each brand, which is overkill, but there's no point in trying to talk her out of it.

"Because the people in the movies do it! Maybe they're onto something!"

When we check out, the clerk doesn't say a word, though she must sense the nervous energy pluming off of Sam because she gives her a small smile as she loads the pregnancy tests into two bags.

This is what we want. We've talked about it. I'll be 32 in a month. Sam turned 28 a few weeks back. We have a decent amount of savings built up. I've already looked at the best options for college funds. We're prepared, but it still feels like we're two teenagers up to no good.

"Hurry, hurry," Sam says as we finish the drive home. "I've been holding it since before dinner because I want to have enough urine for all these tests."

"In my professional chemist opinion, you'll need at least a gallon of urine."

"You're joking, but I actually have it!"

The bags are hefty and loaded down. When I pull into the driveway, Sam hops out of the car and makes a dash for the door. She runs straight for the master bathroom and I follow.

"Should we read the instructions?" I ask, frowning as Sam starts tearing open boxes like a hungry bear who's just stumbled upon a picnic in the woods. "Make sure you're peeing on the right parts?"

"I know the right parts, Ian. Movie people, remember?"

Still, I insist. Each test demands slightly different preparations. Some demand you pee directly on the applicator.

Some want you to dip the end of the test stick in a small cup of urine. Some provide a line. Some spell out POS or NEG. Sam hops back and forth on her feet, clutching her crotch as if she's trying to physically hold the pee inside herself.

"Hurry!"

"Okay, here. This one first."

She pees on it and I pass her another. Then another. We have twelve lined up before she's completely emptied her bladder.

"Damn," I say, hands on hips, assessing our lineup.

She washes her hands with a smug smile. "What do you think, science man? Is that enough data for you?"

I smile and nod before stepping back and sliding down to the ground. The excitement of the last half-hour is starting to take its toll.

Sam stays standing, hands on her hips as she studies the tests. "How long do we have to wait?"

"The first one will be ready in five minutes."

Saying it aloud makes my stomach drop. She turns back to me and I see she's shaking now, her eyes filling up with tears. "What if it's positive?"

I tilt my head and assess her. "We'll be excited."

"And if it's negative?"

"We'll probably be relieved, but we'll also keep trying."

"Maybe your mom is a psychic. You haven't told her we've been trying, have you?"

"No. That was all her."

"She said I was glowing."

I smile. "You are."

"How long has it been?"

I glance down at the timer on my phone. "Thirty seconds."

"Oh god. I feel sick."

"Good sick or bad sick?"

"I don't know. I want this, but all of a sudden I feel like we're in over our heads. It's the same feeling I had when you asked me to marry you."

I understand what she means. We'd be naïve to think this isn't a huge step. Our lives are about to change forever.

"Come sit by me."

I bend my knees so she can fit in the space between my legs. She turns, sits, and leans her back against my chest. My heart thumps against her shoulder blade. My hand wraps around her wrist and I feel her pulse, counting the beats in my head— faster than a hummingbird. I wrap my other hand around her stomach and press there, waiting, expecting. I know it'd be too early to feel anything, but I want to feel something.

"Ian? Do you remember when I dressed up as Hermione for Halloween and you told me I looked like a dweeb?"

I smile and lean my head back against the wall. "Yeah, I tried to kiss you that night."

"What?!"

"Over by the punch bowl, but it was too late. You'd had like four shots and you threw up on me."

"Oh my god. I remember feeling sick, but I don't remember you trying to kiss me."

I glance down and see there are two minutes left on the timer.

"Yeah, well, I wasn't all that smooth. You used to make me nervous."

She laughs like that's completely preposterous.

"I wonder how different everything would have been if you'd actually kissed me."

Completely, but I wouldn't change a thing.

"This is crazy," she murmurs to herself.

Another minute passes and now there are only seconds before that first test is ready. Sam looks down at the time and her pulse punches through her skin.

"Do you want to look together?" she asks.

"You do it."

I'm not sure I can stand at the moment.

Time slows to a crawl as she pushes up and walks over to read the test. Things flash through my mind: nursery paint colors, daycare, diapers, pudgy fingers and toes.

It's a simple, old-school test with two lines for positive and one for negative.

It should take her one second to read it.

The timer starts to beep.

Sam looks down, grabs the test, whirls around, and screams.

Epilogue

Sam

"**M**r. President," I say, nodding in deference as Ian hands me the popcorn.

"Madam Secretary," he responds, equally sincere.

"Ahem, the Speaker of the House needs a refill."

"Wah-wah-wah-wah."

We both look down at Violet, who's pulling up to stand on the edge of the couch. Her chubby-cheeked grin tears straight through my heart.

"Ian, can you believe we're raising such a genius?"

"Not even a year and a half and she's already speaking in full sentences."

In response, she mumbles, "Ma ma ma dog dog."

Obviously, she's speaking in some advanced code. Any robot would be able to decipher her speech and come up with solutions to the world's major crises.

Then she burps and gets distracted by a piece of lint on the floor.

"So wise." I nod, taking the glass of wine he's holding out for me before he turns to grab Violet's cup. "Are you thinking Columbia, Princeton, or Harvard?"

Ian shrugs. "She'll have her pick of the Ivies, but who knows, she might just join the Peace Corps—or a traveling circus troupe."

"Let's not talk about it. It makes me sad."

"That she's going to join the circus? I really doubt that'll happen."

I reach down and pick her up. All I want is one decent cuddle, but she's at the age where she wants freedom, room to roam. She wiggles free and goes back to playing on the floor. "It's just…I don't like thinking about her growing up. She's too little to join the circus."

Ian takes a seat beside me on the couch and tugs me close. I nuzzle into his chest and close my eyes. I can hear the deep breath filling my lungs, my husband's steady heartbeat, my daughter's playful babble—all the sounds of a life I couldn't have dreamed of just a few years ago, mostly because I was busy dreaming about Lieutenant Ian banging me in an army barracks.

"I feel like you're really homing in on the circus thing."

I ignore him. "Today she's babbling at our feet, tomorrow she's swinging from trapeze bars, traveling the country in a train car."

"Again, probably not going to happen."

"Promise me she'll always stay this little." I sound desperate.

He rubs his thumb back and forth on my shoulder. "No can do."

"Promise me she'll always be a mommy's girl."

"Ehhh, *is* she though?" he teases. "Her first word was Dada—that can't be a coincidence."

I have a real, ludicrous urge to cry.

"What *can* you promise me?! Sheesh, my heart is breaking here."

He chuckles and reaches over to tip my chin up so my face is tilted toward him.

"Sam…Samwich…Sam and cheese…"

I blink my eyes open. His blue eyes are inches from mine.

"I can't make promises about the big things, but I can promise you we'll always watch *West Wing* on Wednesdays."

"Obviously."

"I can promise that as long as you're the head of the Oak Hill Gazette, I'll read every issue."

I grip his shirt with a wild plea. "You have to—you're our most devoted reader."

"I also promise to send you the most Valentine's Day bears out of every teacher at the school."

Our tradition still stands. "Thank you. I appreciate that."

"So does the choir director. I think we make up half of his annual fundraising revenue with our antics."

I grin, and then it fades as I realize something.

"You're leaving out one thing," I prod.

He frowns. "What?" Then an idea hits him. "Oh, right: I'll always love you. Is that what you were after?"

I sigh with feigned exasperation, like, *Ugh, you idiot.* "No. Love shmove—I don't care about that. Promise me you'll always be my best friend."

He laughs, tips his head down, and kisses my cheek.

"I thought that was obvious, Hot Lips. Best friends, forever."

EXCLUSIVE BONUS CONTENT

Sam

I can barely believe what I'm about to say, but…this morning, Ian and I are having sex in his classroom. Here's how it went down: Ian left a little note for me on my desk this morning.

See me in my classroom at lunch.

My jaw dropped when I read it. I was sweating all morning, unable to concentrate on my lesson plans or my slide deck. I counted down the minutes until the lunch bell rang, and then I shoved my chair back and not-so-politely encouraged everyone to leave as quickly as possible.

"Mrs. Fletcher, about the grade I got on the qui—"

"Out!" I shooed some over-achieving student.

Who cares about grades at a time like this?!

Ian wants to *see me* in his classroom. That can only mean one thing. He wants me. Bad. My suspicions were correct. He thinks about me constantly. Images of me play through his mind on a loop all day: me walking slowly through the cafeteria. Me laughing in the teachers' lounge. Me, butt naked and propped up on his desk like a stuffed turkey on Thanksgiving.

I fan my face and watch as the last student leaves. My door slams shut, and I wrench the top desk drawer open. Inside, I have a small compact mirror, sample-sized makeup, and...*red lace lingerie*?

Odd, but I don't question it.

This is a dream, after all, and in this dream, I've come prepared. In the blink of an eye, the red lace slips onto my skin, miraculously hidden beneath my simple sundress. I check my appearance in my compact. My hair has never looked better. When Ian sees me, he'll weep.

This dream takes place *before* now. Years ago. I know that. I can feel the zing of anticipation. The hope that finally *finally* something will happen between Ian and me. We won't be stuck in this godforsaken friend zone forever. We'll progress to something hotter. No, *dirtier.*

Oh my god, dream me is a total perv.

Out in the hall, I wave innocently at passersby as I book it toward Ian's classroom.

"Hello, Principal Pruitt. My, what good weather we're having, and I just *love* what you've done with your hair!"

Once Principal Pruitt has turned the corner, I break into an all-out sprint and come to a screeching halt outside of Ian's classroom door. I smooth a hand over my dress, toss back my hair, and turn the handle.

He's waiting for me inside, wearing a confident little smile. He's posed just in front of his desk, wearing dark jeans and a crisp white button-down shirt. Up and down—he tosses a glossy green apple into the air before catching it again and again. It's a taunt.

"Took you long enough."

I bite my lip to keep from smiling too wide. I need to play it cool here.

His blue eyes assess me slowly, *painfully*, and then they slide over to the door.

"Lock it and pull the shade."

Oh. Naughty, naughty.

I do just as he says, and once I'm done, I turn back around slowly to see he's standing and making his way toward me. He takes a bite of the green apple and then holds it up for me. My teeth sink into the fruit, and the tartness makes me shiver.

Ian steps closer, backing me up to the door.

We should talk about this...

That's what I'm thinking, at least. *We're friends. What are you doing? What does this mean?* But Ian wants me, and maybe I shouldn't question it. Maybe, for once, I should just give into the feelings I've harbored deep down inside for him. The ones that keep me awake at night.

Besides, dream me wants this. She wants it badly enough to grab ahold of the lapels of his...*fireman suit*?

Oh god. I'm losing track of the dream's plot. Wasn't he just in a white shirt?

I blink and refocus. We're in Ian's classroom. We're going to break school rules. He's going to feed me this apple and then bend me over the side of his desk.

Ian lets the apple drop to the floor with a total disregard for littering. *What a bad boy.* Then he cups my jaw and brings our faces closer together.

"You must know how much I want you, Sam."

My heart rate quickens. "No. Tell me."

He nuzzles his nose against the side of my cheek and breathes me in. "You undo me. Seeing you in this school every day… Watching you at carpool in the mornings… How efficiently you handle that long line…"

Oh my god, I KNOW. I *am* efficient! I didn't think anyone noticed!

I hold my hand up over his, making sure he has no plans to retreat as I start to explain my ten-point strategy. "It's a simple enough system. If everyone just adheres to the posted signs—"

His lips press against my skin. "But not everyone does. *You* work so hard."

My eyes flutter closed. "I know."

"You deserve a reward."

"I *do*."

"Should I give you one?"

"Uh-huh." I nod, starting to feel a little lightheaded.

Ian's mouth inches closer to mine. We're about to share an earth-shattering kiss that I will never physically recover from. I will be a heap of bones on the ground for the rest of eternity.

Students will have to walk over me to get to their desks.

I tug him closer. His lips ghost against mine. I hold my breath—

Just then, in real life, my phone starts blaring the 1960s classic "I Got You Babe" by none other than Sonny and Cher. This month's alarm clock jingle.

NO.

Already, the catchy melody is crashing through my dreamscape. I keep my eyes squeezed closed and flail wildly for my phone on my nightstand, hoping to silence the alarm as quickly as possible. I want to go back to Ian's classroom. I can still feel his lips. If only…

"We're going to be late if you don't wake up."

My eyes ping open, and there is Ian. The *real* Ian—my husband. He's standing on the threshold of our bathroom, shirtless, brushing his teeth. His pajama bottoms ride low on his slim hips, and his golden-brown chest is an immediate distraction and an instant turn-on.

My cheeks flood with color as I tug our comforter closer to my chin.

"Seriously. We have that staff meeting before first period."

I don't want to get up.

"I was having a good dream," I admit sheepishly.

One of his dark eyebrows lifts suggestively. He wants me to tell him more, and I'm happy to oblige.

"You were in it."

"The space station again?" he quips before turning to rinse and spit. I can't take my eyes off his back—his sloping muscles and provocative lines.

"No. We were at our school."

I hear him choke on the water he's using to rinse his mouth. When he comes out of the bathroom, he's the one blushing. "Where at school?"

"Your classroom."

His eyes widen.

"But it was years ago, when we were only friends. I don't know how I could tell, but I just *could*. In the dream, I couldn't believe it was happening. That we were finally getting together."

He walks over to our bed and tugs down the comforter, climbing back into the warmth and cuddling up beside me instead of doing the practical thing and forcing me to get up. I lean into him, comforted by the familiarity of his size.

"There's no way we could pull it off," he notes, almost sounding dejected.

I prop myself up on one elbow. "You don't think?"

My new position has tugged down my tank top, and Ian's eyes drop to my cleavage. I practically see his eyes dilate with pleasure. The man cannot get enough, seriously.

I prop my finger underneath his chin and teasingly lift up until our eyes lock.

He doesn't look one bit ashamed of himself.

"Why don't you think we could pull it off?" I prompt again. I'm genuinely curious.

"Someone would definitely come knocking... Think about it. When have you *ever* had five minutes of uninterrupted time in your classroom?"

I frown. "True..."

It's always something. A fellow teacher, a student, a vice principal, a well-meaning PTA parent...

"I'd be lying if I said I hadn't thought about it, though," Ian admits.

Ooh la la.

I smile like the Cheshire cat.

"Especially in the old days," he adds.

"Like my dream…"

"Exactly. I did a lot of *dreaming* back then."

Oh. *Oh.* This is too good.

I know that Ian and I are married now and all that—we're about to celebrate our sixth wedding anniversary—but sometimes, out of the blue I'll feel completely gobsmacked by the reminder of what we are to each other. I still can't really believe that Ian Fletcher is mine forever.

I reach out to touch him, drawing my hand over his chest. It's like I'm trying to memorize the feel of him. It's amazing. He's muscled and tan. More importantly, he's mine! ALL MINE!

"We really have to get up now," he says, though his voice has gone a little husky.

"Do we?"

I lean over and kiss his neck, that little spot *he loves* just below his chin. I feel more than hear the deep grown resonating in his chest. He's already crumbling.

"Sam," he warns. "Violet's going to come barreling down the hall any second."

He's right; our sweet daughter refuses to sleep in.

I edge closer so our legs tangle together. "I can be so *so* fast. You know I can."

I'm already climbing up on top of him and pushing him back down onto the bed. His eyes are hooded, his breathing quickening.

It's so easy. He's not putting up much of a fight.

"We have to be up at the school in forty minutes," he reminds me while he gets to work lifting my tank top up and over my head. Cool air caresses my skin.

"No problem."

"We have to—"

I roll my hips, and he closes his eyes for a second, grabs onto my waist, trying to take it all in.

"I should make you wait. I should let you feel this pent-up desire all day," he taunts, his hands roaming up along my sides, covering my ribs before roving higher to cup my breasts. He opens his eyes, and they lock with mine. "I used to have to deal with that misery, you know. You'd come into school wearing my favorite dress, and it killed me," he groans, tugging me down so he can take one of my breasts between his lips.

Oh god.

I'm no match for this. His words and his mouth are a potent cocktail.

"Tell me we'll be like this forever."

He smiles against my skin. "Forever, Sam."

"Nothing will ever change."

He lets his teeth graze my breast, and I shudder. "Didn't you hear that alarm I set for you? *I got you, babe.*"

I laugh and then bend down to kiss him. No restraint. No sense in holding back. We only have a few minutes, and we're going to use every last one of them.

Ten minutes later (not to brag), we're done, showered, and getting dressed when Violet walks into the bathroom with major bedhead, rubbing her eyes and demanding to have banana bread for breakfast.

"How about toast?" Ian counters.

"Toast *with* bananas," she demands.

Ian leans down to kiss her hair. "Got it, kid."

"And orange juice!" she shouts as he heads for the kitchen.

Then she turns and smiles at me, coming over to hug my leg. "Hi."

"How'd you sleep?" I ask her, staring down at her big blue eyes, barely a shade lighter than her dad's.

"Bad," she says with true dramatic flair. "Stuffy fell on the ground."

"Well, we'll have to tuck him in better tonight," I assure her.

"Yes. We have to. And I want to wear a fancy dress to school."

"Okay."

She tries to push some of her long brown hair out of her face, but it just falls right back where it was. We need some cute pigtails, stat.

"Is today Wednesday?" she asks, totally discombobulated when it comes to days of the week.

"Tuesday."

She scrunches her nose. "What's after Tuesday?"

"Wednesday."

"*West Wing* Wednesdays," she says with a shoulder shimmy, having memorized our weekly routine.

I smile. "That's right."

"I really wanted banana bread."

Her ability to ping from one subject to another at lightning speed is truly challenging my pre-coffee brain. "Let's make some after school."

She beams, and I see so much of Ian in her. There's some of me, too, but she's his spitting image. Dimpled, tan, cute as a button. I can't help but pick her up and squeeze her tight.

She laughs. "*Mommy*. Daddy probably needs help with breakfast! And I still need to pick a fancy dress!"

"Then we better get going!"

"Let's go! Let's go!" she urges, wiggling her body in my arms like she's trying to get me to take off like a rocket.

"Are you holding on?!" I warn her.

She grips my arms with her little hands and squeals. "Yes!"

I bolt out of the bathroom and careen down the hall to her bedroom while she loses it to a fit of laughter. "Daddy! Mommy is running in the house!"

"Bad Mommy!" Ian chastises playfully from the kitchen.

I think we're miraculously doing okay on time, but in her room, Violet can't decide on a fancy dress. I hold up every last option, and when none of them work, I eventually convince her to wear a pale-yellow shirt with a tulle skirt. Even once she's wearing it, heading toward the kitchen, she's grumbling about it. Apparently, it barely meets the minimum threshold of fanciness.

"It needs diamonds," she says with a wobbly bottom lip. "None of my dresses have diamonds!"

The travesty.

Ian and I lock eyes and try not to laugh. The audacity of us, not buying Violet dresses adorned with rare gemstones! What horrible parents!

A few minutes later, we've somehow pulled it off. Violet is fed, and she's finally forgotten to be annoyed about her dress. I've made our lunches. Ian's cleaned up the breakfast dishes, and we're running out the door.

I grab my purse and school bag, and then Ian holds out my thermos of coffee and a granola bar. He smiles as I take them.

Right. I forgot to eat.

I sigh with relief. "Thank you."

He kisses my forehead. "Ready to tackle the day, Hot Lips?"

I flush. That old nickname is totally ridiculous, and yet it still does something to me I can't explain.

"What did you call her?" Violet asks with a furrowed brow.

Oh god. We've really piqued her curiosity.

"Nothing!" we shout in unison, failing to stifle our choked laughter.

I think we've gotten away with it, right up until I buckle Violet into her booster seat and she shoots me a little secret smile and whispers quietly, "I know what Daddy called you just now."

"Oh really?"

Please no. The last thing I need is for her to go to school and start calling her teacher or friends "hot lips."

"Snot hips."

Relief floods me as Ian snorts in the front seat.

"Yes, exactly," I tell her, straightening her seat belt. "Snot hips."

"Daddy is *so* silly!" she laughs. "Snot hips! Snot hips!"

And so begins another day in wedded bliss...

Witty banter and slow-burn romance collide in the bestselling enemies-to-lovers romance.

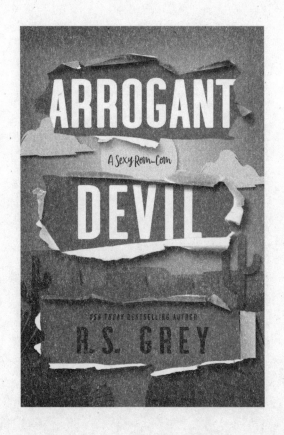

Sure, it could be the Texas heat messing with my head, but there's no way I'll survive the summer without silencing him with a kiss…

Biting banter, fake relationships, and illicit workplace rendezvous— anything goes in this romantic comedy.

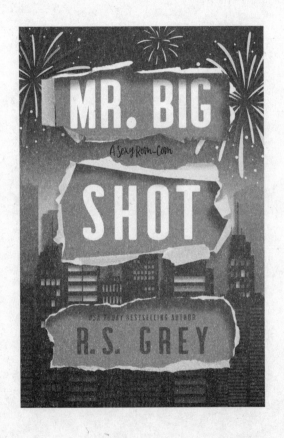

He's the one senior partner I was told to avoid at all costs—just so happens to be the heartless villain I'm assigned to work under.

*Don't miss the exciting new books
Entangled has to offer.*

Follow us!

 f @EntangledPublishing

 @Entangled_Publishing

 @EntangledPub

AMARA
an imprint of Entangled Publishing LLC